Her foot twitched
beneath the blanket

Alan went back to her bed. "Cate?"

Her eyelids fluttered. For a horrified moment, he was afraid she couldn't open her eyes. "Cate," he said again, "wake up. Uncle Ford, why didn't you shout at her before?"

"Shall I try again?" Uncle Ford struggled to his feet, maybe to lean closer to Cate's ear. He might have yelled at his niece, except Dan appeared at his side to help him—or maybe to hold him back.

Alan flashed his son a grateful smile and took Cate's hand. "Wake up. Please, Cate." Asking for things didn't come naturally, and that had been a sore spot between them. But he'd beg freely if he had to. Finally Cate opened her eyes and held them open. He didn't dare look away. Something different in her expression bothered him—some level of detachment.

She studied each person around her bed. Nothing that made her the Cate he loved was in her gaze. She eyed her aunt, uncle, niece, and son with the same strange, dreamy look he'd never seen again.

"Who are you?"

Dear Reader,

Imagine this: You open your eyes and find yourself in a hospital bed, surrounded by strangers who look like a close-knit family. You don't know your aunt or uncle, your niece or even your twin sister. Worse, you don't recognize your own son, and when the man who seems to be in charge claims he's your husband, you realize your own name is a mystery.

This is only the start of Cate Talbot Palmer's dilemma. Soon she discovers she's pregnant with twins, but that she hasn't told her husband, Alan—and she can't remember why. Add to that the tales people recount of the wild Talbot clan she hails from, and you have the kind of family story I love. Cate must figure out who she really is *and* learn the truth about her marriage. No longer the "good" twin, or the woman who never rocked anyone's boat, she wants to live life fully. Her struggle to recover her identity brings upheaval to her family and her marriage.

I hope you enjoy this story of learning to trust a loving stranger.

If you'd like to share your thoughts on this story, please write to me at annaadams@superauthors.com.

Sincerely,

Anna Addams

Unexpected Babies
Anna Adams

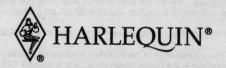

HARLEQUIN®

TORONTO • NEW YORK • LONDON
AMSTERDAM • PARIS • SYDNEY • HAMBURG
STOCKHOLM • ATHENS • TOKYO • MILAN • MADRID
PRAGUE • WARSAW • BUDAPEST • AUCKLAND

ISBN 0-373-70997-8

UNEXPECTED BABIES

Copyright © 2001 by Anna Adams.

Visit us at www.eHarlequin.com

Printed in U.S.A.

To Sarah Greengas, Sharon Lavoie,
Jennifer LaBrecque, Amy Lanz, Carmen Green,
Wendy Etherington, Jenni Grizzle, Karen Bishop,
Theresa Goldman and Michele Flinn—
thank you for reading my unpolished pages.

And to Paula Eykelhof and Laura Shin. Thank you
for the chance and for all I've already learned from you.

CHAPTER ONE

CATE TALBOT PALMER opened her car door and stepped into the sand-blown street that paralleled the beach. Above the small, stucco building in front of her a metal sign rattled like faint thunder in the wind off the ocean. The sign read Palmer Construction, Leith, Georgia.

Her husband, Alan, was inside at his desk. Nearly two hours late for the burned five-course dinner she'd abandoned on their dining room table.

Cate ran one hand across her stomach. The stench of dry, overcooked lamb mingled with ocean salt. She swallowed, her throat almost clenching she felt so nauseous. She'd suggested a special dinner tonight because she'd finally decided to tell Alan the secret she'd been keeping. Thank God she hadn't told him before.

She'd waited for him, staring at a bottle of sparkling grape juice she'd set on the table between their plates as a hint. She'd memorized that bottle while she'd opened her eyes to the facts. She and Alan had both kept secrets for the past sixteen weeks, only she'd been desperate enough to pretend she didn't see what Alan was doing.

Late nights at the office, fierce silences at home, see-through excuses for the cell phone he'd practically strapped to his hand. Most women would suspect an affair, but Alan Palmer had a different problem.

His mother had left him and his father when he was ten because his dad couldn't give her the material things she'd wanted. As a result of that long-ago abandonment and the way his father had used him as a confidant during the divorce, Alan tied his worth to his success with Palmer Construction.

He'd do anything to provide for Cate and Dan, their eighteen-year-old son, but he kept his emotional distance, afraid to risk the kind of pain he and his father had barely survived. His need to protect Cate had pushed her away, because she wanted a husband who would let her help him solve his problems, not pull away when troubles came.

She sprang from a long line of Talbots who'd failed at marriage or any relationship close to that kind of commitment. She and Alan had tried to create the family they'd both craved in their childhoods. Instead, they'd created an emotional divide.

She felt as if she'd already raised Dan on her own. She'd made up excuses for Alan's absences, for his distraction when he showed up late at one family gathering after another. She couldn't start that over again. This time, if she raised a child alone, it would be because she no longer lived with her baby's father.

A car passed her. She knew the driver. Another mom whose son was about to graduate from high school. Cate pasted a smile on her face. After today she wouldn't have to pretend everything was normal.

Wind from the car blew her hair across her face,

and Cate brushed the strands out of her eyes. She refused to wait for Alan to tell her what was wrong with the business. Hurting from the pain of another betrayal cost her more than knowing the truth. She'd make him tell her.

Squaring her shoulders, she marched across the street to the office. Her legs felt like jelly. She opened the frosted glass doors that were engraved with the company's name.

The moment she stepped inside, the temperature dropped. Even in mid-May, the South Georgia heat made air-conditioning a requirement. Cate swiped at perspiration on her forehead. Her hand trembled in front of her eyes.

She'd offer Alan a chance to explain because she still didn't want to leave him. When they were good, they were very, very good.

Alan's voice murmured from the office area. For a moment she hoped he had a late appointment with a client. Then she recognized a tone she always dreaded hearing. She couldn't understand what he was saying, but he was in trouble.

Her anger simmered as every excuse Alan had given her in the past few weeks repeated in her head. She wouldn't have kept her own secret if she'd trusted him.

Not that she could give him all the blame. She'd stayed. She hated feeling dependent, and her relationship with Alan made her feel dependent rather than stronger. When they were bad, they were unbearable.

Striding past models of the buildings and homes the company was contracted to build or renovate,

Cate tried to imagine why her husband had decided his success here meant more than their marriage.

She passed empty offices. Her twin sister, Caroline, who worked as an interior designer for the company, had already gone home.

Alan's office lay at the end of the hall. The air conditioning's whisper cushioned the sound of Cate's feet on the Berber carpet. Suddenly, John Mabry, Leith's chief of police, leaned into Cate's view, his bulk bending the frame of his chair as he crossed his arms behind his head.

"I know," he said on a hefty sigh. "A trained cop had no business losing Jim Cooper in the men's room, but I didn't train the cops who work the Newark airport. Just chill, Alan. We'll find him and your money before you have to shut your doors for good."

The carpet's warp seemed to rise up and trip Cate. Jim Cooper was their CPA, an oily man who always stood too close, tried to talk too intimately. She stumbled to a halt, flexing her fingers against the creamy, patterned wallpaper. The truth came as no surprise, but hearing it in plain words felt like a near fatal wound.

"What if we're already too late?" Alan asked. "I'm working my creditors now as if I were the criminal."

"What?" Mabry said in a sharp tone.

"With my banker's help." Alan placated the other man. "But I don't do business this way, and I don't like knowing my employees may be working on borrowed time."

The scream in Cate's head must have translated to some kind of sound. John Mabry turned to her, surprise widening his eyes. She pulled her hand off the wall. Nearly twenty years of pretending her marriage was healthy had honed her skills. She'd pretend nothing was wrong. Next best thing to acting as if Alan had talked to her about the problem.

"Hey, John."

"Evening, Cate."

Alan's chair squeaked. After a few muffled steps, he came around the door, tall, dark and clueless. "Is something wrong with Dan?"

Startled at his unexpected question, Cate searched tanned features that had thinned over the past weeks to an ascetic sharpness. His problems in this office had distracted him. He'd forgotten their meal and his promise to come home early. Naturally, he only expected her to show up if something was wrong with their son.

"Dan's fine."

A father's fear haunted his eyes. Alan loved the idea of family. He truly loved their son—as much as she did.

"I came because you're late," she said.

He turned a wary gaze on the police chief. "John…"

Mabry pried himself out of his chair. "I'll get back to you later, Alan."

Cate watched the other man leave. With each step he took toward the front of the building, she braced herself to face the reason for her husband's guilty expression.

"Cate." Taking her arm, Alan forced her to look at him before she was ready.

She shook him off. "Don't." All she wanted was

for him to tell her she was wrong. "Why was John here?"

"Please believe I wanted to tell you." He took her hands again. Heat throbbed from his callused palms.

She splayed her fingers over the undersides of his wrists, where his pulse tapped an alarm. A measure of calm came to her despite confusion that had become familiar. "Something's happened. Again."

He tightened his hands, but he couldn't seem to answer her. She studied his face, intent on every nerve, every shadow of guilt that flitted behind eyes that knew her both too well and not at all.

"This time was different, Cate."

"You always say it's different, but it never is." The future yawned in front of her like a hungry mouth. "You keep problems from me because you think I'll leave if the business goes sour."

Sweat beaded on his upper lip. He didn't look well, but she couldn't spare him any more of her empathy.

"I would have told you." He released one of her hands so he could wipe the drops of moisture off his mouth. "I had to make sure I knew how much trouble we're facing."

"I don't trust you." She flattened her free hand over her belly, tracing the mound she couldn't hide much longer. She wouldn't expose another child to a part-time father. "I can't go on the way we are, and you can't change. You never would have told me about Jim. You planned to clean up the mess by yourself."

"I haven't told anyone except Mabry and the bank. Jim Cooper embezzled from the business accounts. He stole from every company he worked for. We've all lost money, and we're trying to find Jim before he knows we're looking for him.''

She fought to control her anger, but reason hadn't worked with him in the past. ''First, you should tell the employees if they're in danger of losing their jobs. Second, I don't work for you, and I'm not a newspaper reporter. You have no right to keep me in the dark. I'm your wife, and I have an equal share in this business. I turned myself into a stay-at-home mom for Dan, not because I'm not intelligent enough to be part of this company.''

''I never said you weren't bright enough to understand the business, Cate.'' He frowned, deep lines leaving furrows between his nose and mouth. ''John told me the police had tracked Jim to the Newark airport.''

''That part I understood. You're obviously worried, and I'm sorry, but I don't know why you won't let me help you.''

''What could you have done?''

''I don't know, but you never gave me a chance. You prefer to suffer alone.''

''I'm supposed to protect you and Dan.''

''Please don't start that old story again.'' She freed herself from him. ''I'm not like your mother. I don't need a house or a car or clothes that impress our neighbors. If the business burned to the ground, I'd want to help you rebuild, but you wouldn't turn to me. You want to protect me, but Dan and I can't count on you if something goes wrong in this office.'' She spun blindly toward the reception area. She had one thought—to escape this building without him—but he kept pace with her as if she were crawling.

"Where are you going?" His stunned tone hurt most of all.

"I told you I wouldn't stay if you hid anything else from me."

"Tell me how I'm different than you, Cate. How often are you at Aunt Imogen's or Uncle Ford's houses? They don't need a nursemaid."

"They're family, and they took Caroline and me in when Mom and Dad didn't want us." Her parents, both officers in Naval Intelligence, had dropped her and her sister off at Aunt Imogen's on their way to an isolated duty station in Turkey. From there, they'd gone on to one unaccompanied assignment after another, and Cate and Caroline had remained with their maiden aunt and bachelor uncle in Leith. "They're both alone and over seventy. I look in on them." And they continued to give her the unconditional love she'd never had from either her parents or Alan.

"What about Caroline? You run to her and Shelly every time they try to change a lightbulb." Her sister had raised her daughter alone since Caroline's husband had abandoned them when Shelly was only four. Alan had never seemed to resent her attention to their extended family before, but desperation edged his tone. "You cushion them and Dan in cotton wool. I'm only trying to give you the kind of care you give our family."

His last, self-serving point pushed Cate too far. She turned on him, but momentum carried her too close to him. His familiar, spicy scent triggered a basic need whose power had always frightened her.

Wanting him so much, she felt weak and angry with herself. "Don't look for someone to blame because you and I failed at our marriage."

He reeled backward, stumbling into a model of the library they were supposed to refurbish. Instinctively, Cate caught his arm before she was certain whether she wanted to shove him or help him.

No, she knew what she had to do. "I stayed for Dan, but he leaves for college in a few weeks. I don't have to pretend you and I are going to live happily ever after. Not together, anyway."

"Cate." His husky plea caught her unawares. He reached for her, his wedding band glowing gold in the building's artificial light.

She arched away from him. Tears clouded her vision, but she grabbed the chrome rail on the front doors. Approaching night had strengthened the ocean breeze, and she had to lean her whole body into the door to open it.

Outside the wind whipped her hair into her eyes. She bumped into a soft figure that had to be a woman. Cate muttered a tear-choked apology and broke for the street. But she stumbled into a parking meter and fell off the sidewalk.

Her right ankle turned over. Pain nearly paralyzed her as her foot skidded through sand. Behind her, a woman's voice shrilled, but the deep blast of a car horn seemed to finish her shriek. Cate straightened, turning. A green sports car, coming fast, froze her.

"Cate!" Alan must have followed her. He was furious, afraid and too far away.

She reached blindly into thin air, twisting back toward the sidewalk. Seconds stretched, defying the laws of nature. Alan caught her hands. She recognized the strength of his long fingers, the breadth of his palms. She grabbed at him, but she couldn't get her feet beneath her in the sand. Holding on to her husband, she peered over her shoulder at the driver.

Intensity crumpled his face. His body lifted in the seat, as if he were standing on his brakes.

They screamed, and time lost its elasticity.

Cate willed her body away from the car. Alan yanked her, but something glanced off her leg, more a jarring thump than real pain.

At first.

Alan pulled her hard against his body as a fire-edged knife seemed to slice through her thigh. Behind her, the car's tires ground into the road and chaos faded to silence.

An unnatural silence, empty of voices or traffic, footsteps or the constant whisper of the ocean. Cate knew only pain and an overwhelming nausea. Panic clutched at her. Was she sick because of the baby, or the torture of her leg? Was she going to lose her baby?

"I've got you. You're safe."

She looked up. Alan's fear fed her terror. She hadn't trusted him enough to tell him about her pregnancy, and now she didn't know how to say the words.

"Focus on me." Alan turned his head. "Somebody call 911!"

Around them, cell phones erupted in a cacophony of beeps. Somehow, Cate found a smile, but Alan stared at her, amazed.

She concentrated on his green eyes. "You've always wanted to save my life."

With his face pale as beach sand, Alan didn't smile back. "Don't talk."

People she knew, Alan's busiest carpenter and Mr. Parker, who owned the Bucket O' Suds, edged into her peripheral vision.

"Look at the blood running down her leg, Alan." Mr. Parker pushed a man-smelling apron beneath her nose. "Maybe you need this."

"Get a damn ambulance," Alan snarled, but then the muscles around his mouth worked as he fought to maintain his composure. "Cate, you're all right."

A resounding roar overwhelmed her silent prayer that he'd keep holding her too close for her to look down and see the blood. Pressure, like a giant hand, seemed to push her toward the ground. "I think I'm not all right."

She was going to faint. First time she could ever remember fainting. Was she dying? "Alan, I— Dan— I want—"

"Dan's fine." Alan's voice cracked. "You're fine."

"I have to tell you..." That strange pressure swathed her in darkness. Only Alan's arms kept her from falling. She forgot what she had to tell him, but she hung on until the darkness swallowed her whole.

DR. BARTON'S CALM infuriated Alan. "After a thirty-six hour coma, we can't know how she'll be when she wakes up. She lost a lot of blood from that gash in her thigh, and she went into shock."

Each word the doctor spoke embedded itself in

Alan like a gut shot. Infuriated that he couldn't help her, he stared at his unconscious wife. Her vulnerable, wounded body rumpled the blanket on her bed. The bank of blinking monitors that surrounded her screeched persistently enough to wake the dead. Alan bit the side of his cheek.

Men didn't cry. So his father had preached, weeping into his beer or scrambled eggs or the ironing they'd both avoided after Alan's mother left. Clutching Cate's unresponsive hand, Alan alternated between an urge to bawl with unmanly pain and an acute need to break everything in the small hospital room.

"She'll wake up," Dr. Barton said, as if he saw through Alan's attempt at stoic silence. "She's healthy—no sign of infection in her wound. We just have to see where we stand. Tests, physical therapy— Excuse me, Alan, Nurse Matthews wants me."

The doctor barely cleared the doorway before Cate's twin, Caroline, slipped into the room.

She shared his wife's fragile bone structure and dark auburn hair. In the old days, only he could tell them apart until Cate had begun using a blow-dryer to straighten her hair into a sleek curtain that brushed her shoulders. She'd looked more like a bank president than a loving creative homemaker. Caroline, a pragmatic businesswoman, never bothered to tame the wild curls she used now to cover her face. Neither of them seemed to see the contradiction in their hairstyles, but maybe Cate had expressed her altered feelings about her life in a not so subtle change.

Alan rubbed his fist against his temple, annoyed

that he hadn't asked her such questions before she'd decided to leave him.

Caroline eased around the bed. "What does Dr. Barton say?"

The sisters were so close they sometimes shared each other's thoughts. If only Cate could sense Caroline's pain, she'd wake up, feeling a compulsion to help her twin.

"Barton says the same thing over and over. We have to wait." He stroked his wife's forearm, grateful for the body heat that warmed her silky skin. How long since he'd touched her? How had he not noticed she was avoiding him, even in their bed? "I'm fed up with waiting." Waiting and thinking about all the signs he should have read as he and Cate traveled to the end of their marriage.

"Where's your dad, Alan? He's the only member of our families unaccounted for in the waiting room, and I think you need him."

Richard Palmer hated hospitals. Sickness scared the pants off him. "You know his phobia."

"I thought he might have handled it for Cate."

She clearly disapproved, and Alan didn't blame her. "He calls our answering machine at home every ten minutes." Alan roused himself. Last time he'd been out of this room, the waiting area had been empty. "Is Dan out there?"

Caroline shook her head. "I sent Shelly to look for him, and she called when she found him carrying a gas can down the highway. They'll come here after she takes him to a service station and then back to his car."

He nodded, twisting his hands on the metal bed

rail. "A full gas tank probably seems pretty mundane to him right now." He and Dan had stumbled blindly through the past two days. Cate anchored their family. Alan only hoped he was taking up enough of her slack to be a good father.

Caroline's eyes seemed unnaturally wide as she tried to smile. "We're all afraid. What if she doesn't wake up? How long are we supposed to—"

"Don't think about giving up." Alan briefly hugged his sister-in-law. "She feels what you feel, Caroline." It was ridiculous, putting such an airy-fairy notion into words, but Caroline met his gaze with Talbot determination.

"Don't you worry." She gripped Cate's hand. "I refuse to lose her."

Caroline's tenacity almost renewed his faith. But it might be too late for him and Cate. Her serious injuries and the possibility she'd never let him try to win her back lingered in his mind.

He'd wanted to make her life comfortable and easy. Instead he'd let her down, and even now, he wasn't sure what he'd done wrong.

The door swished open, and Aunt Imogen entered the room without speaking. Her bare head made Alan take a second look. She habitually wore oversize straw hats that she'd trimmed with flower displays never seen in nature. Today, only her fine gray curls clung to her temples.

Courage in her tired gaze touched Alan. He'd swear she hadn't closed her eyes since he'd had to tell her about Cate. Neither had he, but she looked fragile.

He dragged a chair to the side of Cate's bed. The

way he'd let Cate think he resented her care for Aunt
Imogen shamed him. According to local gossip, the
older woman had been in midheartbreak over an affair with a married navy pilot when she'd taken in
Cate and Caroline. Her emotionally hungry nieces
had loved their aunt back to health, and Aunt Imogen
and her brother, Ford, had shown Cate and Caroline
the only true family affection they'd ever known.
They'd also convinced Alan he belonged to the Talbot clan from the first day Cate had brought him
home. He owed them as much as Cate ever could.

Taking Caroline's hand, Aunt Imogen sat and
smoothed the sheet beside Cate's hip. "I guess you
spoke to Dr. Barton this morning, Alan?"

Before he could answer, Uncle Ford prodded his
way into the small room with the aid of a cherry cane
and his great-niece Shelly's hand at his elbow. Behind them, Dan craned for a glimpse of his mom.

Alan sidled through the others to wrap his arms
around his son's surprisingly broad shoulders. Dan
hugged back, to Alan's relief, but then he quickly
pulled away. Dan preferred a handshake in recent
years.

Alan met Aunt Imogen's questioning gaze. "Barton can't say much until Cate wakes up."

"Until she breaks out of that coma," Caroline
said, as if the coma were an animal that had wrapped
her sister in its vicious grip. "Let's face facts."

"I won't face that word." Aunt Imogen stood, her
expression a faultless display of barely controlled
fear. "Take this chair, Ford. Stop banging that
cane."

Her brother gave her an annoyed glance. "Good

thing I'm not sensitive about having to use it." He patted his sister's hand. "I know you're just worried." Bellowing at a decibel level that compensated for the hearing loss he refused to admit, Uncle Ford nevertheless took Aunt Imogen's seat. "Maybe the racket will wake—" he actually lifted his voice "—Cate."

Her foot twitched beneath the blanket. Alan went back to her bed. "Cate?" Could waking her be that easy?

Her eyelids fluttered. For a horrified moment, he was afraid she couldn't open her eyes.

"Cate," he said, "wake up. Uncle Ford, why didn't you shout at her before?"

"Shall I try again?" Uncle Ford struggled to his feet, maybe to lean a touch closer to Cate's ear. He might have yelled again, except Dan appeared at his side to help him—or maybe to hold him back.

Alan flashed his son a grateful smile and took Cate's hand. "Wake up," he said again. "Please, Cate." He didn't beg easily, and his reticence had been a sore spot between them. He'd beg pretty damn freely now. "Cate," he said again, and she opened her eyes and held them open. Her steady blue gaze made him want to shout, but he knew better than to scare her.

"Are you in pain?" He didn't dare look away. Something different in her expression bothered him—some level of detachment he'd always expected to see. Wives detached themselves, no matter what you did to keep them with you. "Caroline, get the doctor."

As Caroline left, Cate's gaze followed her. She

studied each person around her bed. Nothing that made her the Cate he loved was in that gaze. She eyed her aunt and uncle, her son and her niece with the same strange, dreamy look until she focused on Alan again.

"Who are you?"

The courtesy in her tone chilled him.

Trying to ask her what the hell she was talking about, he choked on his first breath. Confusion threaded the air, like a piece of twine that slipped from body to body. Strangling them all.

Aunt Imogen finally cried out, but then she covered her mouth. Uncle Ford's cane clattered to the floor. Alan reached for both older people, steadying them with hands that shook hard enough to remind him how his father felt about men who gave in to their emotions.

But even his dad would understand this. Cate had left him after all.

THE LOVELY WOMAN with copper hair had raced out of the room, and the others, except for the dark man, poured after her. Just as well. Breathing took such an awful effort, and that many people must use a lot of oxygen.

Why would a hospital let such a crowd mill around a patient's room? She stopped in midthought. She must be the patient. She was in bed.

How she'd come there escaped her, although she felt as if someone had welded a hot metal plate to her right leg. Nausea hovered, as if she were on a boat that refused to stop rocking.

She willed her queasiness away and concentrated

on the man. Watching her from wide, dark-green eyes, he was clearly waiting for her to speak. As if he knew her.

She didn't know him.

She must have been in an accident. Had she interrupted a family reunion? That many people in the same place had to be a family.

She took a deep breath that seemed to fill her head. The truth rocked her. Strangers didn't hang around a hospital bed, even if they'd banded together to rescue an accident victim.

She didn't remember what had happened to her. She remembered—nothing.

At her shoulder, a monitor's steady beep grew more rapid. The sound drew her gaze as she tried to pry her own name out of her blank memory. She didn't seem to have a name.

She knew her name. Everyone knew her own name. It was— She could feel it on the tip of her tongue. She ought to know. The monitor began to ping like sonar.

She didn't know.

Suddenly aware of the man's harsh grip on her hand, she turned toward him. "I don't know you."

"I'm your husband. I'm Alan."

He terrified her. She tried to sit up in bed, but a powerful, formless weight held her down.

"I'll help you," he said.

He wrapped his large hands around her upper arms, but his strength made her feel weak, and she pushed him away.

"I don't need your help."

Stung, he straightened, looking impossibly tall.

"What's the matter?" He reached for her again, but something in her eyes must have shown him how seriously she wanted him to keep his hands off her. He fisted them at his sides.

"You act as if you have some right to touch me," she whispered. "Who am I?" She wasn't sure she wanted to know.

"My wife," he said. "Cate...Palmer."

"Why don't I know you?" She darted a glance at the window. Low clouds hung above a sandstone building. It all looked completely unfamiliar. The glass offered a faint reflection, but she couldn't see the details of her face. "Let me see what I look like. Maybe I'll rememb—"

Before she could finish, he whipped open the top of the table at her elbow. A mirror was mounted inside. With the man's help, she twisted the table toward her, so she could see.

Wild blue eyes stared at her from beneath a mass of dark red hair. She gasped. That other woman— the one who'd gone for a doctor. She had the same face.

The mouth in the mirror opened, and a scream tore the air.

"Cate." His fear-drenched voice scared her, but he tucked her against his body, and she seemed to fit into the hard contours of his chest.

She closed her eyes. Darkness and the man's faint, spicy scent blotted out the mirror, the room, the world as far as she knew it. She didn't want to see herself. She'd lost everything, her past, her sense of identity.

Her life.

CHAPTER TWO

"ALAN, GO HOME. Get some sleep and have a shower." Dr. Barton's voice woke Cate.

She opened her eyes. She'd hardly been out of the coma for a full day, but the doctor's visits interested her. Unlike her family, he wanted nothing from her. She looked from him to the husband she didn't know.

Alan straightened in a metal-and-vinyl chair. "I don't need sleep or a shower."

She lifted her hand to him, but he shook his head, obviously aware she was going to second Dr. Barton's suggestion. She continued anyway. "You need to rest." She shouldn't have buried her face in his manly chest. Her momentary weakness had apparently convinced him she needed a bodyguard. "Nothing bad will happen to me if you leave my room."

He shot a wary glance at Dr. Barton, who nodded. Alan stood, but tension built as he hesitated. Cate didn't know how to respond to him. His deep concern touched her. She found his stubbled chin attractive, his brooding green eyes appealing. She liked the way he smelled, but Alan expected more than the gratitude and simple attraction she felt.

"Do you want me to come back?" he asked.

She'd like to remember why he seemed as uncomfortable with her as she was with him. Had their marriage been happy? "After you rest, if you feel like coming back, I'll be here."

He turned toward Dr. Barton, but his gaze lingered on her as he spoke. "You know where to reach me?"

The doctor moved to Cate's bed, an impresario, showing off his brightest talent. "Cate is awake and healthy and on the mend. We won't need to dive into that pool of phone numbers you gave us."

With a wry expression, Alan trudged to the door, and most of the pressure left with him. Cate sank against her pillows. The gruff doctor shut her door and dragged a chair to her bed.

"Let's talk," he said.

His urgency alarmed her. "Did you find something in the tests?"

"No—well, nothing new, but I've been trying to get you alone since you woke up yesterday. I have to tell you something I don't believe you've told Alan."

She attempted a smile. "Another man came forward to claim me as his wife."

He gave a slight, anxious grin that put her on edge. "We only allow one family per amnesiac." His gaze grew as intense as any of her family's. "I wish I could prepare you for this news, but I must say it quickly before someone else comes in. You're pregnant, and I've been unethical." He patted her good leg. "What a relief to say it out loud at last."

Cate grabbed her bed rails as the world seemed to open up beneath her. "I'm pregnant?"

"Just over sixteen weeks." He went on, as if they should both be ready to talk facts. "You were spotting when you came in. By the time we could leave you to speak to Alan, he should already have asked us about the baby. When he didn't, I began to worry you hadn't told him and that you had a reason for not telling him. I asked Imogen for your gynecologist's name.''

Words escaped her at first. ''How old am I again?''

''Thirty-eight.''

Pregnant, thirty-eight, with a son of eighteen, and she hadn't told anyone about the new baby. Why?

She slid her hands over her stomach. It was round all right. She hadn't thought to ask why. An unexpected protectiveness caught her by surprise, and she accepted a new first priority. ''Is the baby all right?''

''Yes. Your bleeding was light, and you stopped within a few hours. I still would have told Alan if I hadn't tracked down Dr. Davis.''

''My obstetrician?''

''Right. She said you'd decided not to tell Alan yet, so I followed your wishes. However, Dr. Davis needs to see you, so you have to decide how to tell Alan. She'll never make it in here and out again without being ambushed, considering the way your family guards that door.''

Cate's large family overwhelmed her, too. She couldn't see their constant, well-meant surveillance as a joke. ''No one else asked about the baby? Not my sister or my aunt?''

''I wish they had.''

''Did Dr. Davis explain why I've kept the pregnancy a secret?''

''She doesn't know, and I can't promise Imogen

hasn't talked to Alan since I asked her for your OB's name.'' Dr. Barton patted her forearm. ''Try not to worry. I expect Alan would have exploded by now if Imogen had told him.''

''I need to talk to Alan. What was wrong between us?''

''I'm not sure anything was wrong.''

Cate pushed her fingers through her hair. ''Dr. Barton, tell me the truth.'' She pressed her palms together, trying to look self-possessed. She didn't want or need a gentle bedside manner. ''Will I ever know these people again?''

He hunched his shoulders beneath his wrinkled lab coat. ''All I ever say to you or Alan is 'I don't know.' And I don't. Because shock, rather than a head injury, caused your amnesia, I'd say your memory will trickle back.'' Grinning, he popped his glasses from the top of his head onto his face, where they magnified his weary eyes. ''Trickle. That's a technical term.''

Cate tried to smile, but his nonanswer made her head ache. She lifted her hand between them, turning it from side to side. ''I must have seen my fingers millions of times, but I don't recognize them. I scared myself to death when I looked in a mirror and saw my sister's face. My son makes me feel anxious, because he's at an age where he won't even say if he feels let down. I'm responsible for him, but I don't feel that he's my child, and I'm more comfortable talking to you than to my husband.''

''These are the facts. You can't balance them with what you feel, because all your emotions are tied up in your memory loss.'' Dr. Barton folded her fingers between his weathered hands. "I don't know why you'd hide a child from Alan, but he cares about you. He stood a vigil at your bedside no matter how many times I begged him to go home. I thought we might end up having to treat him. That man didn't stay all this time because he felt it was his duty."

Good. She didn't want a dutiful marriage. She wanted passion and commitment, a love that made a thirty-eight-year-old woman want to tell her husband they were having a second child.

Might she have hidden her pregnancy from Alan for a more obvious and insidious reason than a marriage that had wound down to duty? "What if Alan isn't the baby's father? Would you have heard rumors if I was having an affair?"

Dr. Barton sat back as if someone had tried to yank his chair out from under him. "The Talbots have a bad habit of making destructive decisions, but not you, Cate."

"Talbots?" She found no comfort in his vehement support.

"Your father's family. Your Aunt Imogen and Uncle Ford. Before you, the Talbots have tended to live by their own reckless rules, but you've broken that mold, Cate. I've known your family a long time, and I've seen you make healthier choices than the others."

"Explain, please."

"No. You speak to Imogen or Caroline." At his nervous glance, she imagined redheaded women who ran with wolves and men who sought the company of sinners. "You need to rebuild your relationships with your aunt and uncle and sister, not with me."

"You're not hurt because I can't remember you."

He held up both hands. "You have to jump off this cliff. Think of me as a parachute if you jump and you need help getting to the ground, but talk to your family."

Outside her room, a woman's voice paged another doctor over the PA system, and some sort of heavy equipment rolled down the hall on squeaky wheels. Still, Dr. Barton waited for her to behave the way she always had.

Cate covered her face with her hands, but then flattened her palms at her sides. "I can't lie here and wait for my life to happen to me, can I?"

He slipped his hands in his pockets. "I'll arrange for Dr. Davis to see you. Figure out what to tell Alan about the baby."

Memory must shape a person's sense of self. When she tried to think how she should approach Alan, she faced a mental blank. "I think I'll try the truth." She winced a little. "The truth as we know it, anyway."

ALAN DIDN'T go home and sleep. Instead, he asked Dan to join him in an early round of golf at the country club they'd belonged to since Dan had begun to show unexpected talent for the game.

Alan kept waiting for the right moment to ask his son why he was avoiding Cate. Since his golf skills didn't measure up to Dan's, searching for lost balls usually made them talk. Today Dan helped him scour the primordial, South Georgia forest in uneasy silence. He grunted one-syllable responses to Alan's opening gambits. Finally, after they turned in their cart, Alan suggested lunch in the club's excessively Victorian grill room.

After they ordered, Dan sprawled in his wide wooden chair with a look that anticipated a firing squad. "What do you want, Dad?"

His sullen question surprised Alan. Normally, Cate handled these types of conversations. He didn't know where to go when Dan was clearly saying he didn't want to talk.

"Are you angry with your mom? Why won't you go see her?"

Dan rubbed his chin, unconsciously pointing out a little late adolescent acne. "She only woke up yesterday. I had to do some stuff for Uncle Ford and Aunt Imogen."

Was he serious? Did he really think the horses Uncle Ford boarded or Aunt Imogen's errands might be more important than Cate? "But why didn't you stay long enough to tell your mom you were glad she's okay? I know you are."

"You're talking like you think I wish she was still in the coma. I'm not a kid, Dad. I'll go see her." He sat back as their server delivered sodas and small salads.

"Hey, Dan," the girl said.

"Hey. You know my Dad?" Dan generally knew more of the people who worked at the club than Alan or Cate. He'd played enough golf here to earn a scholarship for college.

This time, the girl looked faintly familiar.

"Sure, I know Mr. Palmer. How are you?" she asked.

He was on the verge of losing his mind. "Fine. Nice to see you."

Nodding, she turned away. Dan's smirk mocked his father. "Why didn't you just admit you didn't know her? I would have introduced you again."

"To be honest, I don't have time. I need to go back to the hospital, and I wish you'd come with me."

Dan lifted his soda for a slow sip. When he put the glass down, he wiped his mouth and looked like the kid Alan remembered. "I'll go," he finally said, "but I'm not sure why. She doesn't even know us."

Alan studied him, taken aback. He finally understood how Cate had felt when she'd been the one Dan turned to. She'd handled their family's emotional upheavals and freed Alan to provide material support. He wanted to retire to a safe corner and wallow in his own fear, but this time he was the one who had to put his son first.

"Are you afraid your mom's not going to get well?" He was starting from scratch with a boy he loved more than his own life.

Dan's friend came back and slid their meals onto the table. Even after she left, Dan focused all his attention on getting ketchup to come out of its bottle.

"Son, I need you to talk to me."

"What am I supposed to say? How does she want us to feel about her? She's always been overprotective. She offered my little league coach tips when he yelled at me for rubbernecking. She's chaperoned every school trip I've ever taken. Now, she looks at me and her bottled water with the same interest."

Dan had avoided overt affection for about four

years, but Alan dared to clip his son's shoulder with a loose fist. "Don't underestimate how much she needs you. I don't think she's forgotten us forever, and she's still your mom. You be a son to her, and she'll follow your lead."

Alan felt like a fraud advising Dan when he still hadn't decided what he was going to tell Cate about the business. As he'd chased her out of the office, he'd longed for a chance to start over. He had it now, but it was a bitter beginning.

"Dad, you look worried. I don't want you to keep anything from me."

Alan shook off his indecision for Dan's sake. "Dr. Barton promised your mom will be back on her feet in time to see you graduate."

Dan folded a fry into his mouth. "Will she want to come?"

Alan dropped the corner of his turkey club. "Yes." Cate would have found an answer more convincing than his shocked, one-word response. He tried again. "She'll want to see you graduate from high school."

Dan sounded a youthful, impatient snort. "Sorry, Dad, but I can't really take your word for it." He tossed another fry into his mouth and talked around it. "I'll go by the hospital after practice this afternoon."

Alan didn't pause to enjoy his success. "Thanks, son. I'd better get back myself. How are your aunt and uncle?"

"I stayed at Aunt Imogen's last night after I fed the horses. Uncle Ford came over for a movie and popcorn, and then I walked Polly for Aunt Imogen."

Imogen had recently retired Polly, her old roan mare, from farm work. She'd presented Polly with an extravagant straw hat that matched one of her own. Shocking the neighborhood, but never Cate and Caroline, who loved their aunt for her fabled eccentricity, both Imogen and Polly wore their finery for their nightly walks.

"Did you wear the hat?"

"Sure, Dad, and I took a picture so you could use it for that dorky Christmas card you send out every year."

Cate actually sent the card, but Alan had taken pride in her annual record of their family. He pushed his chair back. "Why don't you stay with Uncle Ford tonight? I'm sure your being there helps them."

"Maybe I'll pick them up after practice and take them to see Mom."

Alan got to his feet. "Sounds good. You want to sign for lunch? I'll see you later."

"Okay." Dan looked up. Strands of his longish black hair made him blink blue eyes exactly the shade of Cate's. "I'm sorry I didn't want to talk. I'm a little scared."

Alan held back a relieved sigh. He felt as if he were luring a wild animal into a clearing. He didn't want to scare Dan into running for cover. "Are you all right?"

Dan immediately thinned his smile. "I just hope Mom is. Soon."

Alan hoped male stoicism didn't run in his family, but he'd protected his own feelings long enough to recognize the steps his son was taking.

Close off. Look tough.

''Take it easy, son,'' he said, wanting to hug his almost grown boy. ''I'll see you later.'' He risked a quick pat on Dan's shoulder and then crossed the black-and-burgundy dining room.

Hurrying back to his car, he checked his watch. He needed to talk to Caroline about her budgets for the medical building, but first he wanted to see his wife. Fifteen minutes took him to the hospital.

He parked in the lot and stared up at the skeletal, half-finished building that overshadowed the hospital. His work site, the new medical building.

Wind blew sand in his eyes, blurring his vision. He wiped a film of sweat off his neck as the early May sun soaked through his clothing. Work continued on the medical center despite the troubled turn his finances had taken. Thoughts of the money he'd owe his suppliers made him sweat some more.

He wanted to tell the suppliers, just as he'd wanted to tell Cate and their employees, about the damage their CPA had done. He hadn't known how to tell Cate he'd failed her by letting Jim steal from them. The other businessmen Jim had duped had decided not to tell their employees until they knew the extent of the problem. He'd argued, but he'd finally agreed to hold off. Deciding to lie to Cate had been shamefully easy.

Maybe her injuries gave him a real reason to hide the truth. Getting acquainted with her family again would be hard enough. Maybe by the time she remembered everything, the police would have found Jim and the funds he'd stolen. Cate might not have to know.

Her accusations came back to him loud and clear

and all too accurate. He'd always followed the same pattern, trying to fix business problems before he had to tell her about them.

He climbed the slight rise to the hospital entrance. Inside, he drank in the cooler air.

The guard who patrolled the lobby stepped forward. Alan knew him and the lavender-haired woman behind the information desk. Formerly kindergarten teacher to half the adults in Leith, in retirement, she volunteered at the hospital. After a curt nod to the guard and his ex-teacher, he evaded their sympathetic glances.

Their pity turned him back into the ten-year-old boy whose mother had deserted him. As his father had disintegrated in front of his eyes, Alan had cleaned and cooked and put on a "normal" face.

After he'd set the kitchen on fire for the third time, their neighbors had stepped in. A Southern staple, the casserole, had begun to show up in its endless varieties, in the hands of their well-meaning friends.

The food, he'd thanked them for. Their looks of commiseration he'd hated so much he'd begun to pretend no one was home at dinnertime. His make-believe often became the truth once his father decided to drink away his sorrows at a bar instead of in front of Alan.

The elevator doors wheezed open, pulling him out of the past. He glanced at the number painted on the pale-blue wall. Cate's floor.

At her door, he knocked lightly before he went inside. To his surprise, she was sitting up, reading a magazine. She looked up, stroking the dressing that bulged against the sheet on her thigh.

"Hey," she said, her tone lush and deep, like the dark river that ran behind her aunt's home.

"How do you feel?" *Idiot,* he thought. Idiotic question.

Cate set her magazine aside. "I want to talk to you about how I feel."

She looked younger than thirty-eight. Far younger. He still saw her as she'd been the day she'd sat in a bed on the floor above this one and held their newborn out to him.

Her wary gaze intimated this wasn't going to that kind of talk. He steeled himself. "Tell me now if something's wrong."

"You're making me nervous. Can you sit down so we can talk eye to eye?"

Wondering how hard his heart could pound before it exploded, he dropped into the chair beside her bed. "How bad is it? Just tell me."

Confronted with the threat of another injury she found hard to discuss, he realized once and for all how they'd changed. Not just because she couldn't remember their past. They'd drifted apart before her accident.

He'd tried to fool himself. He hadn't preserved their love for each other despite all his protection. He'd feared losing her for the same reasons he'd lost his mother. He'd shut Cate out, because he didn't trust her to love the part of him that felt so afraid.

"Alan, I need to know you're listening to me."

Her demand surprised him. She sounded exactly as she had the day of the accident. "You're still yourself, after all."

"Am I?" Interest filled her blue eyes as she held out her hand. "Tell me how."

"What you just said, that you needed me to listen. Just before you got hurt, you were trying to make me understand exactly what you—"

"We argued?"

"I'm afraid so." If she'd given him time, he might have tried to paint a better picture of those last seconds. "It wasn't important."

"But you didn't understand me?"

"We've been married a long time. We've learned a shorthand, but shorthand may not have covered the conversations we needed to have." Jeez, he sounded like a talk show therapist. "What's wrong with you, Cate?"

"It's not serious— I'm not— Oh, I give up." She pushed her hair behind both ears. "I'm trying to tell you gently because I'm not sure you'll be pleased, but I'm pregnant."

He heard but he didn't hear. Alan leaned forward, seeing her as a stranger. Her watchful blue eyes couldn't belong to his Cate. "How pregnant?"

"Sixteen weeks." She spread the gown over her belly, and he saw why she'd begun to avoid his touch.

He'd trusted her with his life, but she'd kept his child a secret. Her betrayal cut deep. "I thought you didn't even want me to make love to you any more." The only time they'd still communicated.

"Why didn't I tell you?" Cate asked.

Rage made him harsh. "Since you didn't, I can't explain." She'd planned to leave, but her decision hadn't been spur of the moment. She'd planned to take his child. His heart stuttered over a few beats. "I can't talk any more."

"But I need to know—"

With his own lie foremost in his mind, he met her tear-sharpened gaze. He didn't trust her tears, but he'd been no paragon of honesty.

"Why are you crying?" he asked.

"Because I don't understand. Were we unhappy?"

"I can't guess how you felt. I remember the past twenty years. I remember when you told me about Dan." They'd celebrated for nine months, until the real party started with his birth. "I would have been happy this time, too."

"JUST PARK THE CAR. Don't stop at the door, boy. I'm no invalid." Uncle Ford's orders bounced around the roof and doors of Dan's car.

Ignoring his uncle, he braked beneath the canopy at the hospital's front door. "I'm stopping here for Aunt Imogen. Will you wait with her while I park?"

"Imogen could best you in a footrace around the parking lot," Uncle Ford said.

"Glad you recognize my talents, Ford. Now get out and let the boy park. Did you bring your cane?"

Dan shot her a grateful glance in the rearview mirror, and she smiled back while Uncle Ford wrestled himself out of the car. He insisted he just used the cane to lure the ladies to his supposedly helpless side.

"We both know I don't need it," he grumbled in what he always assumed was a whisper no one else could hear. People came out of the hospital's vestry to see about the commotion. "Imogen, get out of this car. I'd like to visit my niece before tomorrow morning.''

"Don't mind him." Imogen waved a bottle of vanilla-scented perfume, which she dabbed behind her ears. "He's worried about your mother, but he'd rather snap at us than admit he cares."

Thanks to Aunt Imogen, he was the only guy his age who recognized vanilla at a hundred paces. "I don't mind, but don't go up to her room without me. Okay?''

"I'll hold Ford back, but you hurry." She shoved her perfume back in her purse and followed his uncle to the curb.

Dan parked in the first spot he found and dashed through the lot. Thank God for Aunt Imogen and Uncle Ford. He wouldn't have to talk to his mom with them around. They were still arguing when he joined them.

"Don't tell me not to shout, Imogen. I never shout. Are you suggesting I'm not considerate of sick people?''

"I'm suggesting you put a sock in it before that guard throws us all out.''

Trying not to laugh, Dan herded them toward the elevator. That guard wouldn't tell Ford Talbot to put a sock in anything. Uncle Ford's wild life made him a legend to every man and boy in town.

They crowded into the elevator and Aunt Imogen opened her beaded purse. With pale, pink-tipped fingers, she drew out a small brown paper package.

"Your mother's favorite cookies," she said. "Oatmeal raisin macadamia nut.''

Dan made a face. Worst combination he'd ever tasted. "She'll be glad to see you, Aunt Imogen."

"Watch out your face doesn't freeze like that. I made some chocolate chip for you. Remind me to pack them up before you go over to Ford's tonight." She made a tsking sound. "Chocolate chip. That's a plain cookie."

"Not the way you make them." He meant it. He could earn a fortune off her cookies if he sold them.

Aunt Imogen looked pleased. "You may look like a Palmer, but Cate passed you the Talbot charm."

Yeah? Most of the time he saw himself as a stiff shadow of his inhibited father.

At his mom's room, Uncle Ford used his cane to open her door. His mom was standing at her window. Dan followed his uncle and aunt inside. Just in time to catch the way his mother's bewildered smile lingered on his aunt. When she saw him, her smile faded.

"Dan."

She sounded different. She seemed less worried, but she still looked at him as if she barely recognized him. He'd always wanted her to put a little distance between them, but now, he needed her to know him. Even though he was eighteen—a man—deep in his heart, he wanted his mom.

"I'm glad to see you," she said. "Come in. Let me ask for more chairs. Uncle Ford, take this one." She offered him the only seat in the room, but he pushed it toward Aunt Imogen.

"I'll go to the nurse's station and ask for more. They should have brought more chairs in here anyway. They know you have a big family. Sit down, Imogen.''

''No, I'll go with you.'' She nodded encouragingly toward his mom as she hurried after Uncle Ford. ''Dan and Cate might enjoy some privacy.''

Good thing he *was* a man, or he'd have grabbed Aunt Imogen's skirt as she passed him. Rocking on his heels, he looked at his mom. Tried to think of something worth saying. She limped toward him, and for a second, he thought she was going to try to hug him. Instead, she kept going. He lurched out of her way as she closed the door.

''I have to ask you.'' She held the door shut. ''Why does Aunt Imogen wear a strip of cellophane tape down the middle of her forehead? I swear I saw gold graduation caps and diplomas on this piece.''

Was that all? He shrugged. ''I graduate in three weeks.''

She waited. When he didn't go on, she tossed up her hands in an I-still-don't-get-it gesture.

''Oh, the tape,'' he said. ''She always wears it.'' He put his finger in the middle of his eyebrows and frowned to show her the kind of wrinkles Aunt Imogen was trying to avoid. ''Reminds her not to frown.''

''How old is she?''

''Seventy-something. No one's ever told me. Why?''

She dropped her hands to her sides. ''Well—'' she cleared her throat ''—I shouldn't say this, but she has some wrinkles. And the tape—''

Dan forgot they didn't know each other any more. ''Mom, that's rude.''

She raised both eyebrows. "I guess it was. Sorry."

Just like that, she looked like his mom, except laughter tugged at her mouth, and for no reason he could think of, he laughed with her.

She eased the door open. "She was thoughtful to choose tape to fit your occasion."

"You should see the Santas at Christmas." She laughed again, and he did, too, but he felt guilty about it. Aunt Imogen didn't like to be laughed at.

"I'm glad they left us alone," his mom said. "I was dying to ask, but I didn't want to hurt Aunt Imogen's feelings."

"I think she uses the tape and the hats and stuff to hide how she feels about the gossips in this town. People still spread rumors about that Navy guy."

"Navy guy?" She obviously didn't know. "My whole life is on the tip of my tongue. Not remembering baffles me. I even wondered if I was imagining Aunt Imogen's tape." She tightened the belt at her robe and then offered her hand. "What a relief. Good to see you, Dan."

Dan shook hands with her. "I'm glad to see you, too." For the first time since she'd come out of that coma he meant it. "Mom?"

"Huh?"

He chewed on his lip. He wasn't a guy who clung to his mother, but he'd been so scared she was going to die. "Can I hug you?"

She tilted her head back, startled. "Well," she said, "yes." She opened her arms, but he could see she felt funny about it, too. Then as soon as he put his arms around her, she hugged back. Tight.

"I'm glad you're okay," he said.

"Thanks."

They both moved to neutral corners and avoided looking at each other. But he felt better.

CHAPTER THREE

SHOCKED AT Cate's pregnancy and the fact she'd hidden it, Alan avoided his family that night. He couldn't have hidden his panic at the uncertain future of his marriage, but he realized he had to keep fighting. Dan and Cate and the new baby needed him to save the business and their family.

The next morning, Alan parked in front of Caroline's small cottage. Several miles down the beach from his and Cate's house, the cottage bore the loving stamp of the Talbot women in its neatly maintained appearance and glinting windows. Like all the Talbot homes, the cottage welcomed visitors.

Until today, anyway. He might not be so welcome once he suggested Caroline was neglecting her sister.

He opened the car door and strode up the walk to rap on the door. It swung open. Caroline peered around it and Alan got to the point. "Why haven't you visited Cate?"

"And good morning to you." She stood aside. "Come in, Alan, and tell me what makes you so surly."

Yesterday's news about the baby gave him plenty to be surly about, but he still wouldn't discuss his growing family with Cate's twin. A new thought made him uneasy. As close as the sisters had been, she might already know. He couldn't ask. He didn't want to know if Cate trusted Caroline more than she trusted him.

"Cate needs to see everyone who might help her remember. You didn't go to the hospital yesterday."

"Maybe you didn't notice but she screamed when she looked at her own face after seeing mine."

"She's been there for you, Caroline. All your lives."

"I know. She pretended to be me when I played hooky from school. She helped me run away with my bad husband, and then she picked up the pieces when he left me. She's baby-sat Shelly when my childcare fell through, and she does more than her fair share for Aunt Imogen and Uncle Ford." Caroline paused to draw breath. "None of what she's done changes the fact that my face scares her."

"She sees your face every time she looks in a mirror." He stepped inside the small house. It wasn't so welcoming to a man. Only women lived here, and he felt too large for the narrow hall, the dainty French furniture. "Are you afraid to see her?"

She met his gaze. Not for the first time, this woman who looked so much like his wife but thought so differently disconcerted him. In silence, Caroline led him to the kitchen. She poured a cup of strong black coffee and set it on the counter in front of him.

"I'm terrified. Cate is part of me. We share so many of the same memories I'm not sure who I am without her."

Her frankness only emphasized their serious fix. Caroline had become his friend as he'd fallen in love with her sister. He'd helped her and Shelly when he could, but she'd never confided in him this way.

And now they were going through the same crisis. Who were they when Cate, the glue that had held their family together, no longer knew them?

He closed his eyes. A shout rose in his throat. Pure pain that no one but Cate could alleviate. Only his Cate no longer existed.

"I understand why you're reluctant," he managed to say. "She may not remember you, but she needs you. You are part of each other. You can tell her things about her past that the rest of us don't know."

"I don't know her better than you do, Alan." She took another coffee cup from the cabinet. "I'm only her sister. You're her husband."

Not a very good husband. He'd blamed their uneasiness on the stress of raising a teenager who was about to leave home. He'd assumed they'd find their way back to each other after Dan left.

Not that he'd resented Cate's devotion to their son. They'd both wanted to be better parents than their own. But he'd lost sight of Cate, the woman, in his reliance on her. Over the years, he'd become the provider. She'd been the mom. Had their roles divided them, or had Cate stopped loving him?

"What's on your mind, Alan? Something else is going on." Caroline's conviction reminded him of Cate after she'd seen through all his half truths. "You've never stormed in here before to point out my responsibilities to Cate."

"Help her. Make her remember."

"Make her?" Caroline blanched. "You're thinking she chose to forget? I wonder, too. Who made her so unhappy? You? Me? I've let her take care of me as if she really were older.''

"She is. She takes those thirteen minutes seriously.''

"And twenty-seven seconds.'' Caroline poured coffee in her cup and lifted it to her mouth for a wary sip. "Don't forget those twenty-seven seconds.''

"She never meant to make you think you couldn't take care of yourself.''

"Sometimes I couldn't. I needed her, but I couldn't admit it. I always wanted to prove I knew how to handle my own life.''

Her guilt sounded too familiar. He'd needed Cate to believe he was her knight in shining armor, but he'd tried so hard to be a professional success—and then failed so spectacularly—he'd broken her ability to trust him at all.

Damn it, he'd learn how to win back her faith, but she still needed the rest of her family. "Why don't you take care of her this time?''

She widened her eyes, as if she hadn't thought of the possibilities. That happened when guilt overwhelmed you. "What's to stop me?'' She toasted him with her coffee cup. "I will go. Tonight. Evening visitor's hours.''

He set his own cup on the counter. "I have to go into the office for a few hours. Can you fax me your budget for the medical center interiors?''

"Sure. Why are you working on Sunday, Alan?''

He had no choice. He still had to save the company. Caroline and too many others depended on him for their jobs. "I've spent so much time at the hospital I have to catch up on paperwork. How close are you to the figures we discussed when we started the project? Not over budget anywhere?''

She plucked a pair of glasses from the shelf beside the sink and slid them onto her nose. Cate didn't need glasses. ''I'll get the file now if you want. We're close on window treatments, and I hooked us up with the rugs.''

''Hooked us up?''

She flashed a grin. ''Don't you ever talk to Dan? I worked us a deal.''

Like her, he felt more at ease talking about work, a topic he and Cate rarely discussed. Lately, he'd tended to share tense silence with his wife. Silence couldn't bide easily between two people hiding life-altering secrets.

''I'M DR. DAVIS. I hear you don't remember me.''

Cate looked up from her book, relieved to quit pretending she could concentrate enough to read. A tall woman stood in the doorway, finely dressed in a beige suit that complemented her dark-mocha skin. Her looks were lovely, but the supreme confidence in her eyes brought Cate the deepest sense of assurance she remembered feeling.

''I'm happy to meet you.'' Cate took a get well card from the table and slid it into her book to mark her place. ''Come in.''

The other woman set a file on the nightstand. ''Did you tell Alan about the baby?''

''Yesterday.'' She left out the part where he'd gone and not come back.

''He didn't take it well?'' Dr. Davis reached for

the call button on the cord at Cate's shoulder. "You can't blame him for that?"

"Maybe. Who are you calling?"

"A nurse. I'd like to examine you now that you haven't spotted for several days. Your body has endured a great deal of trauma, and I'd like to make sure the baby's perfectly healthy."

"What do you need me to do?"

"Relax if you can."

Cate tried to disguise her distress. "I'm not sure I could even if I remembered how a pelvic feels."

Dr. Davis laughed. "Good point."

The nurse came, and the doctor began her exam. She seemed dissatisfied with what she found. From her particularly vulnerable position, Cate still tried to be brave. "What?" she asked bluntly.

"Nothing to worry about." Dr. Davis peered over her shoulder at the nurse. "Open Cate's file and remind me of her dates."

The date of Cate's last cycle seemed to make matters worse. Cate fought her increasingly primitive need to remove herself from the doctor's hands. "You're scaring me, and I really need to shove you away."

The doctor straightened, peeling off her gloves. "Don't be afraid. Nothing's wrong, but I need to listen." Taking the stethoscope from around her neck, she placed it all over Cate's belly.

"I think we need an ultrasound."

Cate grabbed her arm, pulling her close with strength that surprised her and the doctor. "You can't hear a heartbeat?"

Humor softened the doctor's wide eyes. "I hear plenty of heartbeats."

Her response made no sense at first. Finally, Cate remembered she was a twin. She dropped back. "Plenty?" she squeaked.

"Just two, but I don't rely on my ears this early on. Why don't we make sure before you pass out?"

"An ultrasound will tell you? Ultrasounds don't lie, do they? I mean I'm not suddenly going to come up with triplets, am I?"

"Try to stay calm. Sudden isn't the way triplets show up." Dr. Davis pulled the sheet up to Cate's waist. "Why don't I use my influence to run the test now?"

Calm? At thirty-eight, with a nearly grown son and a husband she didn't know? "Now would be perfect."

Dr. Davis picked up the large, insulated cup that stood on the nightstand. She shook the cup and then smiled as water and ice sloshed together. "Start drinking this."

LATER THAT EVENING, Cate stared at the ultrasound photo. Two babies. In another twenty-two weeks or so, she'd give birth to twins.

The two small beings on the ultrasound screen had reconnected her to the process of living. She wrapped herself in the happiness she'd felt at watching the two twisting shadows. They needed her, and she resolved to figure out who she was in time to be a good parent to all her children.

And she'd learn to be a wife to her husband. He

wanted their marriage. She must have wanted it, too. Their children deserved two healthy parents.

Someone knocked softly on her door. Cate lifted the top of her table and slid the ultrasound photo inside. "Come in," she called. She smoothed the sheet around her hips and legs and prepared to interrogate her visitor about her past.

Caroline leaned around the edge of the door. Her face still jolted Cate, but another scream seemed inappropriate.

"Do you mind if I join you?" Caroline asked.

"I'm surprised you want to. Come in and let me apologize for the way I acted. I didn't expect to see you in my mirror."

"I shouldn't have run out of here, but I love you Cate. No, don't worry—you know, you used to be better at hiding your feelings—I don't expect you to pretend you feel the way I do, but I want you to depend on me. It's my turn to be the big sister."

"Am I older than you?" Cate asked as Caroline paused to replace a lungful of air.

"By a little more than thirteen minutes, but I've needed you more than you ever needed me." She stopped again, and her face flushed a deep red. "I used to wonder if you wished you didn't have a twin, and now you don't."

"Well, don't sound sad. You're about to settle all your debts. I need a crash course in my own history."

Caroline's instant regret almost made Cate smile. "What can I tell you?" Caroline asked in a wavering tone.

With her new deadline, she had no time for subtlety. First things first. "Why are you so reluctant to talk to me?"

"I'm embarrassed. You rescued me from every jam I ever got myself into. I can't repay you for—"

Cate interrupted. "I know you all loved me, because my close call seems to have turned me into a saint." Saints held no charm for her. She didn't trust the tale, and she needed facts. "Tell me the bad stuff, too."

"What bad stuff?"

"We're sisters. You must have helped me as much as I helped you."

A deeper blush darkened Caroline's high cheekbones. Cate lifted her fingertips to her own face as her twin went on. "You never needed help."

Not true. She probably just hadn't asked for it. "I need help now. Dr. Barton implied our family—the Talbots—are…"

Caroline's discomfort eased as Cate trailed off. "Notorious?" she suggested.

Cate nodded. "I know our parents are deceased, but what happened to them?"

"Dad met Mom in the Navy. They were both intelligence officers, and apparently, the only thing they loved more than imminent danger was each other. They sent us here to live with Aunt Imogen when we were five. The Navy stationed them in Turkey, I think. Some remote place, but it was only their first isolated duty station. They liked the life so much they never came back."

"Never?" Such parenting alarmed her. She felt for the two small girls they'd been. "We never saw them?"

"They came for visits. Brief ones." Caroline shook her head. "But we missed them so much it was easier when they stayed away. When they tried to leave we cried—well, I cried. You pretended you didn't care."

"I did?" She couldn't picture herself as such a tough kid.

Caroline pulled up a chair and made herself comfortable. "Always. You didn't want anyone getting close enough to see how much you hurt." She stopped, seemingly amazed, and reached for Cate's water. "Do you mind if I drink some? It's hot outside."

"Go ahead."

"I never realized you were pretending until I said that just now. I always envied you because you didn't seem to need anyone, but you—"

Cate found she didn't want to know what Caroline thought of her inner workings. Plain facts mattered more. Maybe later she'd be willing to discuss her private thoughts with her sister. "How did they die?"

Caroline's expression clouded. She drank more water and set it back on the table. "In a car accident. They were driving to Nice to fly home for our high school graduation, and they took a curve too quickly. We think they had an argument before they left their hotel because the management billed us for damages."

Cate stared at her for a second and tried not to laugh at the morbid picture.

"I know." Caroline shook her head. "Aunt Imogen's attorney pointed out the tactless nature of their claims, but they still wanted to be paid. My God, how we missed them."

"I missed them, too?"

"You wouldn't talk about it, but someone plants flowers on their graves and keeps them tended. Usually, when I go out to the cemetery, something new is blooming. You must be the gardener, but you always said you didn't know anything about the plants. Aunt Imogen has a killer thumb, and Uncle Ford's still too mad at Dad for dying to do something so kind."

Sadness surprised Cate, knotting uncomfortable tears in the back of her throat. She'd like to see that cemetery, but she had to go by herself the first time. After that, she'd ask Caroline to help her with the flowers. She moved on to their aunt and uncle. "How about Aunt Imogen and Uncle Ford? Dan told me a story about Aunt Imogen's Navy man."

"I don't believe she ever had an affair, if that's what you mean, but like you, she keeps her feelings private. Maybe she'll tell you about him if you ask her in your present condition."

Cate grinned at Caroline's prim tone. "I wondered why she wasn't married, but it seemed rude to ask. And Uncle Ford?"

"He's never made conventional choices. None of us was conventional except you." Caroline swallowed. "Actually, no one was ever sure if Grandma and Grandpa actually married each other. I mean we have a marriage certificate, but the story is, they bought it on the boardwalk in New Jersey."

"What?"

"Don't worry. You and Alan are legal, and you've

never taken a wrong step. You've walked a tight, straight line to give Dan a sense of family you and I didn't get. You've made him strong.''

Tight, straight line? The walls started to close in again.

''In fact, you and Alan have given Shelly a good example. I want her to know someone in our family can make a marriage stick.''

A lasting marriage hardly equated with a wife who'd hidden her pregnancy. How had Alan responded to setting examples? What had she thought about such a responsibility?

''I need to ask you about Alan's father, too. Uncle Ford mentioned that I wouldn't be seeing him inside these four walls.'' She glanced quickly around the room. ''What did he mean? I don't feel comfortable asking Alan.''

''Why?''

Because she didn't trust their relationship. ''Alan's already stressed. I don't want to add to his trouble, but he's— Richard's his name?''

''Yeah, Richard.''

''He's family, too. I'd better know about him.''

''Richard has his quirks.'' Caroline grabbed the water again. ''I don't want to talk about him, either. He raised Alan alone after Alan's mom left when Alan was about ten. I'm not sure what went wrong.''

''I thought you and I were close.''

''We were.''

''I sure hid a lot from you.''

''Just the important stuff,'' Caroline said with a trace of impatience. ''I've never understood what went on between Alan and Richard, and you never told me anything. Of course there was gossip. I've heard Alan did a lot of the stuff fathers are supposed to do for their children, like laundry and cooking. I know Richard had a drinking problem. You and Alan both tried to pretend Richard was a better father than I think he was.''

Appalled and heartbroken for her husband, Cate tried to take this information in. ''Why would we cover for him?''

''Maybe for Dan, or maybe you thought he'd remind me of Ryan, my own runaway spouse. You'll have to ask Alan—or maybe Richard. He's getting married this summer. He must have finally put his first wife behind him.'' Caroline reached for her hand. ''I haven't helped you. You know my worst fears, but I only know hints of yours.''

Cate made herself accept her sister's touch. Dr. Davis and Dr. Barton had both touched her in comfort, and she hadn't minded. Family mattered more. Accepting affection she couldn't return felt false, but she wanted to love her sister so she let her hand rest in Caroline's.

''I have to ask you another question you won't want to answer.'' She felt disloyal to Alan after what Caroline had said about Richard. Imagining her husband as a lost little boy, forced to grow up, hurt her. She had to ask her sister about the state of their marriage, because she wasn't sure he'd tell her the truth. If he'd persuaded her to go along with shielding his father, he must be used to pretending things were ''normal.'' ''Were Alan and I happy?''

Caroline jerked her fingers back. ''How would I know?''

Cate held her twin's so familiar gaze with sheer will. "You're my sister. I took you at your word when you promised I could depend on you."

Caroline looked as if she'd like to run for her life. "You would no more have told me about problems between you and Alan than you would have hired a plane to list them in the sky."

"I have to know."

"You aren't yourself."

"I'm afraid not. I don't trust the way people describe me so far. I was stuffy."

"Not stuffy. Kind."

"So much circumspection sounds unnatural." Cate tucked her sheet around her waist. A walk down the hospital hall might clear her muzzy head, but weakness in her legs, combined with the deep cut on her thigh held her prisoner, and Caroline had backed away when she'd needed her most. "Thanks for talking. I appreciate your effort."

"Wait." Her expression dogged, Caroline propped one elbow on the edge of Cate's bed. "Let me try again. Alan came to my house this morning, and he insisted I see you."

Cate crossed her arms. She still possessed enough of her infamous self-sufficiency to resent Alan's intervention.

"Hold on, Cate. He wanted to make sure I took care of you."

If he knew she needed help, why had he stayed away last night? The obvious answer. She'd dropped a bomb on his head. He needed time to reconcile himself. Not the most romantic tactic, but if he showed up again soon, she'd try to understand. "Alan and I aren't your responsibility."

"Listen to me. You have to listen if you ask for advice. I don't think he'd have come to me if he didn't care." Caroline fluffed her hair. "Why are we talking about this? He loves you. He's been crazy since that car hit you."

"He doesn't act like a man in love. He acts like something's wrong."

"I noticed, but I don't believe your marriage went bad."

Cate plucked at a loose thread on her sheet's hem. "I'm glad my marriage comforts you, but I'd love to know how I felt about it."

"Yeah." Caroline sounded unsure.

And she didn't even know about the twins.

AGAIN, Alan stared at Cate's door. Someone had printed her name on a small, square whiteboard beside the metal doorframe. He brushed away a smear at the end of the *r* in Palmer. Then he went inside.

Favoring her injured leg, his wife turned from the window.

"Cate." He'd expected her to be in bed.

"I almost stopped hoping you'd come, but I didn't want to be flat on my back when we talked." A smile hovered at the corner of her mouth.

He knew that sweet shape as well as he knew his own face. He'd kissed that mouth, frowned at that mouth, dreaded seeing it thin in anger, and waited with held breath for it to smile. A real smile—not like her smile now.

"You knew you could expect me?" Somewhere

inside her remained the wife who'd trusted him to take care of her.

"If you'd stayed away again tonight, I'd have understood you'd made your decision."

No, this Cate wasn't the wife he'd lived with for twenty years. His Cate had never tested him.

"I'm glad I passed."

"I didn't think of it as a trial. When you didn't call or come back yesterday, I assumed you had to think about where we stood."

A cold fist squeezed his heart. "Is that what you've been doing?"

She shook her head. Her bright hair fell over her shoulder, tempting him to slide possessive fingers through the strands before she slipped away from him forever.

"How could I decide anything without talking to you?" she asked in a low voice. Behind her, the night sky perfectly framed her pale skin and tense silhouette.

Her open gaze gave him hope for the first time since she'd run from the office.

"I want to go on together," he said. "You're my wife."

"Don't put it that way, Alan." Emotionally, she distanced herself from him. "I don't want us to stay together because we happen to be married."

"I get the idea you don't want me to say I love you."

Those words didn't belong between them since he'd hidden the business trouble and she'd concealed their baby from him.

She limped toward him, but she stopped beside her

bed and flexed her fingers on the lip of her table. From her knuckles to her nails, her skin faded to palest white.

"I know something's wrong, and saying you love me would only alarm me now." She lifted her chin. "You could tell me what's wrong."

No, he couldn't. It wasn't just that her injuries had given him time to win her back. He'd never been good at admitting she'd always be his deepest need. He'd shown her in the only way he'd known how, providing a good life for her and their son.

From now on, he'd pay more attention to her, become the husband she wanted. His father's decades-old advice rang in his ears. "Give your wife the good things in life. Provide, and provide well, or she'll find a man who can."

"I still don't know why I decided not to tell you about the baby." She slid her gaze away from him. "Don't we need to know why?"

"One day I hope you'll tell me."

Frustration tightened her mouth, but she controlled it. "Tonight I have to tell you I had a test today."

"What kind of a test? Is the baby all right?" Fear nearly dropped him to his knees. Even if he couldn't provide for this child as he had for Dan, he'd love the new baby. He'd be the best father his resources allowed.

"I've scared you again. I'm sorry." Cate hurried around the bed and reached for his hand.

Her fingers felt vulnerable in his, but he couldn't let go. "I should be taking care of you," he said.

"I should have found a better way to say this. Dr.

Davis did an exam today and discovered we're having twins.''

"Twins?''

She nodded. Seconds passed. He didn't know how to respond to twins. The cost, the timing. She'd never understand his panic. Distance came into her eyes. By not answering, he was losing her, the woman he'd loved since he'd learned to love, and the woman he no longer knew.

He threw a longing look at her chair. "Do you mind if I sit?''

She grinned, and he sat without her consent. Was she laughing at him? She didn't respect him for sitting?

"Not that I mind,'' he said. "The twins. I don't mind the twins.''

"You don't have to prove how tough you are. If I hadn't been lying down when Dr. Davis told me, I might have fallen.''

"Twins.''

"Will you tell me how you really feel?''

"Startled.'' He tried hard to think how she'd want him to answer. How he should answer as a decent human being who wanted his wife back, who loved the child they'd already created, and who knew he could love two more when the shock wore off. "How are you?'' he asked her.

She actually seemed to find his lack of assurance comforting. She relaxed her tense stance.

"Glad to see you.'' She squeezed his hand once and then let go to scoot onto the edge of her bed and straighten her leg. "I couldn't tell anyone else before I told you.''

He should be the first to know. He tugged at the hem of her robe. "Do you feel anything for me?"

Her expression was solemn, but full of regret. "I feel responsible."

He let her go. "I don't know what I think about responsible."

She folded her hands. "Let's just be honest and see what kind of relationship we can salvage."

"I want a marriage." He still didn't mention the business. Eventually, she'd understand. Between the twins and her memory loss, he couldn't add to the pressure on her.

He'd been afraid she'd leave if he admitted his lie about the company had caused all their problems. Now, he kept the embezzlement to himself because he wanted to protect his wife and their unborn children. This time, he was right to try to protect her.

CHAPTER FOUR

CATE HARDLY SLEPT the night before she was scheduled to go home. The next day's possibilities ran furiously around her mind. With Caroline's help she'd already begun to collect clues about her life. Now, to piece her past and present into one cohesive puzzle.

Lights from the nighttime traffic danced on her walls as crazily as her thoughts until she began to pick out repeating patterns that calmed her. An occasional jet roared overhead, rousing her when she was getting sleepy. She finally dozed off just before dawn.

A crack of thunder brought her straight up in bed. Its rumble slowly faded, and an early-summer downpour sheeted rain across her window.

She woke each morning, thinking the same question. Would she remember?

Not today. She sensed everything she needed to know, hanging just beyond her reach. No amount of determination brought her answers.

Impatiently, she slid out of bed, but the moment she was vertical, nausea gripped her. She clung to the table, waiting for her stomach to settle. Dr. Davis had suggested saltine crackers, but they only seemed to make her queasier.

Pushing herself to use her weakened legs, she traveled from bureau to bed to pack the small, violently floral overnight bag Aunt Imogen had brought her.

By the time she snapped the catch on her bag, the rain had begun to ease off. Cate perched on the side of her bed to wait for Alan or Dr. Barton. After a few long seconds, she crossed the room to open her door. Then she hobbled back toward her chair. Footsteps in the hall made her look over her shoulder.

Alan stopped in the doorway. His brooding expression suggested strength. His sheer size backed up the claim. He looked from her to her bag. "I came early to help you."

At the slight reproach in his tone, she wished she'd waited. She'd already learned he showed his feelings through service. "The rain woke me early." She pointed toward the hall he dwarfed with his height. "Is Dr. Barton out there?"

Shaking his head, he turned to peer down the hall to his right. His white oxford shirt lovingly caressed the strong, straining muscles of his upper back. Bracing his hand against the door frame, he twisted to look the other way. The worn shirt stretched almost out of the narrow waist of his jeans. Another shake of his head, and rich, dark strands of his hair rubbed his tanned neck. Did he know how good he looked?

"I was hoping Barton might have signed your release papers already."

"No." She tried to sound normal, but hollow, electric bursts of attraction came as a relief. If she planned to stay married, wanting her husband had to be a plus. "Do we have to wait?"

"You're all set?"

She nudged the bag. "I've packed everything except for the magazines and books you all brought me. The book cart lady suggested giving them to the other patients."

"Good idea." Stepping back from the door frame, he looked a touch uneasy. "Why don't you sit and rest your leg? I'll look for Dr. Barton." Alan paused. "Dan's waiting for us in the parking lot."

"Dan?" That put a crimp in her plan. She wasn't sure how she'd react to a home she didn't remember, and she didn't want to risk disappointing her son. They'd formed a tentative bond that day he'd explained about Aunt Imogen's tape.

"He thought we should take you home as a family." Alan paused, his gaze pensive. "If he needs family time because he's been worried about you, I say we all go home together."

She eyed him carefully. They were both Dan's parents, but Alan knew him better. She thought back to the day Caroline had told her she didn't share personal troubles. Her instincts hadn't changed, but she had to take a chance for Dan. "What if he expects me to be comfortable at home? I won't know the house. I don't have a clue about his life or what kind of mother I've been."

Alan tapped the door frame, his gaze bemused. "You don't have to give Dan much. He just wants you home." His deep voice drew a shiver down her spine. Left unspoken in his husky reassurance was a hint he wanted her there, too. "Maybe you should try not to think of Dan as a child. He's trying hard to become an adult."

Dr. Barton appeared behind him, carrying the clipboard that held her chart. Alan moved out of his way, but the doctor stopped, clearly discerning stress in the air.

"Am I interrupting?"

Cate shook her head, still digesting everything Alan had said. "Can I go?"

"Don't rush me. How do you feel? Any morning sickness? How's the leg?"

"My leg's fine, but I feel sick as a dog."

"Sometimes morning sickness lasts and lasts in a pregnancy." He flipped up a page on her chart. "I see the nurse liked the look of your wound last night."

Cate picked up her bag. Alan started toward her, but Dr. Barton stopped him.

"What's your hurry? Cate has to wait for a wheelchair, and you might want to bring your car around. I'll walk out with you." He scrawled notes on the chart. "Cate, I believe I covered all your instructions last night?"

She nodded. "But you can tell me anything you want to say to Alan. I'm not an invalid."

The older man laughed. "You're getting paranoid." His bland smile annoyed her. "Once you're home, take it easy. If you want to exercise, walk on the beach, but take water along. I don't want you to get dehydrated. Call me if you have any questions. Oh, and Dr. Davis asked me to remind you about your appointment with her."

"I have the card she gave me."

"Fine." He capped his pen and held the chart to his chest as he extended his hand. "Good luck to you, Cate Palmer."

She ignored his hand, forgave him for his chauvinistic urge to talk about her with Alan and hugged him. "Thank you for everything."

Alan's bewildered gaze told her she rarely hugged spontaneously. She wasn't surprised after her talk with Caroline, but she didn't like thinking of herself as a woman who withheld affection.

After a brisk squeeze, the doctor released her and turned to Alan. "She's going to be fine. Better than ever. Let's go. I'll tell the nurses you're ready, Cate."

They left, and Cate felt painfully alone. What kind of woman would be better than ever because she hugged her doctor? A frightened one who wasn't sure people would return her affection? Cate shook her head and chose not to be frightened anymore.

STRIDING BESIDE Dr. Barton, Alan glanced back at Cate's door. Her concern for Dan made him feel even guiltier about their fiscal jam. He had to fix it before she found out anything was wrong. He'd made his decision to help her, not to hurt her. He hoped he wasn't kidding himself when he tried to believe she'd forgive him.

"Alan, slow down. You don't have to worry about Cate." Dr. Barton hurried, the sound of his footsteps ricocheting off the pale-blue walls.

Alan's heart thudded in time, but he shortened his stride. "You don't understand."

"I do. She's not the wife you knew, but she's charming, and she wants her life back. She'll benefit by returning to her old habits."

Barton had to be right, and yet... "Is she more likely to remember at home?"

"Seeing the places and people she loved may stimulate her memory, but I can't promise you. Just take good care of her. If she seems down or upset, and you don't know what to do for her, persuade her to call me."

Alan nodded. "As long as she tells me how she feels."

"You'll know. She isn't a complete stranger. The Cate we know is still inside her. Are you afraid you can't wait for her?"

What if he didn't know the real Cate? Maybe she'd never told him how she truly felt. How much had they hidden from each other? Alan lifted his eyebrows. "I'll wait." What else could he do? Except patience had never been his strong suit. "Cate's my wife."

Dr. Barton's thin smile implied he shared Cate's opinion of that statement. What did they expect? He wanted the Cate he'd married. Did that mean he wasn't a good man?

A good man's wife would have told him about their unborn twins. She would have trusted him enough to share news that must have shocked her.

The day of the accident Cate had been angry enough, disappointed enough—maybe even hurt enough to believe he had no right to know about his own children. Why hadn't he realized then how far apart they'd grown?

"Alan, I wonder if I should let you leave without talking to someone. You wouldn't be normal if you weren't unsettled about your future with Cate."

"We have to make a future. Can a stranger tell me how to do that?"

Big talk from the little man who'd been the last to know.

Alan punched the elevator button. His lie about the business was no foundation for a new life. But he cared for his family, and he'd provide for his wife.

Bracing himself to start a future he only half trusted, Alan shook the other man's hand. "I'm grateful for the care you've given Cate."

"My pleasure. I'll say goodbye here because I'm in the middle of rounds, but remember what I told you."

"I will. I'm sorry if I've been abrupt."

"You have a right." The doctor pulled his pen out of his pocket. "You know my phone number, Alan?"

He frowned. "I can find it. Why?"

"If you need to talk, call me. Don't fume about your problems alone. Dan and Imogen and Ford depend on you as much as Cate does."

Barton's grasp of his weakness made him smile. "Good advice. I'll remember."

The elevator doors jittered open, and he stepped inside. He avoided looking at Dr. Barton as he pushed the lobby button. The elevator jerked once before it began to descend.

The doctor might be right. He wasn't himself, but his resolve built with every inch of space he put between himself and Cate's room. Never, in all their marriage, had she leaned on him easily. She'd always held parts of herself back as if she had to force herself to share. Now, with their past and her memories beyond her reach, even she needed him. If she leaned on him, he'd support her.

He stepped off the elevator in the lobby to find Dan sprawled in a big chair. "I thought you wanted to wait in the car," Alan said. "Why didn't you come up?"

Faint color dusted Dan's fuzz-covered, youthful cheeks. He shrugged with his mother's reserve. "I thought you'd want some privacy. Besides you had to come through here sooner or later. Where's Mom?"

"Waiting for a wheelchair. Why don't we get the car?"

Dan tossed him the keys.

Alan caught them. "You can drive if you want, son."

"I always make Mom nervous."

"You're a sensitive guy." Alan garnered a sheepish grin from his son. Side by side, they pushed through the glass doors into light, warm rain and a rumble of dying thunder. "Where did you park the car?"

"This way," Dan said and started toward the parking lot.

As he followed, Alan resisted an urge to tell his loose-limbed son not to slouch. He'd parked Cate's SUV in a spot not too far from the entrance. They got in and Alan started the engine.

He parked beneath the canopy at the hospital entrance. A nurse pushed Cate through the doors in a wheelchair. His wife's stiff posture suggested she remained a woman who accepted assistance only under duress.

"Boy, she's pissed about the wheelchair," Dan said.

"Have you ever said the word *pissed* to Mom or me before?" Alan opened his door. "Don't say it around her."

He circled the SUV. Rain had turned the air into a humid sauna that began to curl Cate's hair. Searching the buildings around them, Cate let him take her arm as she rose.

The nurse nodded. "You'll find Dr. Barton's instructions on that paperwork I gave you, Mrs. Palmer. Don't hesitate to call us if we can answer any questions."

"I think we'll be fine. Are you ready, Alan?"

He opened the door and helped her inside the front seat. When he reached for the seat belt, Cate dropped her hand on his.

"I remember how these work," she said tightly. She twisted to look over the seat. "Morning, Dan."

"Hi, Mom. How do you feel?"

"Perfect. I'm glad you came with your dad."

"Me, too."

Alan quickly joined them. He met Cate's nervous smile. At least he knew the world they were starting over in. The hospital was the only place she knew.

Her blouse trembled over her breasts. Her heart must be running like a fugitive train. "Have you guys eaten breakfast?" she asked.

"Are you hungry?" Grabbing a chance to do something tangible for her, Alan turned the key in the ignition again. "We'll take you to your favorite diner. Can you miss a couple more hours of school, Dan?"

''I'm starving,'' he said, as if that answered the question.

''Sounds like a yes to me.'' Alan pushed some telepathic reassurance Cate's way.

Her gaze lingered on him, a soft touch he'd missed as he'd miss food and drink and air to breathe. He turned his attention back to the road, the better to avoid killing his growing family.

Maybe the diner would spark a memory for Cate. It was, after all, where they'd shared their first meal together.

WIND SLAMMED RAIN against the windows, and Dan stared at the backs of his parents' heads, pretending he didn't see how scared they were. He'd like to tell them to cut the crap and act normal, but if he did, they'd work harder to convince him nothing was wrong. His mom and dad never admitted they had problems. They seemed to think his brain might explode if someone told the truth about their happy little family.

His mom went around fed up half the time, and his dad thought he was Captain Fix-it. Divorce hung in the air. He no longer doubted his mother and father would split up. Mom couldn't pick his dad out of a police line up. How could she love him?

And Dad. Big bad Palmer Construction came first. He'd kill to protect the business he'd built from scratch with his first set of tools and an ancient backhoe. How many times had Dan heard that story?

His mom turned in her seat again. ''What does this diner serve?'' she asked, her voice lighter than air.

Why couldn't she just be real? Like that day at the

hospital with Aunt Imogen and her tape? She'd talked to him that day, as if they were friends. If she was going to make a big deal out of being his mom, he'd go back to school.

He ground his teeth as he tried to answer, ignoring the spurt of fear for her that made him so angry. "It's called The Captain's Lady, and they serve the usual stuff for breakfast. Grits, eggs, pork products." Dan caught his father's stern expression in the rearview mirror and moderated his belligerent tone. "Still love bacon, Mom?"

She leaned toward him, her surprised smile startling him. "I do," she said. "Bacon, mmm."

"Even the hospital's version?" his dad asked.

"Are you kidding?" She turned to him, looking young. "They don't acknowledge bacon exists. Caroline and Aunt Imogen smuggled in a BLT. The tomatoes came from Aunt Imogen's greenhouse. She said the tomato plants in the garden are blooming already."

"You remember the garden?" Dan's voice squeaked with hope. He cleared his throat and concentrated on achieving a deeper tone. "Aunt Imogen loves having you work with her."

"Caroline said she had a killer thumb. I thought that meant she wasn't a good gardener."

His dad laughed. "That's why she likes your help."

Cate shrugged. "She told me everything about it, from tomatoes to cornstalks and all the organic fertilizer Polly provides. She gives an amazing fertilizer speech." She tossed Dan a wicked grin. "Do you suppose Aunt Imogen will make me wear one of the hats?''

"How do you know about the hats?" He'd thought she'd pined away in her hospital bed, waiting for her memory to come back. Someone must have talked.

"Another chat with Caroline," she said. "I hear you've been walking Polly for Aunt Imogen."

"I don't wear the hat, okay?"

"Okay." This teasing glance didn't belong to his mom. Some other woman had snatched her body. "But I heard Aunt Imogen requires the wearing of the hat. She must have made you the exception. I'll ask her why when I see her."

"You do that." Okay, his mom was a pod person now, but he couldn't hold back a grudging laugh. He'd always wanted her to be his friend. Just not this friendly.

Suddenly she straightened. "Look at that." She pointed through his father's window, her face reminding him of the time his cousin Shelly had stumbled into the locker room. The whole time he was shoving her out, she'd claimed she didn't know "golf guys" changed after a match.

Instead of sweaty guys switching from khakis to normal clothes, the ocean grabbed his mother's attention. At the tail end of the storm, waves slammed across the sand onto rocks that bordered the sidewalk.

"Stop the car, Alan." She leaned into his dad's shoulder. She was wearing a short-sleeved sweater, and her arm looked thinner.

Could she be sick on top of this amnesia thing?

Naturally, they'd hide it from him. He was "too young" to understand real bad news.

His dad hadn't stopped the car. "What about the rain, Cate? You don't want to get out?"

"I want to see the ocean. Please stop, Alan."

The second his dad parked at the curb his mom jumped out. Dan and his father sat in silence that was thick enough to cut.

"She's not her old self, is she Dad?"

"Not yet. How about you? How are you handling the changes in her?"

"I'm eighteen."

"Huh?"

"Not a baby. Don't pretend I don't get it."

"If you understand, you're a better man than I."

He meant it as a joke, but it wasn't the kind of joke they usually made. Together, they stared through the window at his mom.

The wind tossed her hair straight up into the air. She lifted her face, as if she were sniffing the ocean.

Whitecapped waves churned up blue-gray water. Low fog shortened the horizon, but the ocean looked exactly as it had during every storm of his life.

It hypnotized his mom.

Finally, she turned her head toward the wildlife sanctuary. Those trees looked taller and greener than he remembered.

Jeez.

When his Dad got out, Dan opened his door, not too sure what else his mother could change for him.

Then she moved again. Using both hands to brace herself, she leaned over the sidewalk railing and pointed her body toward the ocean.

His dad eased behind her and dropped his hands on her shoulders. He curled his fingers slowly around her arms as if he expected her to push him away.

His mother turned to his father. The wind pushed her sweater against her body and outlined the curve of her stomach. A paunch.

She'd never had one before. In fact, she'd lost weight since her accident, but her stomach looked huge.

He might not be the most observant guy on earth, but he'd seen enough pregnant girls at school to recognize the shape.

"Mom?"

Absorbed in each other, his parents ignored him.

A baby explained a lot. His mom's recent astounding ability to throw up for no apparent reason. The tension that had filled his house for the past few months.

The nearly silent arguments they never thought he'd heard. They'd argued more often in the weeks before his mother got hurt. How long had they known about this new kid?

"*Mom.*"

And they turned.

He opened his mouth to ask what the hell were they thinking, but his voice wouldn't work. Who needed a baby? Damn fine graduation present.

"You're pregnant." His accusation shamed him almost as much as the prospect of what his friends would say. Couldn't his mom and dad have waited until everyone went away to college?

"Dan, I—we meant to tell you." His mom broke away from his dad, but he spun out of her reach.

"I'm going to school," he said.

"Dan," his father barked as if he were still twelve years old. "Talk to us."

Dan turned on his heel. What were they? Blind? Even at eighteen a guy didn't want people to know his parents had sex. He had a right to complain.

"You want to talk? Fine. When did you ask me if I wanted a kid around?"

CHAPTER FIVE

DAN SPRINTED UP the sidewalk in the direction they'd come from. Helplessly, Cate turned to Alan. His disturbed gaze made her even more worried about their son.

"Let's go after him," she said.

He hesitated, his mouth tight. "We should give him time. If we drag him back, we'll be lucky if he grunts at us." He took her hands and flicked a brief, perturbed glance toward the ocean behind her. "You're soaking wet. Let me take you home, and I'll pick Dan up after school."

"He left his books in the car. I saw them on the back seat. Are you sure he's going to school?"

Alan urged her back to the vehicle. "Don't borrow trouble."

His abrupt tone shut her out, and she resented his high-handedness. "You and I share responsibility for Dan," she reminded him. "Doing nothing can't be right."

"Try to trust me. I know him, and you don't right now. I'll take care of him."

"What if you're wrong?"

"I'm not wrong. Let me take you home."

She followed him to the car, her heart and her gaze lingering on the boy who hadn't yet reached the top of the hill. He rounded the curve in the road above them without looking back, and she lifted her shoulder to try to brush the rain off her face.

"I wish I hadn't made you stop," she said.

"He's embarrassed because we had sex, Cate."

She stopped where she stood, appalled, and Alan widened his eyes at her.

"I'd have felt the same when I was his age."

He didn't understand. What distracted her was trying to picture a world in which she had sex with Alan—made love with Alan.

The rain blurred her vision as she looked him up—up a lean, strong chest and broad shoulders. She looked down his narrow waist and long legs that stretched the faded denim of his jeans taut.

"Does that picture in your head do anything for you?" His thready voice seduced her, but his straight, thinned mouth kept his own desires a secret.

She tried to put herself in his shoes. His wife of twenty years had forgotten him. His son, who'd stepped out of character to ask for a family homecoming, disliked the idea of becoming a big brother at eighteen. Alan's family had changed entirely in the past three weeks.

Her head began to spin. Would he want her to be attracted to him, or would he want them to get to know each other again? She couldn't guess, but he was still waiting for her answer.

"The idea of intimacy with you unsettles me," she said.

He hunched his shoulders. "Lie to me once in a while, Cate." He curved his mouth in a self-conscious grin. "I can take it."

His words and his tone only strengthened her physical awareness of him, but thinking of a stranger as a lover felt a little wicked.

His sun-darkened face and arms made her wonder if his tan ran beneath his shirt. It was only May. Caroline and Aunt Imogen had told her he worked at all his building sites.

He released her hands and walked ahead of her to open the car door. "I'll make you breakfast at home." He waited.

Cate looked one last time at the now empty sidewalk. What had they done to their child?

She went slowly to the car, but paused with the open door between her and Alan. He couldn't know what trusting anyone cost her.

"Tell me he'll be all right." Her depth of need surprised her. Terribly aware of the wall between her past and her present, she didn't want Dan to pay for mistakes she might have made.

Alan's expression softened, and he touched his fingertips to her cheek. "I'll make sure he's all right."

She caught her breath. She wasn't asking him to let her perch on the sidelines. "Dan needs us both. I need you to help me be his mother again."

Insight deepened his gaze. He nodded, and their emotional connection became as tangible as the warmth of his skin against hers. "We'll make sure," he modified.

She caught his wrist and absorbed the feel of rough hair beneath her palm. His effort to understand drew her closer to him than she'd meant to go. His scent wrapped her in a fantasy of marriage with a sensual, safe stranger.

"Dan is worried about his family," Alan said. "He'll be fine if you and I are all right."

She laughed. So much for hearts and flowers and daydreams. Her heartbeat slowed appropriately. She hoped he wasn't always this practical.

ALAN STOLE a glance at Cate. The tip of her nose peeked out of the fall of her hair. If she was still worried, she hid it in a close study of the beach cottages they passed on their way home.

They might survive this crisis after all. She'd asked him to help her enter her life again, and he felt stronger because Cate needed him.

As he turned up their driveway, she drew in a quick breath and pointed to the tall, narrow white house they'd restored together. It was just home to him, or would be now that his wife was sharing it with him again. Through Cate's eyes, he saw how the bright-pink wild, rambling roses had grown to tumble across the front lawn. Bronze daylilies crowded the door.

He stopped the car. "It's beautiful." The unfamiliar word felt strange in his mouth.

Cate's hair whispered against the seat as she turned to him. "You sound as if you're seeing it for the first time."

"Maybe not the first time, but I've taken it for granted. You're in this house, the part of you I can't forget." His loving wife who'd scrubbed every separate pane of glass, who'd scraped and shaped the old plaster, who'd painted and repainted walls until she'd pronounced them perfect.

"The part you wish would remember you?" Cate prompted.

"I guess that depends on why you forgot."

"Dr. Barton didn't talk to you about shock and the amount of blood I lost?" She sounded as if she suspected the doctor might have given her a different story.

"That's what he told me." He hastened to relieve her understandable fear. "But I've researched memory loss on the Internet. I know about stress. What if Barton's wrong, and you forgot because you don't want to remember?"

"Tell me what stress I was under."

Annoyed with himself, he reached for the remote control attached to the visor above the windshield. He pressed the button that opened her side of the garage. His truck and Dan's car were parked in the other two bays.

"The usual stress. Dan's about to leave for college. You've never been home without a job of some sort, whether it was school or taking care of Dan." Another stressor occurred to him. "And you're pregnant, but I didn't know about that."

She clasped her hands in her lap. Her gaze rode him hard as he pulled into the garage.

"Why didn't I tell you?" she asked. "I can't believe I would have chosen to try to replace Dan. And I don't think I would have let myself get pregnant without your knowledge."

He tightened his hands on the steering wheel. Her tone asked him to let her off the hook. "You stopped using the Pill last year. We must have made a mistake. Don't waste time worrying about why you didn't tell me. We'll deal with the answers when they come.''

Cate slid her hand beneath the weight of her hair, leaning her nape into the palm of her hand. He rubbed his own hands together, remembering the soft texture of those dark red strands against his bare skin.

"Sometimes," she said, "I feel as if you know something you aren't telling me. You don't have to protect me. I'm not fragile.''

He didn't answer. He couldn't lie to her outright. "Alan?''

Looking at her, he knew his eyes begged her to take him on faith. She nodded slowly.

"Let's start our life again," she said.

Brave words. In the past weeks, he'd struggled each day for a respectable measure of courage. Hers came from sources he'd underestimated. Nodding, he pulled into the garage.

They stopped and Cate opened her door. Her leg seemed to give as she climbed out. Watching her grab for support, he felt as he had watching Dan run up the sidewalk away from them. He ought to do something before the worst happened.

"Wait, Cate. Let me help you.''

"I'm fine." She waited for strength to return to her injured thigh.

He got out and opened the back of the SUV to get her bag. As she pressed her hands to the car, her nervousness bounced off the walls.

"Over here." He opened the door and waited for her to precede him down the vine-covered, latticed walkway that led to the kitchen. Her intense concentration drew him, but he tried not to watch her. The last thing she needed was to feel like a bug under his magnifying glass.

"I'm home," she said.

He hadn't expected her to think of their house as her home already. His own legs threatened to give.

Cate flashed an apologetic glance. "I keep repeating that in my head. I thought I might be more convinced if I said the words out loud."

Reality again. He was starting to dislike it. "Do you feel up to exploring?"

"I can't wait." She plucked the keys from his hand. "Which one?"

"The brass one next to the car key."

She opened the door and walked inside ahead of him. Two years ago he'd insisted they renovate the kitchen. She stopped now at the butcher block island and revolved in a slow circle, bemused at the stainless steel fixtures, all state-of-the-art, all sturdy and useful.

"Why does this place look like a restaurant?"

He almost dropped her bag. "That's what you said the first time you saw it."

She turned her head so fast her hair swung beneath her chin. "Sorry. Am I insulting you?"

He shook his head. "I talked you into these appliances to make your life easier. You refused to hire a maid service to help you."

"Help me what?"

"Take care of the house and Dan, do the cooking, give you more free time."

"I must have had a lot of free time. Why didn't I work?"

"When you got pregnant with Dan, we agreed he

should have a stay-at-home parent. You were the more logical choice, because I'd already finished my degree.''

She tugged at the hem of her sweater, silently conceding they were about to start parenting small children all over again. ''Did I plan to look for a job after Dan left? Do I have a degree?''

How did she feel about being with the new babies? Maybe he should give her time to get used to their family before he asked. ''You majored in history, but you were working toward your teaching certificate when you left school after Dan was born.''

She turned away from the island. ''I don't recognize myself when you all talk about me.''

Alan's world slipped a little, like a foundation incorrectly laid. After twenty years, he'd believed he knew all about Cate. ''What don't you recognize?''

''Obviously, women choose to make homes for their busy husbands and teenaged sons, but how would I stay home with so little to do around here?''

Little to do? How about taking care of their family?

She laid her left hand on his forearm. He stared at the narrow band on her ring finger, at the diamond she hadn't wanted. He'd insisted, because the sapphire she'd liked hadn't said the same thing as a diamond. People might have thought he couldn't afford proper rings for his wife.

''What did I say that scared you?'' she asked.

He shook his head. ''I wonder if you were bored with me—with our life—before the accident. After all, you still think the kitchen looks like a restaurant.''

"I wish I hadn't said that."

He twined his fingers with hers, and she didn't pull away. Did she notice she'd let him touch her? "Say what you feel. Ask me anything. I want to help you, but I can't promise I won't be disturbed when you tell me something I didn't know about you."

Shrugging, she gently disentangled herself from him. Her smile flirted a little. "I hope I keep on disturbing you. I'd rather not be the only one who's confused." The tender curve of her lips made her look more like his Cate.

His heart responded, but he checked his involuntary response. "Why don't we take your things to our room? I'll show you the way, and then you can explore the rest of the place while I cook."

"Do you cook often?"

"Hardly ever." With his answer, he realized he should have eased more of her burden around here. "We'll take those stairs." He pointed to white wooden steps tucked into the corner beside the pantry.

Cate climbed ahead of him. Her perfume drifted back from the damp strands of her hair, the knit of her sweater.

"You'll want to change out of those wet clothes," he suggested on the second-floor landing. "Our room is the first door on the left."

As she took in the narrow hallway, he saw its shadowed closeness for the first time in years. She hung back, as if she shared his unexpected claustrophobia.

"We should have discussed sleeping arrangements before now," she said.

A rush of resentment surged through him, but he opened their bedroom door. He was determined to be strong for her.

She followed him inside, carefully avoiding the four-poster and the overstuffed vine-printed chintz armchairs that guarded their wide bay window. A reading lamp hovered at the corner of her chair. She'd loved this room.

He also avoided the furniture they'd used all their married life. He wouldn't let his need to hold her again turn into immature anger. "You're asking me to move out?"

"No, this is your room. It's strange to me." She stopped.

Well, he probably looked stricken.

"It's comfortable," she improvised, confused about what mattered to him. "But unfamiliar. I'll move out until we know each other again."

He did know her. Some caveman instinct that startled even him suggested he ease her to their bed and remind her in all the ways he knew she loved.

"You stay here," he said and then cleared his throat. If she'd known him at all, his husky tone would have betrayed the erotic images in his mind. "I'll take the guest room."

Stubbornness she'd never shown before firmed her mouth. "Why should you sleep anywhere besides your own bed? You don't have to be a gentleman."

"I'm not," he said. "I want you to remember. Maybe, if you stay in a room you loved, surrounded by belongings you've chosen, your life will come back to you." And she'd return to him. Unless she remembered his lie about the business.

For a moment he didn't care if she remembered what he'd done as long as she remembered the rest of their lives together. The company mattered, but they had children who'd need both their parents, and he wanted Cate to remember loving him.

"I'll move my things and call the high school to make sure Dan showed up."

She relaxed her obstinate expression. "I knew you weren't being entirely straight about that."

"I'm sure he went, but it's still raining. He might need dry clothes." He was only doing what Cate would have done before. Most of what he'd done for Dan since her accident, came from a single question: "What would Cate do?"

"Can't you call from here?" Her gaze reached the telephone on his side of their bed. She picked up the receiver and held it out to him. "Do you know the number?"

"Listen, Cate, this time I could use a break. I'm willing to do what you want about our marriage, but I'm not happy about separate rooms. Let me go downstairs and call Dan's school." He stopped as she looked at him with a pinched face. "You don't know Dan any better than you know me, but you'll go the extra mile for him. I don't mean to sound jealous, but I wonder how you can care for him so much when you don't know either of us."

She twisted her neck, flexing her muscles. Once, he would have stepped behind her to massage her tension away.

"I guess I'm trying to be a mom," she said. At his lifted eyebrow, she held up her hands in submission. "All right, Dan thinks he's grown-up, and you think he's mature, but he's still young enough to look like he needs me. Dr. Barton told me about implicit memory—an emotional reaction that comes from feelings I've had before. Maybe I react to Dan because I've loved him. All I know is, he needs me.''

Alan needed her with a yearning that went so deep in his body he had to force himself not to shake like a scared child. ''I'll call the school,'' he said, unable to believe she'd want to know how he felt.

She put her hand on his arm, and he jumped, but then he stood still, meeting her gaze. Her mouth was vulnerable. Her eyes beseeched. ''I'll learn to be your wife, too, Alan.''

''I don't want you to learn.'' He bit the inside of his cheek until it hurt. ''I want a wife who loves me.'' He felt naked.

''What if I don't remember? I can't promise to fall in love with you.'' She took both his hands in hers and pulled them against her stomach where the babies they'd made together were growing. ''But I want a real marriage.'' Her dark-blue eyes glittered with life he'd never seen before. ''And I want it with you. I'm willing to believe I might come to feel love enough to make our marriage real again.''

''For the children?''

''For them. I won't lie to you, but I don't want to throw the past away just because I don't remember it. I want to know what I can feel for you if we give each other time.''

He wasn't a man who talked about maybes. He believed in reality, like concrete and steel. He carried her bag to the chair in front of his cluttered desk.

When he turned, she was still watching him. Her

soft tone and intense gaze promised a future he craved. But would she try so hard if she knew he'd failed her in their present?

He'd feared losing Cate for most of his married life. She'd always said she wanted to share the bad times, the problems he'd tried to hide as well as their successes, but he hadn't believed she'd want to be with him if he couldn't give her things—like this house, the car in the driveway.

Nothing had changed. He couldn't lose their company and keep his wife.

He needed a few more days, maybe a few more weeks. "I'll get the school's number from my briefcase and check on Dan. After I call, I'll let you know what they say."

"You don't have to handle me with care, Alan."

He held on to the desk chair to fight off another bout of shaking. She knew something was wrong. "I'm not. My dad is joining us for dinner. He said he'd like to see you now that you're home."

She lifted her chin. "What's wrong with your dad?"

He could have kicked himself. She didn't remember his father. "He can seem somewhat irresponsible before you know him well."

"Is he irresponsible?" Again, she knew something. Knowledge made her tone sound aggressive.

He nodded at her. "Who talked to you about my dad?"

"Caroline." She admitted it right away. He had to admire her courage. "I asked her about him. She didn't gossip. She said he'd had a drinking problem and that you took care of him."

He breathed deeply. "I didn't realize Caroline knew so much." He hoped Cate hadn't betrayed his family secrets.

"You think I told her?" Cate looked surprised. "She said I kept all important information to myself."

He shrugged, pretending it didn't matter. "Your clothes are in that wardrobe." It towered over the room, but her rosewood wardrobe was more delicately carved than the cherry behemoth that housed his clothes across the room.

"What will you do with your things?" she asked.

"Move them to the guest room." He paused at the door to the hall. "Settle in. You must be tired, and I can take my clothes out after you rest. We'll have to tell Dan about using separate rooms."

She opened the wardrobe door, but eyed him absently. "Why not tell him the truth?"

"After he's discovered we've had sex, we should tell him we won't any more?"

With an open laugh he'd never heard before, Cate turned from perusing her clothes. "Let's not *promise* that," she suggested.

CHAPTER SIX

CATE WOKE, gasping for breath. Her pounding heart made her reach for her chest. She listened to her own breathing, unsure what had made her wake so suddenly.

She stared at the shadows that stood sentinel duty around the dimly lit room. Furniture and memories she couldn't decode. She hadn't planned to sleep, and she wasn't sure if she'd slept through the whole day. The rain had returned, and with it, darkness.

Willing her heart to slow, she crept toward the edge of the wide bed. From somewhere outside her room, came the tinkling of dishes and the murmur of deep male voices. Richard must have arrived, because she recognized Dan and Alan, but she heard a third voice.

She bent to inspect her hair in the vanity mirror. Fluffing the flattened strands, she took stock of her makeup. Pretty much gone, but she waved her hand at her sleepy face. The Palmer men would have to take her as she was.

She hurried down the same narrow stairs she and Alan had climbed earlier. In the kitchen, her husband turned from the stove, an iron frying pan in his towel-covered hands. Dan sat alone at the table. Richard wasn't in the room.

"You didn't have to come down," Alan said. "I planned to bring you a tray."

"I'd rather eat with you."

Dan stood slowly, as if he weren't sure how she'd approach him. Painting a smile on her face, she met him halfway across the room.

"Dad told me to tell you I'm all right, and I'm sorry I ran off this morning."

His approach lacked aplomb, but she studied the circles beneath his eyes and decided there was more to him than he was letting them see. "I understand you might need time on your own, but are you really all right?"

"I just didn't expect a baby."

"We didn't have time to tell you the other unexpected news," she said, glancing at Alan. He hesitated, looking as green as she felt, but finally he nodded, and she turned back to Dan. "We're going to have two babies. Twins."

"How do you plan to do that, Cate?"

She whirled. The man who'd spoken stood at the other kitchen door. In looks, he was a mix of Dan and Alan. He shared the same tall, lean body type, but his hair was salt and pepper and resembled piano wire.

He looked her up and down. "You're a strong woman, but I don't think even you could order up a couple of kids."

His comment about her strength distracted her. Tales of her former saintliness had made her suspect she'd been something of a doormat. "They're on order already," she said. She smoothed her sweater over the mound that had begun to grow at an astounding rate.

"Mom, don't do that." Dan stared, as if he expected an alien creature to emerge from her belly.

"We're talking babies," Alan said, losing patience. "They won't hurt you, Dan."

"And two of them don't make the event more special." Dan snatched a cabinet door open and took out plates. "I'll finish setting the table. You stay and talk to Mom, Grandpa."

He disappeared down the hall, but Richard appeared to side with him. "More kids? You want more?" he asked, as if he couldn't fathom why.

"We're having more." Alan shook his head. "And Dad, we haven't asked for your advice."

"How long have you known?" Richard eyed Cate's stomach with trepidation that matched Dan's. "Not that I blame you for trying to hide your pregnancy. Aren't you two old enough to know better?"

"You love Dan, Dad." Alan's voice placated. "You'll love these babies, too. Calm down."

"I guess it's none of my business if you want to saddle yourselves at your ages." Richard held out his hand to Cate. "I probably don't need an introduction."

"You must be Richard." She shook his hand because Alan seemed to believe he possessed redeeming qualities.

"I'm sorry I didn't see you while you were in the hospital."

"Alan explained."

"My son despairs of me, but I just can't stand

being around all those sick people." He shuddered. "I don't know how you dealt with them."

"I was sick enough to fit in."

Alan began to slice the contents of the pan he'd set on the counter. "I don't think Dad understands how shallow he makes himself sound," Alan said.

Cate took a deep breath. The physical therapist at the hospital had taught her relaxation techniques. Sadly, she never could remember if she was supposed to breathe in through her mouth and out through her nose or vice versa. She tried both ways. Neither worked.

Oblivious to her surprised feelings of dislike, Richard pulled her to a chair and helped her into it. More assistance than she needed, but she reminded herself he was Alan's father. And Alan cared for him.

"I don't think I'm shallow," Richard said. "I just know my limitations. Knowing exactly what you can and can't do makes you a stronger person. I just don't pretend I can be someone I'm not."

"That *sounds* right," Cate said, and literally felt her husband trying to hold her back with a warning gaze.

He lifted the pan again and carried it to a marble slab on the island. "Help me serve this frittata, Dad, and drop the subject."

"All right, if you're determined to be foolish."

Cate grabbed a stack of silverware from the counter, an excuse to flee the kitchen and her father-in-law. "I'll take this to the table."

She'd looked around the house before her nap, but she'd been so tired, it still felt unfamiliar. A narrow hall that split the living spaces ran all the way through. Two doorways down, she found Dan rearranging plates on a long, oval table in a turquoise dining room. Cate stopped in the doorway.

"These walls are bright," she said.

Dan looked up. "The paint is historically accurate. That's what you told me."

A whitewashed fireplace at the end of the room drew her. The wood flooring creaked as she crossed. She brushed her fingers against the painted plaster that bordered the fireplace. Even lit by electric candle sconces placed around the walls, the paint was hideous. Cold and unwelcoming.

"I insisted on this color?"

He nodded. "What do you think of Grandpa?"

She caught the back of a chair. "What do you mean?"

"You don't bother to hide how you feel any more. I'll take the silverware."

But she only gave him half, and then they started in opposite directions around the table. "I don't get your grandpa. Is he always so free with his opinions?"

"You'd rather he lied?"

"I guess not, but he's so cheerful, and every word out of his mouth offended me." She stopped for a careful study of her son. "And why do you and I get along better when we're alone?"

He didn't answer at first. All his attention seemed focused on the knife he arranged beside a plate at the head of the table. "I'm sorry I left this morning. I was mad. And I hate to be as honest as Grandpa, but I'm glad I'll graduate before anyone else finds out about the babies."

Cate finished her share of the silverware. How would a more natural mother respond? "You want us to keep the twins to ourselves for now?"

"Yes." He took glasses from a sideboard. "I guess I sound like Grandpa to you."

Dan might love his grandfather, and she wouldn't alienate him with her negative first impression of Richard. An impression that probably had a lot to do with what Caroline had said about the way he'd treated Alan. "I don't know the man well enough to have an opinion, but about the twins, Dan? You guessed from seeing my clothes. Your friends might be as clever as you."

"Wear something loose to my graduation," he said. "Do me that favor, Mom."

"I will, but I'm not ashamed, any more than I would have been with you."

He knocked a glass over. The sound focused her on the anger that distorted his face.

"You don't remember me," he said. "You don't know if you were ashamed of me."

She made her voice gentle, trying to ease his anguish. "I'm willing to bet I wasn't." And she'd bend over backward to prove he was important to her, whether she remembered him or not. His need was as obvious as the hollows beneath his eyes and his perpetual touchiness.

In silence, he glared at her, but she refused to be perturbed. Behind her, footsteps heralded Alan holding a serving dish and Richard carrying a pitcher of ice water. Richard smiled absently in Cate's general direction as he began to fill the glasses.

"I love breakfast for dinner," he said. "Thanks for asking me to stay, son."

Alan, more sensitive than his father, seemed to diagnose the atmosphere. "Have we interrupted, Cate?"

She hesitated. She'd be furious with Alan if he hid something as important as Dan's asking her to pretend she wasn't pregnant. But she didn't want to discuss her son in front of Richard. "Grandpa" might be as harmless as Alan and Dan seemed to think, but they loved him. Her concern for Dan was too personal to share with Richard.

"We were talking about this paint." She slapped her hand to the turquoise plaster. "I hope you're not attached to it, Alan, because Dan and I plan to change it. What color do you think, Dan?"

His open mouth expressed surprise, but he went along with her change of subject. "I like forest green," he said. "Like your truck, Dad."

"Your truck?" Cate echoed. "We're going to copy the paint from a work truck?"

"I don't think I'll have a difficult time finding a chip to pry off. They'll be able to match it for you at the paint store." Alan grinned as he set the serving dish on the table. "I made a salad, Dan. Do you want to bring it in?"

"Okay." Dan's grateful glance warmed Cate as he shot past her. He obviously loved Richard, but he must not have wanted to discuss his sibling rivalry issues in front of the older man.

"I'll get the salad dressing." Richard followed his grandson. "Did you make the vinaigrette I like, son?"

"You'll find it on the counter." Alan began to serve while Dan and Richard were out of the room. "Want to tell me what really happened with you and Dan?"

"Not now. I promise I'll tell you after your father leaves. I really need to know about Richard. How much time has he spent with Dan? Is he a nice—"

Alan put his finger across his lips and glanced toward the doorway. Cate nodded, more frustrated than she'd been since she'd awakened from the coma. He was too careful with her and with Richard. His wariness hinted at a past that had begun to feel ominous.

"Let me get your chair." Alan pulled one out for her and she took it. She looked up at him, and his smile confused her more. She liked the curve of his mouth, the reassurance in his gaze.

"Salad, Cate?" Richard came in, ready to serve.

"Please."

"This is a first." He put mixed greens on her plate. "Us waiting on you."

"You like Dad's vinaigrette, too, Mom." Dan passed her the crystal decanter, and she poured. They all waited until Richard set the salad bowl on the sideboard and sat in a chair opposite Dan's.

Cate sliced a bite of frittata with the edge of her fork and tasted. After an experimental, ambrosial chew, she beamed at her husband. "Delicious," she said as soon as she could talk.

Alan opened his mouth, but his father beat him to the punch. "Alan did almost all the cooking when he was a boy. After his mother left us."

This time she didn't bother to finish her bite. "From the time he was *ten?*"

"Dad, let it go." She'd never heard the harsh note in Alan's voice before. Was he protecting his father, or did he still feel the pain of his mother's leaving?

"Do you ever see your mother?" she asked.

Again, Richard answered first. "She made no effort to stay in touch, and I began to think Alan might be better off without her. I didn't want her to leave him more than once."

Cate turned to her husband. Two broken people had raised the man she'd married. Had their neglect forced him to be strong or merely damaged him?

Tonight's conversation with Richard had told her one thing. Alan still kept his own secrets. She glanced at his lowered head. Her instincts had been right. He was holding back.

He stood up, and everyone at the table stared at him. "I forgot the bread," he said. "I'm going to the kitchen to get it, and when I come back, I'd be grateful if we could leave my past where it belongs. I'm not the one who needs to remember."

He left, and Cate looked from her father-in-law to her son. They returned her startled glance. Cate pushed her chair back.

"He can be so emotional," Richard said.

She turned on him, Caroline's information and Alan's own refusal to talk pushing her to defend her husband. "Don't try to make Alan sound less a man." She glanced Dan's way and held back on the rest of her advice for Richard. "It sounds as if he's been carrying a man's burden since he was ten years old."

Her melodramatic speech echoed embarrassingly in her mind as she headed for the kitchen. Maybe

Alan didn't need her protection, but she took their marriage and the relationship they were trying to build seriously.

She half expected to find him slumped over the counter, trying to put his world back together. But no, he was cutting slices of bread off a crusty loaf. He looked up.

"You're limping more," he said. "You should stay off that leg."

"Are you all right?"

He stopped cutting to look at her in surprise. "I understand the humiliation that drives my father. My mom convinced him he wasn't man enough to be her husband. For all I know, he may still believe her, but I don't want him to upset you."

"Do you want some butter for that?" She went to the fridge and pulled out a tub of margarine.

"You always liked garlic toast, Cate. Do you want it now?"

She grinned at him. "If it keeps us out here longer, I sure do."

His smile lingered on her face. Her heartbeat sped up, but then he opened the tub of margarine. "You're different," he said as he scooped out a dollop of margarine.

"I might be," she said. She turned toward the dining room. What really drove Richard Palmer? He couldn't be unaware he'd hurt his son as much as his errant wife had. Looking back at Alan, she lowered her voice. "I'm stunned *you* turned out so well."

He froze. An oversize blob of margarine dripped off his knife, onto the counter. "You'll have to explain that."

"Maybe I'm overreacting, but from the way your father talks, you were raised by a wolf."

Alan widened his eyes. He looked one hell of a lot like Dan when he stared at her in shock, but his shock switched to stunned laughter.

"Don't laugh. I wish you were more concerned." For himself. "Don't you ever want someone to take care of you?"

He sobered. "I'm fine. I like things the way they are."

"With my mind a blank, and your father—" She broke off. She couldn't just blurt her opinion of Richard to Alan, either.

"My dad is hardly wolflike. More a puppy you just can't train."

Cate disagreed, but she kept it to herself. "I'll help you with the toast."

"No, thanks. I don't even trust you with a butter knife in your mood." He stopped spreading margarine to glance at her. "I'd better try to stay on your good side."

THE NEXT MORNING, Dan dressed for school and started downstairs for breakfast. On his way past the guest room, he noticed his dad's pajamas on the floor.

Now, what? What happened after parents decided not to sleep together? Behind him, his mother's door opened.

"Dan?"

"Go back to bed."

"I'm tired of sleeping. Have you eaten breakfast?"

If she was going to split up his family, he'd rather she stopped talking to him as if she had to help him blow his nose. "I'll get my own."

She tugged the neck of a long T-shirt that reached almost to the knees of her pajama pants. "I'll make my own, too. Mind if I join you?"

"Sure you want to?" He jutted a thumb toward the guest room. "Looks like you'd rather be alone these days."

Her skin turned bright red. "We forgot to tell you." She wrapped her hand around her throat—also bright red. "We decided to sleep in separate rooms until I remember more. You can see I'm nervous about sharing a—room with a stranger?"

She seemed so different, he forgot he and his dad were the strangers. She was like someone he'd never known. "I guess I get it. You can come on down if you want."

He made coffee while she hunted down ingredients to make pancake batter. She didn't ask for help, and she found everything she needed. When she finished the batter, she stood over the griddle built into the stove.

"Are you sure you don't want some?"

He relented. Her cooking tasted better than his. "If you have some to spare, I'd take a pancake."

"Thanks," she said dryly. "Maybe you can find the plates. I don't remember where I saw them."

She'd opened every cabinet in the kitchen. He wasn't surprised she'd forgotten which one held the plates. He took out two and set them on the table.

"We always eat in here unless we have company," he said.

"Good. It's a long way to the dining room." She flipped the first pancake. "Thanks for going along with me on the paint in there last night."

He nodded, a little guilty for being mad at her about the separate rooms when he remembered she'd made up that story to protect him. She turned to him when he didn't answer, and he nodded again.

"Will you really help me paint it?"

Was she trying to baby him into a relationship? "You don't have to think up busywork to spend time with me."

She looked surprised, really surprised. Maybe she was faking it to trick him into a mom-son activity for old times' sake.

"I want to paint," she said, "and I thought you might help me. You're taller than I am."

"What if you like the blue-green paint when you remember everything?"

"I don't care about historical accuracy. We live here, and that room feels cold."

"Everything had to be 'appropriate' before. It was one of your favorite words."

He'd never been so up-front with his mom. She'd wanted him to look happy. He'd never been sure she wanted to know how he really felt. "You tried to convince me life runs by rules."

She twisted her mouth in disgust. "Saint Cate again. I don't necessarily want to be inappropriate, but surely you can have some fun and still follow rules. Whatever they are." Balancing the first pancake on a spatula, she carried it across the room to him.

He wouldn't have been more startled if she'd

hoisted the stove on her back and trotted it up the stairs. "I can get you a serving plate for that," he said. His involuntary offer surprised him. "You've made me more correct than you are now."

"So lighten up." She looked from the pancake to him and tipped it onto his plate. "I'll bet you'd like a couple more?"

The "lighten up" suggestion bugged him. "You could try to cook more than one at a time."

She'd already headed back to the stove, but she turned, holding the spatula as if it were a weapon. "How do you know? Did I make you do the cooking here?"

"Grandpa really spooked you, didn't he?"

"He gave your father too much resp— Never mind."

"You can be honest with me."

"We didn't make you responsible for cooking and housework at such a young age." She flinched. "Did we?"

"Yeah, right. You made me wait a year longer than any of my friends to get my driver's license. I'm about to leave for college, but I've never had a party without you or Dad in the house. Dad even 'supervised' me every time I balanced my checkbook for the first year."

"How long before you leave, Dan?"

Like always, she only listened to the part she wanted to hear. Still, he was glad she didn't want him to go. "I'm taking summer classes."

"Why?"

"I want out of school. I'm ready to be on my own."

She turned her back on him. She still didn't want him to see how she felt.

"Who's Saint Cate?" he asked.

"I am—or I was, and I really can't stand her." She grabbed a towel off the counter and wiped at her face.

Was she crying? If his dad found out, he was dead meat. He took her shoulders and gently made her face him.

"Why are you crying?" His voice squeaked again.

"What if you go before I remember you? I'll never really know you."

"Cut it out, Mom. You don't have to see me every day to remember who I am." He put his arms around her, but hugging her felt weird. He patted her shoulder. Girls liked that. Moms must, too. "I'll only be an hour away. If you remember, you can call me."

He felt like an idiot, so he went to the stove. She was still sniffing into the towel as he picked up the batter. "I'll do this," he said. "I've mastered the art of three at a time, and I'm going to be late for school."

She nodded. "Whatever. Listen, if I pick up the paint, we can start painting."

"Tonight? I have practice."

"Golf?" She moved out of his way. He avoided looking at her face—a real mess. "How about tomorrow night?"

His mom didn't cry, and she didn't let him cook pancakes. Why did she want to paint with him? "Okay, if Dr. Barton says you can."

"He said to rest when I'm tired. I'm not tired."

He poured batter on the griddle. "How many for you?"

"Two, thanks. Dan, are you happy here?"

"Well, yeah. This is home." What'd she think? She just pissed him off with this forgetting thing. That and he couldn't get divorce off his mind.

"You'd say if something bothered you? I know I'm not the mother I used to be, but I want to take care of you."

"I don't need you to take care of me. Mom, could you sit at the table? You're making me burn these pancakes."

She limped over to the table and pulled back her chair. As she was about to sit, the phone rang. He waited for her to answer. Damn it, this was her house. He'd cook pancakes, but he wasn't pretending she didn't know how to answer her own phone.

"I'll get it," she said.

Guilt gave him second thoughts as she made her way toward the phone on the wall beside the back door. Her leg must hurt pretty bad.

She picked up the receiver. "Hello? Oh, hi, Alan. I didn't expect to hear from you."

She turned toward the wall, as if she wanted to keep him from hearing. His dad always called home during the day.

"Tonight?" She twisted the phone cord around her wrist. "What time?" After a pause, she turned slightly. "Yes, he's still here. I'll tell him. What? We're making pancakes." She laughed, but she sounded funny. "He took over. No, I won't forget to tell him." She waited. His dad must have said something. "Okay," she said. "Bye."

She hung up the phone, and he flipped the pancakes onto a plate. "What are you supposed to tell me about tonight?"

"Aunt Imogen and Uncle Ford asked us to dinner. We're supposed to show up with appetites at six-thirty."

"I'll go from practice." He took the stack of pancakes to the table. Then he sat down and shifted his onto the plate she'd already given him.

She didn't even notice his bad manners. She just reached for syrup. "I'll move the furniture out of the dining room today."

"Leave the heavy stuff, Mom."

"Don't worry." She looked completely unlike her old self, smiling at him as if she were about to tell a joke. "Why break my back?" she teased.

Her question made a lousy joke. His mom would have broken every bone in her body before she'd ask for help.

"Dad will blame me if you move the furniture." That should fix her.

He poured syrup on his own pancakes. At least the rest of the family would be at dinner tonight. Let someone else take a shot at this new version of his mom.

ALAN WATCHED shadows drift across his desk. He was already late getting home if he and Cate were going to make it to Aunt Imogen's in time for dinner.

The men he'd invited to meet with him and John Mabry remained stony. Each slumped in varying postures of defeat in the leather chairs that had cost him two hundred fifty-three dollars and some odd cents apiece in his company's flush days.

Howard Fisk owned the hardware center. Shep Deavers ran his family's plumbing supply business. Brian Henney had landscaped almost every project, large and small, that Alan had ever worked on.

All these men had trusted Jim Cooper with their books, and they all faced the prospect of losing their businesses. More so because they depended on Alan's jobs for many of their contracts.

"New bottom line," Mabry said. "We tracked Jim to Maine. He spent two weeks with his computer and Internet access to accounts all over the States. From there, he rented a car that the Wheeling, West Virginia police found disabled with a flat tire on the side of the road. If he stayed in Wheeling, he used a false name."

"You have no idea where he is now," Howard said.

"Thanks for the obvious, Howard." Shep also looked forward to the dependent faces of a large family when the news became public. "I'm starting to agree with Alan. We have to tell the people who work for us."

"No," the others chorused.

"Once we lose control, our businesses go under." Brian repeated this refrain at least three times during each of their meetings.

"How long before you catch up with Jim again?" Alan asked.

"Hard to say." Mabry shifted. "As soon as he uses a form of payment or identification we or the FBI can track, we'll find him."

"And if we're all broke by that time?" Shep asked.

"I don't know what to tell you. The money hasn't gone out of the country yet."

"So you can still get it back?"

"Possibly. We don't know what he's done with it."

Alan disliked Mabry's answer. "How are we supposed to placate creditors with a possibility?"

"We'll prosecute Jim Cooper, but you all know where you stand better than I do. I'm doing my job, Alan."

"I wonder if you forget how many jobs will disappear from this town if the people in this office lose their companies."

"That's not fair. I know you have a lot on your mind, Alan, but I'm not sleeping any better than the rest of you."

Mabry was right. The business meant more to Alan than ever, because he'd never be able to explain to Cate now. Her concern last night had surprised and pleased him, but he could see this new incarnation of his wife going for his knees if she discovered the business problems he'd hidden.

The intercom on Alan's desk buzzed. With an eye on his watch again, he picked up the receiver. He'd promised to be home half an hour ago. "Yes?"

His secretary's voice came over the line. "Cate just called. She said she'd be happy to drive to her aunt's by herself if you're going to be late."

Already late, he was grateful she'd put it that way instead of complaining. "Can you call her back? I'd rather she waited." Dr. Barton hadn't said she shouldn't drive, but she'd slept most of yesterday. Visiting her family might tire her again.

"I don't have anything more to tell you," Mabry said, catching on to Alan's end of the conversation.

The other men stood. Alan grimaced, caught between frustration at being unable to change his business situation and relief at being able to go home to Cate. "Tell her I'm on my way," he said to his secretary.

After a round of handshaking, he saw the men out and went back to his desk to gather up paperwork he'd have to do at home. He stuffed everything in his canvas briefcase and left his office.

Caroline's door was shut. She'd already gone. Alan hurried to the front door. He should have called Cate back today, asked her how breakfast had gone with Dan. After his father'd left last night, she'd told him Dan had asked her to keep her pregnancy a secret. He'd like to know if they'd discussed it this morning.

On the street, he unlocked his truck and tossed his briefcase inside. Traffic out to their cottage was fairly light, but as he turned into his driveway, the front door opened and Cate hurried out, her limp less noticeable already.

Her filmy, pale-blue dress hid her pregnancy. She looked deceptively delicate as she draped the thin strap of her small purse over her shoulder and waved at him. He got out to open her door.

"You don't have to do that," she said, waving him off.

"I wanted to. I'm glad to see you."

She stopped at his side. "Me, too."

The shine in her blue eyes shallowed his breathing. For a moment, he believed she was going to kiss him the way she used to when he came home from work. A slight breath whispered through her lips and she curled her fingers around his forearm.

A squeeze of welcome hardly cut it, but he settled for what she offered. Ahead of him lay free time to remind her she'd married a good husband who was glad she'd come home to him.

She slid into the passenger's seat. "Aunt Imogen called a few minutes ago."

"I'm sorry I'm late."

"Don't worry. She offered to come get me, but I told her you were on your way." She reached for the door handle. "She mentioned something you and I have to discuss."

"What?"

"Get in." She closed the door and waited for him to walk around the truck. After he started the engine, she turned, curving her good leg onto the seat between them.

Something different gleamed from her eyes, a serenity he hadn't seen before. Ever. He marveled at her. Despite everything, this woman had found peace that had always eluded her.

"Why are you looking at me like that, Alan? As if I'm the stranger. Dan does the same thing."

"You're happier than I've ever seen you."

Her laugh seduced him, low and full of self-awareness that made no sense in light of her amnesia. "I finally have something to do," she said. "Unfortunately, you have to help me."

Would she respect him if he killed the truck's mo-

tor and fell outside onto his knees to beg her to let
him help her? He'd grind his knees on the road for
a couple more of her smiles. "What can I do?"

"Dan's graduation," she said. "How does he want
to celebrate? Have we already chosen his gift? Do
we need to rent a hall? I searched my desk to see if
we'd made any preparations, but I couldn't find anything. We have to make decisions. Fast."

Decisions about arrangements they probably
couldn't afford, definitely shouldn't attempt right
now. He'd felt less pressure facing Chief Mabry and
the other gullible fools who'd trusted the CPA they'd
all used for nearly twenty years.

He didn't have to lie to them.

CHAPTER SEVEN

"SHOULDN'T WE make sure we know what Dan wants?" Alan's guilt nearly choked him. Worrying about spending money on such a momentous day underscored his failure to provide. Backpedaling to keep Cate from finding out they had a problem made him feel like a slug.

"I don't think Dan will say. Aunt Imogen tried to pump him, but he won't tell her. Did we discuss a gift before the accident?"

"A golf school," he said. "I'm not sure why he wouldn't talk to Aunt Imogen, but he gave us suggestions."

They could still afford the school—barely—but they'd be foolish to spend that much money. For the first time, he wanted to tell Cate the truth about their finances. But he was still afraid to burden her with the stress of their failing business.

"What's a golf school?" she asked, somehow oblivious to his tension.

"A week of one-on-one instruction with a pro at Myrtle Beach. All the golf he can play outside of class time."

Cate sat back, so happy she made him want to give the present to Dan. "Perfect," she said. "I can't wait to see his face."

"I'm sure he knows which gift we'd choose."
What a hole he'd dug for himself. Alan took her
hand. "What if we had to ask Dan to wait for the
school until maybe fall?"

"But isn't he starting college soon? Is the golf
school full?"

"I'm actually thinking of what we can afford."
Disgusted, he let her hand go. He couldn't tell her
the truth yet, so he'd find a way to do what she
wanted. "Never mind. I'll make the arrangements."

"If you're not sure about the cost, we should explain to Dan, but let's try to arrange the school for
him, Alan."

He'd almost rather she'd argue for her own way.
But Cate had never played those kinds of games, and
a bad case of shock couldn't transform her completely. "I'll look at our finances again and we can
talk."

"Okay," she said. "What about a party?"

"Let's leave that up to him." Alan turned off the
beach road and headed across the marshy wetlands
into town. An egret wafted into the air to race along-
side them on the ribbon of beige road. He felt like
that bird, trying desperately to keep airborne. "Dan
may have made plans with his friends."

"Drinking and orgies?"

Alan stared at her. She burst into laughter. "I'll
bet I looked like you do now when Aunt Imogen
suggested those possibilities to me. I'm glad I was
alone."

"Aunt Imogen? I can't believe she's ever heard of
an orgy."

"Because she's my maiden aunt? She strikes me as a woman who made her own choices in her time."

"I suspect she still makes her own choices." He reached for sunglasses as they turned into the setting sun, and their windshield framed Leith's skyline. "Look at the town." He pointed toward the rounded dome of the courthouse, the church spires and the intricate Eastern design of Leith's synagogue. The sun, dropping out of sight, bathed the buildings in pale orange. Close at hand, tall pines and Southern hardwoods, maple, oak and cypress rose out of the black dirt.

"It's beautiful. I wish I could remember my past here."

"I can't imagine how you feel." Asking her seemed like an intrusion, since he felt unsure how much of her life she was ready to share. He wished she'd tell him anyway.

"The frustration makes my head ache," she said, giving him what he wanted as if it were the simplest response in the world. "I see the extra thought you give to every word you speak to me. Everyone treats me as if I'm about to break. I have a life to get on with, but I don't know how or where I'm supposed to start."

"You have started. Dinner with my dad last night, and tonight with your family. You're concerned about Dan. You're attached to Aunt Imogen and Uncle Ford. You had a good visit with Caroline in the hospital."

"And I care about you." She dropped her hand on his arm, her tone infused with a warmth he hadn't heard in a long time.

When she brushed her fingers over the hair on his wrist, her touch raised the skin beneath her hand. He felt like a teenager.

She tilted her head toward the window on her side of the car. "I can't get your father's visit out of my mind. He's not even embarrassed he made you an adult so he could wallow through his loss."

"I'm glad you came to my rescue last night," Alan said, slightly embarrassed. He was supposed to be his family's guardian angel. "But Dad did the best he could. Let's not psychoanalyze him now."

"He makes me nuts when he laughs about it. No guilt on his conscience, huh?"

"He has nothing to feel guilty for. I grew up. I'm a responsible adult."

"And you've been one since you were ten. You don't tell me the truth, Alan."

"Cate." He let his tone ask her to drop the subject.

She took the hint. After a while, she leaned forward to look through his window. Her hair fell over her shoulder, soft, silky, its sweep lending her chin a vulnerable curve.

"Why are we going around the town?" she asked.

"Aunt Imogen and Uncle Ford live on the other side, out by the Leith River."

"They share a house?"

"No. Your aunt lives in the family home. Your uncle lives in a house he built when he left."

"On the same property? What was his point in leaving?"

"He wanted his own place and he needed a barn. He still boards a few horses. Most of all, he didn't want to be beholden to your grandfather. He and your grandma never agreed with the way Uncle Ford lived his life.''

Cate plunged her fingers into her hair and shoved it away from her face. "You wouldn't believe what one of the nurses told me about Uncle Ford. Don't ever mention Las Vegas or carousels to him when he's in a confiding mood. I wouldn't be surprised to learn I spring from vampires and villains.''

The old Cate had used particularly weak humor to hide her discomfort. "Are you nervous about seeing them again?'' he asked.

"I want to see them, but they all have something to say—usually all at the same time, and everyone watches me as if they're on the lookout for the exact moment my memory comes back. Even I'm starting to expect a lightning strike.''

He braked and pulled onto the shoulder of the road. Cate faced him, her expression raw, and he curved his hands around her shoulders. At first she stiffened, but after a second she relaxed, as if she were relieved to feel human contact. With a sigh, Alan pulled her into his arms.

She smelled of Cate, some sort of spice he'd never been able to name, the soap she'd ordered from a store in town for the past several years, and the shampoo he'd left in their bathroom.

She buried her face in his throat, and he shifted in the seat to make her more comfortable. No doubt she felt his heart pounding against her. His exposed feelings made him restless. He needed her more than she needed him.

"What was wrong between us, Alan?''

"We were both afraid.''

"Of what? Didn't we want to be together?"

"We don't want to be hurt." He lifted her chin so he could look down at her. "I won't ever hurt you on purpose."

She stared into his eyes, surprising him with a hunger that might possibly match his. "We're still keeping secrets."

"If you think so, why aren't you upset?" He pressed his mouth to her forehead, a chaste kiss when his body ached from being against her soft curves. "Maybe you can learn to believe me."

"I'm trying, but you're going to have to tell me what you're hiding before I get frustrated." She twisted, until she was facing him, and she looped her arms around his neck.

Where had his Cate gone? And why had this temptress stepped into his life? She was willing to trust him until he could tell her the truth. God, what freedom that gave him.

She wriggled. "The steering wheel," she muttered.

Swallowing a groan at the pleasure of her firm breasts against his chest, he slid his hands between the steering wheel and her back, both to cushion her and to position her body away from his arousal.

"Can we stay like this for a few minutes?" She pressed a kiss to the bottom of his chin and he gritted his teeth.

ALAN'S HEART thudded against her cheek. She'd turned to him for comfort, but comfort held no attraction. Simply being in his arms, she learned each sinew that met hers, from neck to waist.

She lost track of his pulse, because she had to concentrate on holding her own respirations at a normal rate. She was drowning, swimming against a tide of overwhelming power. Her arms and legs grew heavy, languorous with delicious need.

His desire for her spoke more loudly than his silences. She had to take so much of her life on faith. Why not believe Alan would tell her what he was hiding when he learned he could trust her again?

She pulled away from him only because her family would worry if they stayed much longer on the side of this lovely road.

Alan opened his eyes, startled. His pupils were almost as large as his deep-green irises. She pressed her palm to his cheek, feeling powerful because he wanted her. "We should go. The family will send out search parties."

"All right."

But he didn't move, and she didn't urge him again. She wanted more of what he'd given her, desire and human connection, a touch she might have taken for granted once. Could any woman take so much for granted?

Alan finally helped her back to her side of the seat, not bothering to hide his regret. "We'd better move. You know who Aunt Imogen will send?"

She shook her head, mystified.

"Dan," Alan said with distaste.

"I'm not sure he'd approve of finding us parked in a nearly compromising situation."

Alan's laughter came out of his throat in the low purr of a jungle cat. "Might do him some good. He'd realize we're in this marriage for the long haul." He started the engine and immediately ground the gears. She jumped, and he looked at her, amused. "Sorry about that. My mind is elsewhere."

She laughed. "Don't apologize to me. It's your transmission. I'm not sure I'd have the strength to move the stick right now."

He stopped the barely moving truck. "I didn't imagine you wanted me, too?"

"Imagine? You surely didn't have to imagine."

"Why didn't you—"

"What? Tell you?" She scooped her hair off her damp nape and held it in a ponytail to cool her skin. "How could I have said it more plainly?"

"You asked for separate bedrooms, so I think you have to say the words when you're ready for a relationship."

She preferred their unspoken communication. Did the strain around his mouth come from hurt feelings because she'd rejected his company in her bed?

"I feel the same as I ever did," he said. "I want my wife back."

His wife. Why did he have to claim her like a piece of furniture? "When I hear you call me your wife in that tone, I want to run."

The last trace of tenderness fled his expression. Remorse swept through Cate. His claims made her claustrophobic, but she might have found a kinder way to tell him.

He pulled back onto the road. His truck ate up the pavement as he pushed it to greater speed.

A concession might be in order. After all, she'd talked about working on their marriage, but she'd insisted on separate rooms. She'd put Alan off at any sign of commitment stronger than talking about it.

She stared out the window at cypress trees that seemed to hold up their skirts to avoid the kudzu vines that crawled from limb to trunk and limb again, making for the sand-rimmed road. She sympathized with those trees, but if her husband wanted her and she wanted to be his wife, she was in no danger if she reached out to him. He proposed caring for each other, not lifetime bondage.

She started innocuously. "Will we get there before dark?"

"In a few minutes. The sun will still be up." His tone was brittle, but then he cleared his throat, answering her effort with his own. "I'll show you the river behind Aunt Imogen's house."

She snatched at his compromise. "Did we spend much time at Aunt Imogen's?"

"Sure. Dan used to play in the attics and Uncle Ford's barn. He and Shelly and I built a tree house in the pines near the river."

"Is it still there?"

"Some of the floorboards, bits of the walls. The kids got too old for it about five years ago."

"I'd like to see the tree house, too."

"We'll ask Aunt Imogen to hold dinner a little longer."

"Thanks. Something will make me remember." She had to remember, because the nuances of her family relationships were killing her.

At a narrow break in the crushed shell, Alan turned onto a wide, sandy path that turned out to be a road. An arch of Spanish-moss-laden oaks embraced across the sandy drive, forming a sieve for the last of the sun's rays.

Cate peered through the squat tree trunks at a long, low white house and a red barn. Both relatively new. "Is that Uncle Ford's place?"

"Yes," Alan said. "And next we'll come to Aunt Imogen's."

Excitement made her lean forward as the road twisted in a last curve to reveal a whitewashed home. Two storys, shutters in dark blue and wide navy double front doors, sheltered in a wide porch.

Several cars sat at strange angles in the graveled driveway, but no one waited outside. Cate was glad. She wanted a few more minutes with Alan. As soon as he stopped the truck, she opened her door and jumped out, ignoring the jolt to her injured leg. She hurried around to take her surprised husband's large hands.

"Show me that river," she said. "Before the others see us."

Smiling startled agreement, he splayed his hand across her back and turned her away from the house. Glad she'd taken this chance, she leaned into the curve of his arm. At the back of a verdant yard, dotted with colorful flower beds and iron sculptures of strange animals, Alan opened the gate in a white picket fence.

Loose leaves and long pine needles scattered in front of their feet as they walked. Cate couldn't have found the path through the dense shrubbery, but Alan's step was sure. The greenery grew thickly right to the edge of the wide, dark-green river.

"How deep is it?" Cate liked the sound of the water lapping at the other bank, thirty feet away.

"This part is about twenty feet, but the current is fast. Don't swim alone."

"Is it clean enough to swim in?"

He nodded. "But it's too fast, Cate."

"Don't worry. I really asked you down here as an excuse." She draped her arm around his waist. "I wanted to talk to you for a minute more. I'm sorry I can't seem to be the woman I was."

He peered down at her, and she felt his heart again, beginning to pulse against her shoulder. "I'll try to stop pushing you."

She bumped her head against his chest. "You'd better keep pushing. I don't want to be content with the status quo until we're back to normal."

He lifted her chin and looked into her eyes. He wasn't the stranger she'd seen at her bedside when she'd awakened from the coma. He'd fathered her children, cared for her, and he was willing to wait for her. He needed her to be his wife again.

"How far can I push?" he asked on a slow, thick note that gave her courage.

Desire rushed at her with the speed of the river's current. But the kind of connection he needed required a leap of faith. Then again, if she could leap for Dan and the twins, she could leap for their father.

She breathed deeply of his musky scent. "I'm not sure...."

He leaned down, his eyes open, uncertain. Suddenly, he focused his demanding gaze on her mouth. She couldn't restrain a nervous smile. Alan's ragged groan seeped between them, and then he brushed her lips with his.

It wasn't enough. She cupped his face between hands that trembled, and he caught her fingers and deepened the kiss.

At the sweet, provocative stroke of his tongue, her legs trembled.

She was falling, but Alan's strength held her.

When he lifted his head, she freed her hands to wrap her arms around his neck. His smile, charged with erotic awareness, brushed her face like another kiss.

"Nice," he said in a thickened voice.

She pressed her face to his chest, luxuriating in the friction of his cotton shirt against her cheek. "You're a master of understatement. A talent I didn't expect."

"We'd better go inside. In a minute or two."

"We could." She ran her hands up the strong muscles of his back, exploring. This man was her husband. She couldn't guess how much she'd loved him, but his kisses implied a mutual knowledge that intrigued her.

"Dad?" Dan's voice betrayed confusion. "Mom?"

Cate turned, but Alan held her, sliding his hands down her arms.

Relief washed Dan's face at finding them together. "Sorry," he said. "Aunt Imogen saw you walk around the house. She thought you might have come down here, and she sent me to ask you to come in so everyone can say hello before we eat."

"Thanks." Alan moved to Cate's side. "She means they'll look for us if we don't go in."

Deeply aware of his long, lean body sheltering hers, Cate stayed within the circle of his arm. Together, they climbed the slight rise to reach their son.

"I brought a friend," Dan said. "Phoebe Garner. Do you remember her, Dad?"

"That girl who lives up the street from us?" Alan asked, and Dan nodded.

Cate eyed her son with interest. What did this girl mean to him? Why would he bring her to the first family function they'd attended together?

"We're all in the kitchen." Dan opened the screen door on a wide back porch.

They stepped into a jungle of tropical flowers. More fecund than sweet, the aroma went straight to Cate's unreliable stomach. She took a step backward, but Alan caught her.

"I know." He held her back as Dan entered the house ahead of them. "This porch garden creeps me out, too. Makes you think of poison."

"I just feel sick. Alan, remember I promised Dan we wouldn't mention the twins."

The crowd within the pale-yellow kitchen surged toward Cate the moment she crossed the threshold. Instinct pushed her back toward the ominous garden for safety. She put her hand behind her, hoping Alan would take it, but maybe he couldn't reach her. She held still, accepting embraces from strangers who clearly loved her.

Only one person steered clear of the throng. A willowy girl with spiked blond hair, who wore a flimsy tank top and skintight jeans. Bemused, Cate took in the barbed wire tattoo around her upper arm and the three studs and two rings that glittered in each ear. Sporting that much hardware, she must start quite a party at airport security points.

"Hello," Cate said when everyone else had finished their greetings and gone self-consciously silent. This girl looked like the kind of Talbot everyone had warned her about.

"Mom, this is Phoebe." Dan broke free from the milling crowd and took Phoebe's arm just beneath the barbed wire. "You've met, but Mom won't remember you, Phoebe."

"Hello, Mrs. Palmer. I was sorry to hear you were hurt."

She wore another stud on the tip of her tongue. And she wasn't even a reckless Talbot. Cate looked from her son, whose taste ran to golf shirts and khakis to this girl, who seemed his opposite. Curious about their relationship, she tried to read the body language between them.

Dan's gaze conveyed affection, but how much, or how deeply it went, she couldn't say. Recognizing her curiosity was making her rude, Cate finally shook Phoebe's outstretched hand.

"Hi. I'm glad to meet you again."

"Aunt Imogen, we'll walk Polly for you." With a smirk on his face, Dan reached for the straw hat festooned with Carmen Miranda-like fruit and flora that hung beside the door. "Phoebe, you get to wear this."

She planted it firmly on top of her blond spikes. "Cool. Did you make this, Miss Talbot?"

"I did. Would you like one of your own, Phoebe?" Aunt Imogen's tape was plain today. Kind of disappointing, but her finery couldn't have matched Phoebe's anyway.

"I'd love a hat, but I think I can show you a thing or two about decorating it."

"Chains are too heavy," Aunt Imogen said in a dry tone. "But I'm willing to learn, girl. I'd like to find out what's behind all your metal. Does it give you courage for your frank talk?" Aunt Imogen flicked a glance at Cate. "She pulls no punches, and she's termed us stereotypically suburban."

Phoebe merely laughed, and Dan turned her toward the porch. "We'll be back in time to eat, Aunt Imogen."

"Wait." The older woman grabbed an apple out of a wire basket that hung above the counter. She tossed the fruit to Dan. "Give this to Polly, and don't you two eat it and spoil your dinner."

"Okay." Dan polished the apple on his shirt and opened the door for his friend. "Don't talk about Phoebe while we're gone."

"I doubt we'll be able to resist," Aunt Imogen said.

Caroline followed them to the door. Cate stared at her sister, distracted as always by the sight of her mirror image.

"Are they dating?" Caroline asked. "I'd die if Shelly brought home—"

"I think she's a looker," Uncle Ford bellowed.

Like the rest of her family members, Cate took shelter from his loud voice at the farthest edge of the small kitchen.

"Oh, good grief. I'm not that loud. You all and your delicate ears."

"I like Phoebe." Aunt Imogen ignored her brother. "She's a wise girl, and she must have a strong sense of herself."

"If she's not covered in metal to hide from the rest of the world," Caroline suggested.

"She's probably going to be valedictorian," Shelly interjected. "Dan's lucky she's in his study group."

"She looks experienced," Cate ventured. "But I guess I'm jumping to conclusions because of the tattoo and all those earrings."

"They played together as children, Cate." Alan leaned against the counter, splaying his long legs before him as he reached into the basket for another apple.

"They aren't kids now." Aunt Imogen filched the apple from him. "We're about to eat."

He glowered good-naturedly before he met Cate's gaze. "I'm surprised Dan brought Phoebe tonight, but I've never heard you or him suggest she might be anything more than a friend."

"From what everyone says, I was overprotective."

A communal "Yes" rebounded off the walls. Even Uncle Ford flinched from the volume.

Cate took their teasing in stride. "I must have trusted her. We'd better get to know her before we prove she's right about our suburban attitudes."

They all gaped at her as if she'd sprouted a new head. This time they weren't teasing. She shivered. How to understand a former self that seemed like a figment of her family's collective imagination? Alan came to her, worry imprinting his handsome face.

"Dan's a good kid. You've been a loving mom,

and I'm not surprised you don't judge a person by her looks.''

"Thanks for reassuring me.''

With new familiarity, he pulled her close. His affection propped up her self-confidence. She hoped she hadn't been bad for Dan, but she'd try to show greater belief in his judgment from now on.

The doorbell chimed, and Aunt Imogen turned toward the sound. ''That will be your dad, Alan. He's bringing Meg.''

"Meg?'' Cate echoed as the family moved en masse to greet the latecomers.

"Meg Hawthorne, his fiancée,'' Alan said.

"Oh, yeah. Caroline told me he was getting married.''

Alan took her arm, holding her back when she would have followed the others. ''Will you be all right?''

She tilted her face to look into his eyes. He silently asked her to remember his dignity. She knew him well enough already to comprehend the question.

Girding herself for battle, she squared her shoulders. ''I remember my manners. Bring him on.''

CHAPTER EIGHT

"AUNT IMOGEN, why the plain tape tonight?" Dan's voice cut through the conversation that echoed in the dining room.

Alan waited to see how the older woman would respond. Her tape was an eccentricity, but Aunt Imogen had a few, and she might be sensitive. Seated to his left at the end of the table, she glanced at Cate on her other side before she answered her great-nephew.

"The first few days your mom was in the hospital, she stared at my tape as if I'd lost my mind." She pressed her hand to the back of Cate's head, and her tenderness for his wife swept Alan with the wide, comforting brush of her affection. "I'm not nuts, just vain, and I hate those wrinkles."

Cate allowed her aunt's hand to remain. Still flushed from the bone-shaking kiss they'd shared outside, she fascinated Alan. His awareness of her was so strong he almost believed he could feel her body heat from across the table.

He shifted uneasily in his hard chair. Memories of Cate's arms around his neck, the innocent press of her body, aroused him. He wanted to take her home, make new memories like the one they'd conjured by the river.

"I think your tape's great, Miss Talbot." Phoebe, at Dan's side, curled her index finger into the tip of her thumb, to signify a hearty okay. "I especially admired the Santas last Christmas."

"Hey, that was my favorite, too." Dan shouldered Phoebe. Her smile faded as she looked into his eyes. Startled understanding replaced her warm friendship.

Where was that relationship headed? Dan had been dating a rather timid unpierced brunette at spring break.

His judgmental thought caught Alan short. Like Cate, he'd never prejudged a person based on looks, but Phoebe provoked the protective instincts Cate's family had teased her about. He'd never been Dan's primary caregiver before, but now that he was, he'd do it right, and a young woman who looked as if she investigated alternative lifestyles alarmed Alan. He must have turned into a god-awful prude.

Looking away from Dan, he bumped into Cate's uneasy gaze. She shrugged almost imperceptibly.

Once he'd have considered the worst that could happen. So what if Dan walked on the wild side with an iconoclast? Phoebe might show him life offered more than golf. A couple of piercings—eleven or so, by Alan's count—didn't make her Mata Hari.

All the same, he'd better schedule another talk with Dan. They hadn't covered safety issues in a while. He hated those talks. Discussing such private matters turned them both into mumbling zombies.

"Dan." Alan's own father's voice boomed cross the bounty of fried chicken and fresh peas, corn on the cob and home-baked rolls. "I don't believe I've met your lady friend."

Meg, self-assured, smoothly groomed, and crisp in a linen suit that had thus far withstood the South Georgia humidity, reached across the table to shake Phoebe's hand. "I'd like to introduce myself." Phoebe and Dan had barely made it back into the house before dinner. "I'm Meg Hawthorne, and I like your look."

"My look?" Phoebe withdrew her hand, as if she didn't actually want anyone to like it.

"I do, too." From across the table, Cate stunned Alan. "You don't give in to peer pressure, do you?"

Surprisingly self-conscious in the center of everyone's attention, Phoebe appealed to Dan with a glance.

"I don't let her golf with me." His tone teased her. "All that metal glinting in the sun distracts me. Plus, I can't get her tattoo out of my mind."

"How is your golf going, son?" Richard leaned around Meg. "I always wanted your father to take up extracurricular activities."

Familiar anger tightened Alan's muscles. He pretended not to mind his dad's talk, but he slid his gaze away from Richard Palmer. Being angry with his father got him nowhere.

There was more to the story than he'd told Cate. He'd run their house, pushed himself through school and pretended nothing was wrong. One afternoon, just after he'd graduated from high school, he'd noticed Cate as she'd walked past a construction site where he'd worked for someone else.

She'd become his extracurricular activity. Being with Cate and eventually building their own family.

A mother, a father and a son who'd never had any reason to be ashamed.

Richard cupped his chin, stroking thoughtfully. "But I guess I kept Alan pretty busy at home."

"Busy how?" Phoebe asked.

Alan studied the storm gathering in Cate's eyes. She had loved his father, understood his weaknesses. She'd grown up with her own secrets, the way her parents had left her, rumors of her aunt's affair with a married man, Uncle Ford's renowned talent for chasing half the nursing staff at the hospital, because he'd chauvinistically claimed they understood a man's needs.

In an unspoken collusion, she'd gone along with Alan's tendency to hide the truth. If Richard hadn't fallen in love with confession in his middle years, no one would ever have learned the truth about his paternal failures.

Richard turned to Phoebe, glad of an audience. "My son balanced our checkbook from the time he was ten years old."

"Why?" Phoebe's irreverent expression both charmed and disturbed Alan. She was too young to be so cynical. "Couldn't you manage your own accounts, Mr. Palmer?"

"Do we have to talk about this?" Cate interrupted with deceptive softness.

"I trusted him." Blind to Cate's meaning, his dad tried to defend trusting a ten-year-old with the family finances as a mark of his good judgment. "Alan was so precise I turned that responsibility over to him."

Cate's impatience grew, and Phoebe looked uncomfortable. "I shouldn't have asked," the young girl said.

Cate shook her head. "No, you didn't do anything wrong. I should pick my times better. I apologize for—"

"Cate, I sense you're upset with me. I know I wasn't the best father, but I love my son. Don't you think the fact I can see myself as I was is penance enough?"

Alan gave Cate credit for trying not to respond. Her skin flushed bright red, and her eyes glittered as if she were holding back tears. "You're lying to yourself if you think your behavior now makes things up to Alan. You treat his childhood as a joke, but I don't believe turning my husband into an adult at the age of ten was funny." She gulped a breath, and her calm voice spooked Alan as she stood up. "Excuse me. I didn't mean to ruin dinner."

Alan found himself on his feet at her side. She wasn't going anywhere without him. She'd been too ill to get this upset. Intent on getting her out of the house, he still caught a glimpse of his father's alarmed face.

"It's okay, Dad. You and Cate will settle this, but right now, we need air."

With nothing except her eyes, Cate told him she didn't want company. He didn't care. He had to prove, if only to himself, that she could depend on him.

She was annoyed with his father for a few bad decisions. She'd lose her mind if she found out about the company from someone else. And he'd lose Cate.

She pulled away from him and marched through

the kitchen, to the porch. Alan followed on feet that
felt like the cement blocks he'd soon not be able to
afford.

Beside the screen door, he switched on the soft
lights that illuminated the yard. The wooden porch
steps creaked beneath Alan's feet as Cate broke away
from him again, and he hurried after her.

Spanish moss dangled cool, spindly fingers
through her hair. She slapped it away as she headed
toward the river. Anger had conquered her limp. She
turned on him.

"I don't understand why they put up with your
father. How many people in this town know how he
treated you?"

"It's all in the past."

"He slaps you in the face with the past." She
threw her hands in the air. "Why do you put up with
it, Alan?"

Her harsh question made him flinch, as if she
thought him less a man because he wanted a relationship with his father. "I love him. I'm willing to
take what he can offer. That's all."

She calmed immediately. "I'm sorry. I didn't realize."

"My mother took a lot of him with her. Or maybe
when she left I saw him the way he really is, but he
did stay, and he keeps trying to be a better father to
me."

"I still don't know how you stand it. If I believed
I couldn't trust someone I loved to see to my best
interests…" She licked her lips. God, her lips had
felt full and firm and pliant beneath his just an hour
ago.

Had he kissed her for the last time? The marriage-breaking secret he'd kept squeezed his chest. She'd believe he'd hidden the truth for selfish reasons. And maybe he had in the beginning.

Alan shook his head. A cool night breeze off the river lifted his hair and cooled his heated skin. All of his childhood, he'd pretended life was normal. Cate alone had learned parts of the truth, but even to her, he hadn't confided the depth of loneliness that made him want to give her everything she needed. What if she still couldn't understand?

"I have to tell you something, and you're not going to like it."

"What?" Cate wrapped tight fingers around his arm, and he wondered what the hell she heard in his tone.

"A secret I have to tell you." He wanted to believe in his own courage, but fear of losing Cate forced him to say the words that might end his marriage. "When you walked in front of that car, you were leaving me because our business is in trouble, and I hadn't told you." She'd claim she was leaving because he'd lied to her, but he knew the truth. She'd been afraid of living without the good things his hard work brought them.

He didn't blame her. Women feared doing without.

She formed an O with her mouth. Only when she inhaled, did he realize he'd stopped breathing.

"I don't believe you," she said.

"I didn't want you to worry, but you'd made a special dinner, and I was late——" He broke off as he grasped what that special dinner must have meant. "You were going to tell me you were pregnant."

"Was I?" She looked relieved. "Are you sure?"

"I'd bet," he said, "but you walked in when I was talking to John Mabry, the police chief, and you must have heard us. I'm losing everything I worked for, everything that was important to us."

"What are you talking about?" she demanded, sounding riled again. "Why would I leave you when you needed me most? You're not making sense."

When he needed her? She thought he couldn't handle his own problems? He fought a surge of resentment.

"How bad is the business?" she asked. "I'd never abandon you."

"I don't need your help at work."

Cate widened her eyes and he tried to backtrack. "The business is what I do."

"You do the business, and I run your house? I take care of your son?" She molded her hands around her belly. "I carry the babies?"

Cate never used sarcasm, and she never got this upset this fast. "Have you remembered something, Cate?"

"No, but I'd give a lot to remember, so I don't have to depend on you to mete out the truth."

A body shot. "If you know yourself, why do you think you waited to tell me about the twins?"

She dropped her hands. "You want the truth? From what you said about your handling the company, I suspect I thought you'd like me barefoot and pregnant. You want to be the guy on the big white horse who saves the day, and you think I'd get in your way.''

"You're wrong." But he couldn't admit his deepest fear, that she'd think he wasn't man enough to support her. He saw no reason to let her in on his craven cowardice now.

"I'm wrong?" Her tone openly criticized. "Then you tell me the truth.''

His own temper finally showed up. "We agreed from the time Dan was born that you'd be home for him, and I'd take care of the company, but every time something goes wrong, and I do what I'm supposed to do—I protect you—you act as if I've been unfaithful."

"Every time?" She raked back her hair, unmistakable challenge in the familiar gesture. Known ground between them shifted.

"Let's stop now. You're still not well." He reached for her, but she pulled away. In the back of his mind, he'd dreaded this moment for as long as he'd known he loved her.

"I depended on you to tell me about my life, but now I think I made a mistake trusting you.''

"See it from my point of view. You're pregnant. You've forgotten me. I even wonder if I'm the reason you forgot everything. Was I supposed to tell you things that could make you worse? I just wanted a chance to make our marriage right again, to take care of my family.''

"Our company employs my sister. Think of Dan. Think of everyone who deserves a warning if the company is going to fail.''

"I agree with you, but I have to go along with the

other company heads involved, and they don't want to worry their employees or our creditors more than we have to. The police believe we're going to find Jim.''

''Who's Jim? What's happened?''

''He's our CPA, and he embezzled company funds.'' How many more times would he have to admit he'd let that scum dupe him?

''So I shouldn't worry my pretty little head? You let me babble on about starting a new marriage, and you hid the truth from me?''

''How could I drop everything on you in that hospital room?''

''I thought you might have—'' She cut herself off, her hesitation dripping discomfort. ''I thought you might have loved me, no matter what secrets we were both keeping. I don't know who I was before, but I refuse to live with a man who lies to me. Even now, you don't see me as your equal partner. Look at the way you've talked about our responsibilities—yours at work and mine at home.''

''I'm trying to protect our investments.'' He inhaled deeply. ''I believed you were too ill to know.'' And, frankly, he didn't want a marriage that felt like an extension of his business.

''Fine.'' She circled him, her hands wrapped around her belly. ''When you're ready to plan a joint solution you'll find me here.'' She turned back for one scathing moment. ''I can't believe people think the Talbots screw up their lives.''

''Meaning I have? Because we don't run our home like a business merger? When we got married we promised we wouldn't repeat history. We both made keeping our family intact our first priority.''

"You changed your mind." She walked away.

Fear and rage froze him. He was ten years old again, and his mother was walking out, just as graceful, just as determined, just as indifferent to pain that shredded him into small pieces.

Sheer will held his voice steady. "I'm asking you not to do this."

"If I can't trust you, I can't stay with you. Please don't come inside. I'll explain to Dan that you've gone home, and I want to stay with Aunt Imogen and catch up."

"What if I don't come back?" No woman was going to control him. If he gave up one more piece of himself, who would he be?

"Don't threaten me, Alan. You made a choice I don't respect, and now I have to trust Aunt Imogen and Caroline to tell me the truth."

As the screen door swished shut at her back, he clenched his teeth on a groan of pain that struck from his scalp to his toes.

On THE PORCH, in the dark shelter of Aunt Imogen's crazy garden, Cate breathed deep and willed her heartbeat to slow.

Had she just thrown her marriage away? She couldn't shake the last harsh image of Alan's stricken expression.

When she'd finally entered the kitchen, Caroline and Aunt Imogen met her with a cup of chamomile tea and a healthy helping of concern. Shelly pulled out a chair at the table.

"Where's Dan?" Cate asked.

"He took Phoebe to The Zombie Zone to listen to music," Shelly said.

"Is that a bar?" Cate shot each woman an anxious look. How tolerant were these Talbots?

"They don't serve alcohol," Caroline said. "Bands have come from all over the state to do a few nights at the zone since we were kids."

"And Richard and Meg?"

"I'm afraid we may have chased him out of the house," Aunt Imogen admitted. "I don't believe I ever saw him through your eyes before, and he appeared to dislike us looking at him tonight. Ford took him and Meg up to his house with their dinner. He asked me to tell you he was sorry."

Guilt and relief mixed in Caroline's thoughts. "I'm the one who should apologize. And Alan and I planned to talk to Dan about his graduation party when we got home tonight." A wave of nausea flip-flopped her belly. "Do we usually end an evening this way?"

"Not you, Aunt Cate," Shelly said. "Mom and I have. Remember that time I rode Polly and then didn't put her back in the barn?"

"Polly isn't a riding horse," Aunt Imogen explained.

"She was that day," Shelly said brightly. "But then she strolled through the porch door while we were eating dinner, and we had to chase her all the way to Uncle Ford's barn."

"I think the screaming made her bolt for familiar ground," Aunt Imogen said.

"And once we persuaded Polly the screen door

hadn't killed her, Mom dragged me home for a serious chat. I still say two weeks was too long to ground me for that, Mom.''

Caroline didn't say anything. She just came around the table and put her arm around Cate.

Their kindness made her self-conscious. ''I'm sorry I lost my temper.''

''No need,'' Aunt Imogen replied.

''Don't apologize,'' Caroline added.

''I'm not even sure what happened.'' Shelly balanced her hip on the chair.

''Alan and I talked about things we should have discussed weeks ago.'' Cate met her aunt's gaze. ''If you don't mind, I'd like to stay here a few days.''

''What about Alan?'' Aunt Imogen asked as all three women eyed Cate sharply.

''I need some time to myself.''

''I'd love having you. You need spoiling.'' Aunt Imogen looked doubtful, but didn't push.

''I am spoiled. I've been waiting to find out about my life, but I can't sit back any more.'' She wiped her arm across her eyes, relieved that her aunt and Caroline and Shelly were willing to be patient with her need for privacy.

Shelly looked at her watch, the canvas band barely held together by thick black thread she'd obviously used to mend it. She pushed away from the chair. ''Maybe I'll go look for him and make sure. What do you think, Mom?''

''I think it's a school night, and you need to be home at a decent hour. Do you have homework?''

''I had to translate a page of Voltaire, which I could have done in my sleep. I finished it in study hall." Shelly flounced toward the door. "I'll be home by ten. And maybe I should warn you Dan's made plans for graduation. We're going to a couple of the same parties." She grinned over her shoulder. "But feel free to figure out what presents you're going to give us."

Her sneakers squeaked on the hardwood floors. Cate stared from Aunt Imogen to Caroline. "Why does Dan always seem on the edge of losing his temper, but she looks like she's about to laugh from absolute joy?"

"I think I'm lucky," Caroline said.

"Maybe I should hope the next two are girls," Cate said before she remembered the "next two" were supposed to be a secret.

"What two?" Aunt Imogen asked, frowning so hard Cate half expected her tape to eject from her forehead.

"I'm pregnant. I wasn't supposed to say anything because Dan's ashamed, but I think I'm going to be sick anyway, and you'd probably guess."

"Or rush you to the hospital." Caroline hugged her tighter. "My guess would have been concussion, not a baby. You said you're having two?"

"Twins."

"I knew one of us would." Caroline let Cate go and clapped her hands together. "This explains the green tone of your skin lately."

Studying her sister, Cate saw where Shelly got her joy. Maybe in the next few days she'd find out why Caroline tried to hide hers.

"I hate to burst your bubble with reality, girls, but

now I have to know why you're here instead of with Alan, Cate?''

''We finally told each other the truth about some important problems we have, and I don't know if I can stay with him.'' She was too tired to paint a pretty picture, especially for her sister and her aunt.

''You don't have to be afraid,'' Caroline said. ''We're on your side.''

''Slow down.'' Aunt Imogen flattened her hand against Cate's nape. ''I can't agree with taking sides. Cate and Alan will work out their problems with each other. I love you two, but we Talbots historically run away from ugly situations, and I already helped you leave your marriage, Caroline.''

''As I recall, Ryan left me.''

''But I let you run to me, and I never suggested you fight to stay together. How many times do we have to throw love away before we learn to fight for it?''

Her unabashed passion about love startled Cate. She turned to Caroline, who quirked a smile Cate couldn't help returning. Her bond with her sister flirted at the edge of her consciousness. She felt Caroline turn toward Aunt Imogen at the same time she did.

''Laugh at me all you want if laughing makes you look like you belong together again.''

Caroline stood up and took cups from a cabinet above the sink. ''Start the coffee, Aunt Imogen, and we'll explain to Cate that my situation was different. Ryan Manning's plans didn't include marriage. And then you can tell us both if you chose to be alone because you loved someone else's husband.''

Cate stared at an echo of pain in the older woman's eyes. Aunt Imogen seemed to read Cate's mind.

"Don't worry. I've always been just as blunt with you. I should have explained the whole story a long time ago. Gossipy people in this town will tell you that Whitney Randolph and I had an affair. I don't care what they say. We didn't. When we recognized our feelings for each other, he asked for a transfer. He was a pilot out at the Naval base."

"I've been meaning to ask someone about that. I kept hearing the planes when I was in the hospital. Did you ever see him again?"

"Never." Her sadness made Cate's heart ache. "We agreed we couldn't even keep up with each other through my friendship with his wife. We both loved her too much."

"He might have been the one," Caroline said, but then snapped her mouth shut.

Cate eyed her in surprise. "Do you believe that we might have a 'one,' Caroline?"

"Not since Ryan, not for me anyway. Ryan simply didn't want to be a husband." Caroline glanced at the door through which her daughter had exited. "Or a father."

Cate shot a look at their aunt. "I hate to talk jargon, and I know our father was your brother, but don't you think Caroline and I would have made wiser choices if our parents had wanted us? I think that's what makes me so mad at Richard. I don't even remember my mother and father, but I feel abandoned because I know they chose the Navy over us. I think parents should live with their children and take care of them."

"Cate, you have to make your peace with Mom and Dad again." Caroline came away from the counter to hover around the table. "I'm sorry you have to start over, but you're a good parent and your marriage has lasted no matter what was wrong with it. You've made your choices, not Mom's and Dad's."

"And don't measure Alan by his father or my brother. Alan wants it all," Aunt Imogen said. "I haven't watched over you both all these years without seeing how much he loves you."

Cate held her tongue. With a few words she could disabuse her aunt and her sister of their mistaken assumptions about Alan. She'd forgotten him, but he knew her enough to be sure she wouldn't be able to endure his patriarchal attitude. The damning words refused to come.

Cate bit her lip. Apart from his lie to her, Caroline had a right to know her livelihood was in danger. She'd have to convince Alan to tell her.

Her continued loyalty to Alan bewildered her. She turned toward the night beyond the kitchen windows, and her feelings remained ambiguous. She'd sent her husband home in the middle of a quarrel. She remembered the day Caroline had told her their parents died after an argument.

Why couldn't he have been honest? "Why has he kept so many secrets from me?"

"About his father? Don't you think you might be overreacting?" Aunt Imogen asked softly. "Was he supposed to deliver a soliloquy on the past the moment he realized you couldn't remember? I imagine he's had other matters on his mind.''

Cate let them think Richard was her beef with Alan. ''I need to understand him.'' She smoothed her hand over her stomach, still terribly aware she'd kept an important secret of her own. Alan had learned early to depend only on himself. He'd had no choice with Richard. No one to talk to, even when he was afraid.

Aunt Imogen pulled her close. ''You've already learned something. You miss him. His answers to your questions are important to you.''

Cate agreed. ''But I resent him like crazy.''

''I'm relieved you're not really sick.'' Caroline seemed to consider the subject of Alan closed. She went to the counter and started the coffee herself. ''I knew you were hiding something from us all these months.''

''Before the accident? Why didn't you ask?''

''I told you in the hospital, some questions are off-limits between you and me because you're the big sister.''

''Being deathly ill is one of those bits of information I'd consider too personal to share?'' The incredulous question burst out of Cate. She couldn't have held it in if she'd covered her mouth with both hands. ''We're part of the oddest family, and I think we make trouble for ourselves.''

''Well…'' Aunt Imogen's astonished expression inferred it was about time Cate figured that out. ''We may be unusual, but we're lovable. Give us a chance, and you'll see.''

CHAPTER NINE

A WEEK LATER, Cate had caught up with Aunt Imogen's gardening, including a judicious trim of the people-eating plants on the porch that looked even more menacing now that she'd pruned them back. Even Aunt Imogen thought they waved their tidy little branches in search of revenge when she walked by.

Cate moved on to painting the porch, but she felt those plants behind her while she worked. When she finished, she picked up her paintbrush and the small can of paint and searched for imperfections in the walls. Finally satisfied, she entered the house, where Aunt Imogen handed her a glass of lemonade.

"You finished already? Can you change the oil in my car now, Cate?"

Cate avoided the extremely inviting lemonade and took the brush and paint to the sink. "I can try, I guess."

"Those paint fumes have gone to your head. You don't recognize sarcasm?"

"The fumes have gone somewhere." Cate grabbed her stomach and ran for the bathroom. Afterward, she hung over the sink, splashing cold water on her face. By the time she returned, Aunt Imogen had cleaned the brush and put the leftover paint away.

"All better?" she asked. "Are you hungry?"

"No," Cate groaned. "How can you ask?"

"Well, you don't have the flu or anything. I figured you might be hungry if you aren't really sick. I've never been pregnant."

Cate hugged her aunt. "You should have been. You're a loving mother to me."

"You've always said that." Her aunt beamed. "I think you're going to remember something soon. When did you last call Dan?"

"This morning." She glanced at the white clock on the wall above the stove. "I promised myself I'd call him when I finished painting."

"I'll give you some privacy. After you talk to him, have a shower, and I'll let you take me to town for lunch."

"I doubt I'll speak to him. They aren't returning my messages." Not that she'd expected Alan to call her back.

"You can't give up," Aunt Imogen said. "I'm going to choose a hat for our outing."

There was a promise that struck fear into the hearts of strong women. Cate nervously dialed her home phone and got the machine that apparently erased messages as soon as she recorded them. She was sick of hearing her own voice.

Cate hung up the phone and slumped at the kitchen table. Truthfully, she wanted to hear Dan's voice. Or Alan's. Especially Alan's. She missed them. How were they getting on without her? She secretly hoped they were just as miserable as she was.

She sagged forward until her face touched the table. The wooden surface cooled her cheek. She closed her eyes and imagined her loneliness as a dark wave of nothing that seemed to swallow her whole. She'd felt better with Alan and Dan. She was supposed to be with them, flipping pancakes and fighting for her independence.

She loved her aunt, treasured the new memories they'd made together with Uncle Ford and Polly and the houses of her youth, but her life lay in the house Dan and Alan were sharing.

"Cate? Honey, are you sick again? What's wrong?"

"Nothing." She straightened and wrapped her arm around her aunt's waist. "They'll come to Dan's graduation, won't they?"

Aunt Imogen tipped Cate's chin. Her gaze indulged her forlorn niece's. "Dan has to be there."

"But Alan will go, too, won't he?"

"You miss them?"

"I can't trim one more plant, mow one more blade of grass or paint another picket in your fence. I've been pretending I didn't feel as if I've misplaced a major part of myself. Why didn't Alan at least stay to talk when he brought my clothes over?"

"Because you told him you didn't want to live with him right now. A man takes offense as easily as a woman, you know."

"I do know." Cate rose and took the tattered phone book off its shelf. "Even Richard. I owe him an apology, too, and I won't put it off any longer."

"Do you want more privacy?"

"Yes, please. I'm humiliated that I put it off so long."

"You don't have to look up the number. I wrote it on the back page."

Cate turned the book over and opened the back page. Aunt Imogen had scrawled phone numbers at wild angles in every blank space she could find. Cate looked at the book's cover again. "1984?"

"Do you know how long it takes to transfer those numbers every year? I add any new ones in the back."

"Okay." Cate finally found Richard's number and began dialing. She put off the last digit until Aunt Imogen left her alone in the kitchen.

He answered right away, as if he kept the phone in his pocket. "Is she home yet?"

"Richard, it's me, Cate."

"I thought you were Alan. Did you forget his number?"

"I called to apologize." She suddenly recognized what he'd said. "Has he called you to talk about me?"

"Just to tell me he misses you, as if I didn't know. Do you want me to call him?"

"No," she said, too vigorously. "I want to apologize for the way I behaved at dinner."

"Don't waste another thought on that night. I'm sorry I rub you the wrong way, and I miss your friendship."

"Were we friends?"

"I thought so. Now, I wonder if you put up with me for Alan's sake. You and I should talk our problems out."

"I don't think that's a good idea until we're more used to each other," she said. She didn't see how he could explain his past away. "But I want us to get along."

"As do I."

"Next time we see each other, I'll be polite."

"And I won't say a word about my son."

"That might do the trick, Richard, but I won't hold you to your promise."

"I'd like you to promise you'll come to my wedding."

"I promise." She hoped she'd occupy a pew between Alan and Dan.

"And warn me before I annoy you so much you change your mind."

She laughed. "You've been generous about this, Richard."

"I can be, you know." He turned his head from the phone. "Cate," he whispered, reminding her of Uncle Ford's attempts to be furtive. "Meg says to tell you hi."

"Say hello for me. I have to take Aunt Imogen to lunch, but I'm glad you were home."

"Me, too. Bye, Cate-girl."

He hung up while she marveled at the affectionate pet name. She turned to find Aunt Imogen in the kitchen doorway, tying the ribbon of a peony-covered straw hat beneath her chin.

"Skillfully accomplished," Aunt Imogen congratulated her.

"Thanks. Now I'm ready to take Alan on. He might ignore my calls, but he can't duck me at our son's graduation." She squared her shoulders. "Do you mind if we make a stop in town? I noticed Shelly's watch is all beaten up, and I want to buy her a new one as a graduation present.''

TEN DAYS AFTER his mother left home, Dan took his place in the line of graduating seniors. Silent, waiting in front of the Leith Community Center, he stood alone in the milling group of over a hundred. He refused to look for his parents in the crowd that streamed past to take seats in the overheated auditorium.

His mother hadn't bothered to see him. Why should he look for her? He'd be leaving in a little over five weeks, just after the Fourth of July. He'd tried to talk to his dad, who'd said the argument wasn't Dan's problem.

Right. It was only because it would have made him seem like a girl that he hadn't asked Aunt Imogen to put him up, too.

Except that would have meant rooming near his mom. He could have turned to Uncle Ford, but the horses lived in cleaner quarters than his uncle.

So he'd stayed at home with his furious father. They'd both ignored the phone. Maybe his dad thought like he did, that his mom would come home if she couldn't get them on the phone.

He'd stumbled through finals. He hardly remembered them. And he wondered why his mom didn't care how she'd screwed up their family. She couldn't remember her past. Fine, but all these years, during one silent battle of wills after another between his parents, he'd convinced himself they'd never split up.

Wrong again.

"Hey, whassup?" Floral perfume accompanied the question, a breath of fresh female that made his knees lock.

He turned. Phoebe sported a new ring today, this one through her eyebrow, gold that shimmered next to the silver ring she'd already worn there.

She followed his gaze and touched the new hoop. "Cool, huh? Graduation gift from my father's sister. He and Mom nearly collapsed over the cheese eggs."

At Phoebe's house, breakfast would never be a meat product and eggs. "I like it," he said. What he wanted to do was pull his "friend" into his arms and lick that scent off her.

"What's wrong with you?" She patted his arm, totally not getting it. "Still upset about your mom? She'll come home. Mine always does."

"But do you ever think your mom won't?"

"I think when my mom and dad decide the sex has slowed down, they pick a fight. My mom walks out, and at the exact moment they'd explode if they had to keep their hands off each other, she strolls back into the house. My sister and I have seen every movie Hollywood ever made because my mom always times her arrival so we can make the matinees."

"My mom never walked before."

"She didn't know the value of a good break." Phoebe linked her arm with his, and her perfume seemed to seep into his skin. "There she is."

"I don't give a damn. Phoebe, is that smell you?"

She pulled away, forgetting his mother. She felt

what he felt. Her eyes grew full of feelings he'd never connected with Phoebe back when they'd hunted turtles or chased crabs down the beach together.

"I told you that night when we left your aunt's, Dan, I won't let you use me to teach your parents a lesson. You know I scared them both silly, so I look pretty good to you."

"My mom liked the way you looked." He laughed at Phoebe's grimace. "You don't want someone her age to like the way you look, do you?"

She glared at him. "I don't like you letting her walk into that auditorium without acknowledging her. She was flagging you down, man."

"Mom has my dad," he said.

"No she doesn't." Phoebe eyed him curiously. "She was alone. You expected them to come together?"

"To my graduation? Yes." Damn right, he did. "I ought to walk out this time."

"Not a chance." She gripped his hand. "If I have to stand this kid stuff, you're standing it with me. You'd better be in your chair when they call your name, Dan Palmer."

"Or what?" What could she do to the Amazing, Invisible Palmer?

"Don't try me."

He'd never been a person who tried. He'd let life push him around. Why change now when it was getting so good? He took a deep breath that almost turned him into a crybaby.

Jeez, he missed his mom.

PERSPIRATION PRICKLED between Cate's shoulder blades. She arched her back as she craned to see over the whispering families around her. She'd come early, hoping for a glimpse of Dan. A glimpse was all she'd had.

Phoebe had seen her. Cate was sure she had, but she either hadn't alerted Dan, or Dan had decided to ignore his windmilling mother. She'd probably embarrassed him.

"Hey, sis. Did you see your boy outside?"

Cate forced a smile as she turned to Caroline, who must have entered the row of seats from the aisle opposite the one Cate had used. "I saw him, but I think he ignored me. How's Shelly?"

"Nervous, and so hot she put on shorts under her gown. I hope she doesn't trip. If Aunt Imogen sees her shorts, I'm a dead woman."

Caroline shook her hair away from her face, and Cate wondered why she reached for a blow-dryer every morning when her hair could look as loose and free as her sister's dark auburn curls.

Caroline slipped into a chair one seat over from Cate. "I don't believe he ignored you. He asked me to tell you hello. Phoebe was with him, and you know, I don't care if she's valedictorian. She scares me. If a guy who looked like that came calling for Shelly, I'd move."

"Because of the way he looks? That seems odd coming from you."

"Why from me?" Caroline settled a small envelope purse, more chic than anything Cate owned, on her lap.

"Look at us. I don't think anyone could tell us apart, but are we the same person?"

"No." Caroline's answer came with alacrity. "You're nicer than I am, but I'm more determined."

Cate studied her sister's slightly angular bone structure. She certainly held her faintly pointed chin at a firm angle. "I'm not that nice. I left Dan when I swore I wouldn't hurt him." She missed Alan, but abandoning Dan had been wrong. He couldn't get used to the idea of his new siblings, and now she'd busted up his life a week before he graduated from high school.

Caroline relaxed against the uncomfortable, slatted wood chair, but Cate felt the strangest sensation— her sister's confusion. After a moment, Caroline straightened again and pulled her hair off her neck, searching fruitlessly for the slightest hint of coolness in the humid auditorium.

"I thought I had us pegged. Was I wrong?" Caroline asked. "Maybe we've worked with equal single-mindedness toward different goals."

"What were yours?"

"Making a living that provided for my daughter. Shelly was only three when Ryan left us. I've been grateful to Alan for the work, and I think we make a good team, but I should have been home more."

Cate endured a slight jab of jealousy. "You and Alan work closely together?"

"I've designed the interiors for every building he's ever put up." Caroline looked proud. "We've made a name for ourselves, because we specialize in designs architects have used since Leith became a playground for the rich and famous in the late nineteenth century.''

''Sounds expensive.''

''We aren't cheap,'' Caroline said, ''but we use the money from new construction to work on projects we really love. The renovations. More and more, people buy cottages like yours. They used to be plentiful along the coast, but these days, their owners mostly have them moved here.'' Caroline laughed. ''The muckety-mucks who turned up their noses at Aunt Imogen after that whole Whitney episode are even angrier now with our family, because we don't boycott new owners who buy the land our high-and-mighty citizens sell. Then, the new people—nouveau riche, according to some of our local snobs—have the nerve to move an old cottage here, or have one built to contemporaneous blueprints. Nouveau riche cheek by jowl with old money. I like the work. I don't care how it comes to us, and I'm grateful to Alan. He's always been there for Shelly and me.''

Cate shifted restlessly. Her sister was so much more sure of her husband than she was. ''Why do you suppose Alan didn't tell me all this?''

''Did you ask him?''

Caroline's blunt response raised Cate's hackles. ''I don't know what to ask.'' And she didn't know which of his answers had been lies.

''Have you been happier without him?''

Cate didn't want to answer. Alan came to mind at times that shook her. When she was sound asleep, she woke with his name on her lips. When she thought of Dan, Alan stood with him in her mind.

She couldn't talk about the grief that swamped her at those moments.

"I've wondered about him."

"He's been a bear at work. No matter what he did, he loves you. You're better off fighting it out than pretending you don't care."

"You sound like Aunt Imogen."

"I shouldn't have taken your side against Alan." Caroline leaned into Cate's shoulder. "But when push comes to shove, you're my first concern."

Cate nodded at a stranger who spoke her name before she turned in her seat, the better to see her twin. "What if he lied to me, and I can't trust him?"

"What if he decides he can't forgive you for leaving him? I know you don't remember him. I know Alan is a grown man, but he hasn't forgotten how his mother left his father, or their agreement to not have a relationship. He's lived by that agreement. What if you remember him, and you decide you want to work on your marriage, but it's too late?"

Her relationship with her husband was too private to discuss with Caroline. "Tell me about his mother. How did they decide not to see each other? Richard implied he didn't let her see Alan."

"Maybe when he was younger, but when Alan was in high school, she came to tell him she didn't want people to know she had a son his age. She told him not to look for her when he was old enough to act without Richard's approval."

Her heart ached for an Alan who faintly resembled their gangly, almost adult son. "I told Richard I was sorry for the way I treated him, but I don't understand why Alan let either one of them get away with what they did to him.''

''Do you see Alan begging anyone to love him?''

''No.'' Except he had begged her not to leave him. He'd let her see his pain, and it had been as real as the ache she felt now for the husband she didn't remember marrying, the father of the babies growing inside her and the son whose life passage they were celebrating separately. ''Have you seen him yet, Caroline?''

''No, but when he comes, give him a chance to explain.''

''I'll ask him to sit with us.''

''He said he had to stop by the office on the way over here.''

He must not have told Caroline about their business problems yet, so Cate had an excuse to talk to him.

''Rosalie Danvers, I was talking to you.'' From the back of the room, Uncle Ford's voice boomed. Cate and Caroline turned in their seats.

''He's always had a thing for Rosalie.'' Caroline waved at Aunt Imogen, who'd entered behind Uncle Ford.

Adorned with the cap-and-gown-embossed tape today, she wriggled between seats to take the chair between Cate and Caroline. ''I thought I'd stand out with my tape, but Ford, running after that Rosalie, makes me look nice and sane. Did you arrive in time to talk with Dan, Cate?''

''He didn't see me.''

''I saw him. They look as if they're about to revolt out there, where I must say they're getting a nice ocean breeze. I hope when they complete the refurbishment on this place, they take care of central air.''

"Refurbishment?'' Cate said.

Caroline leaned around Aunt Imogen. ''They gave the contract to one of our rivals. A company from Brunswick, but they've fallen behind. The renovation was supposed to have been complete by today.''

Asking if that company shared Alan's CPA might have put ideas in Caroline's head, but Alan's secret wore on Cate. She changed the subject. ''Why did you wear the tape today, Aunt Imogen?''

"For Dan. He mocks me for it, but I finally realized he was grown-up when I caught him looking at my strip of tape, and then he looked into my eyes with love.''

Cate envied Aunt Imogen a little. ''I think I understand what you mean.'' She turned back. ''I wish I'd talked to him.''

"We'll catch him after the ceremony.''

"If he wants to see me,'' Cate said in a low voice.

Aunt Imogen looped her arm around Cate. ''He wants to see you. Maybe he doesn't know how to tell you. With the twins coming, he may feel displaced. The coincidence of your being pregnant just when he's leaving home might have damaged his self-esteem.''

Cate looked from her sister to her aunt. ''Remember, he doesn't know you know.''

"You'd better tell him we know soon, or we're going to look like dopes. Have you looked in a mirror lately?'' Aunt Imogen stretched to search the crowd as Cate's ego tried to recover from her ambush. ''Where is that Alan?''

"I thought he'd be here by now," Cate said. All around them, the elderly speakers crackled with the initial strains of *Pomp and Circumstance*. "Maybe he's closer to the front."

"No, I looked for him while I was waiting for Ford to talk Rosalie into sitting with him." Aunt Imogen shook her head. "I can't believe he'd be late for this."

"You say that like he's late a lot."

"You'll have to talk to him about his punctuality."

"Or lack of it. He should be here for his son."

"You're not looking for reasons to be angry with him? I know you're wary of living with a stranger you feel has betrayed you, but you've been open with me, Cate. Give him the same chance."

"Shhh, here they come," Caroline said.

Aunt Imogen stood, and Cate followed. Caroline reached around their aunt to squeeze Cate's hand, as if they'd both worked hard for this day. Cate longed for the richness of a past, the events and images Caroline still knew.

She'd stopped on her way to the auditorium to pick up a disposable camera. She pulled it from her purse and searched each graduate's face, hoping she'd recognize Dan beneath his navy-blue cap. These young adults looked more young than adult today.

She saw Shelly, who grinned with her customary joy. Cate took Shelly's picture, and at last she saw her son. His green eyes, as large and deep as his father's, caught hers. After a long, painful second, Dan smiled a faint smile that made Cate's day. She'd begun to care for him, not just because everyone told her he was her child, but because Dan mattered. Stinging tears made her blink, and Dan looked away.

In the nick of time, she remembered the camera and snapped a picture of him walking. His serious, thin face, sober beyond his years, made Cate's decision. She had to ask Alan if she could come home and find out what kind of life they had left.

She didn't want to cause the kinds of problems for Dan or the twins that she and Alan had yet to get over. She'd like Dan to trust the woman he eventually chose to marry, not to poison their relationship with mistrust he'd learned at his parents' knees.

Dan took his place at the front of the velvet-roped seats with the other graduates. As he sat, she caught sight of Richard a few rows behind Dan. They nodded at each other. Cate divided her attention between the speakers, as they opened the ceremony, and the doors, closed now against any slight promise of coolness, as well as the threat of late-arriving guests. As seconds ticked past, she grew so anxious to see Alan burst through the doors at the back that she lost track of the goings on in the front of the auditorium.

Then a voice caught her attention.

"I remember that first day of school, my blue Tiger Woman lunch box, the terrifying home perm my mom put in my hair, and the black nail polish I insisted on."

Phoebe's voice, clear and light and flying on strength that lifted it above the audience's laughter, made Cate glad the young woman was Dan's friend.

"Since then, I've learned about reading and math, chemistry and botany and the stars. I've made new friends, lost old friends and wished I were friends with people who didn't want to be my friend. I've hurt my parents, skinned my knees and learned to drive. Most of all, I've learned how to live, and like my fellow graduates, I'll take these life lessons into the new world that opens up to me today.''

A tear surprised Cate, dripping from her cheek to the top of her hand. Dan probably shared some of Phoebe's memories. Her speech probably evoked memories in every human being in this huge room.

Not in Cate. To her, the past was empty. Why hadn't she stayed to fight for her future with Alan?

She turned away from Aunt Imogen and Caroline, unwilling to expose her loneliness. She'd been angry because Alan had lied to her, because he hadn't defended himself against his father's flip confessions. But she'd also forgotten that a man whose parents had abandoned him emotionally and physically would hurt most if his wife deserted him. She couldn't keep leaving if she meant to stay.

After Phoebe's speech, the principal began to call students to the podium for their diplomas. With each name, Cate forgot her new will to work her marriage out with Alan. How could he risk disappointing Dan?

She tapped her feet to keep from swearing at fate and Alan and her own frustration on her son's behalf. Light slashed across her face. She turned to find its source.

Alan stood just inside the door he was easing shut. Relief hit her in a wave, but Alan's intense expression changed relief to awareness.

She turned and followed his gaze to the back of their son's oblivious head. He loved Dan.

He lifted a video camera and added the whirring of its mechanisms to the low hum of the other parents' cameras. Aiming at Dan, he continued to shoot and then he turned the camera on Shelly.

"Thank God," Aunt Imogen said.

Startled at her vehemence, Cate realized she didn't quite know her aunt as well as she thought. She'd believed in Aunt Imogen's faith in Alan.

"Not that I doubted he'd get here in time to see Dan cross that stage," Aunt Imogen said.

"Does he know how good a friend you are to him?"

Her aunt's mouth curved in an acknowledgement of Cate's teasing. "I suspect he does."

"Shelly Imogen Manning," the principal called.

Aunt Imogen and Caroline linked hands, and Cate covered their hands with hers. As Shelly left the podium, she waved her cap, and they saw flowers hand painted on the mortarboard. Aunt Imogen cried, while Cate and Caroline laughed, and the principal continued calling students in a reproving tone.

"Daniel Ford Palmer," he finally intoned.

Standing, Cate found herself making a woof sound that nearly brought the whole proceedings to a halt. The room rustled as every person in it turned. From closer to the stage, Uncle Ford stood and copied Cate's approving bark. Off to her left, Alan did the same.

Aunt Imogen dried her tears to join Caroline in laughter, and the rest of the room copied them. His face flaming, Dan slouched up the stairs to take his diploma from the principal's hand, but then he turned toward Cate and woofed with her.

She subsided into her seat, tingling with pleasure. This was what being a Talbot felt like. Misbehaving in public. And not caring.

She veered her gaze from Dan to Alan and felt a sense of connection. Disturbingly undefined toward Alan. But Dan—her pride, the sheer happiness that washed through her as she studied the planes of his young face. That had to be a mother's love.

Walking back down the aisle, Dan stopped inches from his father. Alan's face seemed to crumple. His mouth tilted at a painful angle that exposed his lack of control where Dan was concerned.

She needed to believe in Alan's ability to lose control. Everything she'd learned about him told her he'd tried to peg her into a slot that made his life safe. To continue in their troubled marriage, Cate needed to believe he could care for her if she didn't fit the slot.

She lifted her camera to catch him hugging Dan, but then she lowered the camera, unable to look away from them. In her mind, she saw herself walking down the row to meet them. Before she could convince herself not to go, she was on her feet.

Neither saw her. She was two, maybe three steps away, when Alan said, close to Dan's ear, "I'm sorry I'm late again, son."

Dan laughed, but Cate's feet stuck to the floor. "It's okay, Dad. I'm used to waiting for you." He turned slightly to include Cate in the conversation. "And here's Mom, mad at you already, so at least we don't have to worry there might be an argument because you're late."

She noted Dan's sarcasm, but she'd forgotten to

be annoyed with Alan until Dan repeated Aunt Imogen's opinion of his promptness. Dan and the twins deserved a father they could count on. "Should I go back?"

Alan pulled her close. Her shoulder connected with his chest, and she felt him shiver.

"I'm tardy," he said. "I didn't miss the ceremony or commit a crime. Come on, you two. Let's go outside before they have the football team throw us out."

"I'm not sure I should," she admitted. She'd have to explain the amount of grief she planned to give him if he ever showed up late for another family occasion.

"But you want to come with me. I saw."

Dan pushed ahead of them, his ears as red as his face. "Do you have to rattle the family skeletons in front of everyone in this town? Just post the divorce papers on your Web site, Dad."

"Cool it, son."

Alan kept a firm grip on Cate's arm. Determined not to add public brawling to their sins in Dan's eyes, she gave in.

Alan leaned down as Dan shoved the auditorium door open. "I know you're upset with me, but today belongs to him. You can take me apart after he leaves for his party."

"Parties." Mindful of Shelly's announcement that ugly night at Aunt Imogen's, Cate hadn't mentioned Dan's plans in the phone calls he hadn't returned. She relaxed against Alan. "You have a deal."

Their son jerked his cap off and unzipped his

gown, ignoring interested stares from parents who'd
sneaked outside to smoke or escape the heat.

"Should you go back for the end of the ceremony?" Cate asked.

"It's too hot. If you can stand each other for a
whole hour, I want an ice cream cone." He tossed
his cap to his father, who caught it easily. "Who
knows?" Dan said. "You may never get to buy me
ice cream again."

Nonsense. His school lay hardly more than an hour
north on a fast road, according to Aunt Imogen.

"I'll bring all you can eat," Cate said.

A little thing like distance couldn't force her to
lose touch with him now. To become his mother
again, she'd yank her old life back on like a suit of
clothes—even if it no longer fit.

Dan turned back, his expression baleful. "Sounds
great, Mom. Don't forget my favorite bib."

CHAPTER TEN

SUNLIGHT GLINTED off his wife's dark-auburn hair. Perched as far away from him as she could manage on the bench they shared, she attacked her peach cone with zest. She'd loved Nonie's Hand Dipped Ice Cream Parlor since her Uncle Ford had staked Nonie the nest egg that put her first, small shop up on the boardwalk.

When Dan came along, their family visits had assisted Nonie with her ambition to move into larger quarters, which Alan had built. He turned to Cate, but whatever inane remark he'd been on the verge of saying about their family history with Nonie's ice cream died on his lips.

With the tip of her tongue, Cate dragged a trail through the melting, frozen treat. As if she sensed his interest, she glanced his way. A drop of peach lingered on the corner of her lip. Alan forced himself to look away.

Maybe he wasn't as bad as she thought, but he certainly had illicit designs on a woman who no longer knew him from Adam. Didn't matter. He hadn't forgotten her.

The ten days he'd lived without his wife had taught him one thing. He had no idea what his wife wanted from him, and he wasn't likely to stumble onto the key to her heart and mind. When she'd told him to leave, he'd thought he might die. He hadn't gone home, because he hadn't wanted Dan to see him in such a defenseless state.

He'd parked about a mile from their house and wandered into the dunes. He'd needed several hours to work himself from the age of ten, deserted, unloved, unwanted, back into manhood, where he had a choice about the amount of grief he took from a woman. Even a woman he loved. And how could he stop loving Cate?

Wandering their empty house, he'd realized Cate was different since the accident. She hummed now. All the time. Melodies that lingered in his head and annoyed him for days at a time.

Until she'd taken her songs away and turned him into a guy who thought with his broken heart. This new Cate made him crazy, where his Cate had tried to make him happy.

"Dad, you're melting." Dan held out his hand. "What is that? Mississippi Mud? I'll take it if you don't want to finish."

Alan bit a chunk of chocolate and nuts and marshmallow. "It's good," he said.

"Are you going to eat it?" Dan stood, digging for change in his pocket. "I think I'll get one, too."

With a bemused look on her face, Cate watched him walk away.

"Hollow leg," Alan said.

"I'm envious. Too many of these." She paused for a lick that sent his thoughts on another erotic wild-goose chase. "And Dr. Davis will fire me as her patient."

"How do you feel?"

Her stomach seemed to have grown in the past week. The mint-green dress that belted at her back draped in clinging folds around her distended belly.

"I'm fine. A little dizzy this week, and my back aches."

Peach ice cream dripped down her wrist. Once he would have eased over and cleaned that for her, but now he passed her a napkin. "Is that normal?"

"For a woman carrying twins?" She lifted her arm to her mouth and caught a small fleck of peach with the tip of her tongue. "I'm fine. I see Dr. Davis next Thursday." She glanced at him, and the lust in his gaze must have taken her aback. "What?"

He couldn't take a breath to answer. His mind filled with the ways he might show her here and now she belonged to him. They'd never been able to resist their strong attraction. He hadn't changed.

"Are you all right, Alan?"

He coughed, and then he pitched the rest of his cone into the garbage can that sat beyond the next table.

"Ice cream go down the wrong pipe?" She scooted over and pounded his back with her non-sticky hand.

"Cut it out." Her complete oblivion tried his patience, and he captured her fingers, so she couldn't return to her corner. Time to get to the point. "Are you coming home?"

As she hesitated ice cream dripped back down her wrist. This time he cleaned her arm himself.

"Phoebe's speech convinced me I was hasty. I

planned to ask you if I could come home, but your present mood scares me a little.''

Her teasing was out of character. ''You are no one I know,'' he said.

''I don't know who I am, either, but I'm trying to figure myself out. Do you want me to come home with you?''

He'd risked everything. He'd told her the truth. Now she wanted him to beg her again. ''You always said I could trust you to stay if I was honest. You left.''

''I don't know about always from before the accident, and I'm sorry I left, but I'm asking you to start over.'' She glanced toward the door, eager to finish her piece before their son returned. ''Before we agree on anything, I need to know you can change, too. I didn't like what Dan said about being used to waiting for you.''

''I was late because I met with Jim's other clients. We argued about hiring a private detective to see if we can get a quicker response than the police are giving us.''

''Did you warn Dan you had a meeting?''

''As a matter of fact, I spoke to Caroline this morning.''

Cate sat back, shocked. ''You told her about Jim?''

''No.'' But he'd have to soon. Far from improving, his business seemed to be going downhill fast. Whispers had started among the businesses that held notes he and his colleagues had to pay. ''I told her I had to stop by the office.''

"What's your priority, Alan? The business or Dan and the babies and me?"

"Without the business, how do I provide for you and the children?" He tasted panic as he realized what kind of changes they'd both have to make if he couldn't save their company.

"I'll help you," she said. "We can salvage our lives, but you have to be willing to share the problem with me."

It wouldn't come to that. "You and our family are my priority, but that means I have to take care of the business."

"Then you can't promise Dan won't have to wait for you any more?"

"What are you talking about?"

"I don't want to be his only parent." A chunk of ice cream slid off the top of her cone. With a tense grimace, she scooped up the mess in a napkin and carried the whole cone to the nearest garbage can. "I have to believe you'll be on time for family events like Dan's graduation."

"I tried. Why are you asking me to make promises I might not be able to keep? I don't want to let you down."

"Trying isn't enough." She sat at the edge of the bench. "I don't remember Dan. I don't share any of the memories Phoebe spoke of—but you didn't hear the valedictorian at your son's graduation."

She had a point that went straight to his heart. "Maybe I should have rescheduled the meeting." Especially since they hadn't managed to agree on a course of action.

"Didn't any of the others have children here to-day?"

"I get your point, Cate."

She wrapped her arms around her belly. "Am I nagging?"

"No." He slid to her side and dropped his arm around her. "I feel guilty because you're right."

"We have to provide for Dan and the twins, but I don't know why you want to carry all the responsibility."

He rested his chin on top of her head. "You are pregnant, not that I mean pregnancy makes you less able to work, but you don't need extra worry. Anyway, I won't be late next time."

She relaxed, as if she believed him. While he marveled at her trust, her scent climbed his body, awakening every nerve in its path. Broken only by the whispery chat of waves breaking ashore, and the distant hum of cars driving past the boardwalk, several seconds passed between them. More satisfying than any they'd shared since before she'd stormed into his office.

"We should have stayed at the community center to see Shelly," she said.

"We'll go by Aunt Imogen's before we go home."

She nodded, rubbing her face against his chest. Need for her surged through him so fiercely he had to clench his teeth to keep from groaning. He wanted her home. In their house. He wanted her to himself.

He leaned back to peer into her gorgeous, fathomless eyes. "We'll probably see my dad there, too. He tells me you negotiated a truce."

She looked anxious. "I want to understand Richard, but I feel protective of you."

Gratitude made him press his lips to her forehead. Maybe he could get used to this Cate who was so determined to take care of him. He kissed her again. Her skin, firm and warm beneath his mouth, tasted just slightly of salt. From the spray off the water or perspiration? He shouldn't have kept her in the sun this long.

"Where's Dan?" He turned, and his son came through the shop's door as if he'd waited inside for some sign they were ready for company.

Dan took a bite of his already half-eaten cone. "Are you guys ready? I have places to go."

"Yes, you do," Cate said. "Aunt Imogen's house. You can let them wish you well while I pick up my things."

"You're coming home?" A huge grin curved his mouth, but he straightened it out fast. "I guess I can go by Aunt Imogen's. I'll see if Shelly needs a ride tonight."

"Dan, you won't drink and drive?" Cate broke away from Alan to join their son as he headed for the car.

Alan allowed himself a grin that felt at least as big as Dan's had been. His Cate still lurked inside the rabble-rouser who'd possessed his wife's body.

Dan made a show of teenaged forbearance. "We made reservations for dinner, and then we'll probably end up at someone's house listening to music."

She couldn't complain about that. Of course, she couldn't remember how they'd celebrated her graduation. On a blanket in the dunes not far from where they lived now. He still had a soft spot for those dunes she'd refused to revisit.

CATE AWOKE like the dead on Judgment Day. A shrill tone had tossed her from an unusually peaceful sleep. The alarm system. She groped the tangled sheets, but she was alone. Then she remembered. She was glad to be home, but still unready to share her bed.

She scrambled to her feet and hurried to the hall. Her door squeaked a loud protest as she opened it. So much for surprising their intruder.

"It's me, Mom." Downstairs, Dan tapped out the code that reset the alarm.

Cate waited for him to climb the stairs. "Did you enjoy yourself?" she called.

"Yeah. I'm just going to watch a little TV. Night."

She waited. Was he alone? She'd noticed the way he looked at Phoebe. Dan's feelings were definitely strengthening into a more serious emotion than friendship.

What did normal mothers do in this situation? Snooping felt wrong, but what had she and Alan taught Dan about behaving responsibly with a girl-friend?

She should have asked Alan. She glanced at his door. Was he asleep or merely staying out of her conversation with Dan?

Ridiculous. Ask tomorrow. Dan hadn't said he'd brought anyone home. He probably hadn't.

"Night," she finally called.

"Are you still up?" Dan sounded amused. "Don't worry, I'm alone down here."

Busted. "Good night," she said in a crisp voice, but she laughed as she closed her door.

She crossed the room and slid back into bed. Even in the house's more than efficient air-conditioning, her bedclothes felt too heavy. She kicked the sheet down her legs, until it covered only her feet.

Lying in darkness, she recounted the day's events and she let herself hope. She and Alan had shared a quiet dinner in a house that had felt strangely empty without Dan. Ending the evening on a nearly perfect note, Dan had teased her about her uncontrollable maternal response.

Her sense of well-being should have let her sleep, but insomnia crowded her. She turned on her side and flipped on the lamp beside the bed. She saw the room as a place she'd made special for her and Alan.

She pushed her feet over the edge and padded to the bureau. Behind all the other family pictures, holding pride of place, sat a photo of her and Alan on their wedding day. She looked impossibly young, blindly adoring, as she took her husband's face in her hands.

Had she ever been a woman who could believe so completely? How could she allow herself to become that woman if depending on Alan took all her will-power?

The hope that had felt like a lifeline melted away. She searched the room for something familiar to cling to, for courage to make herself part of her family again.

Her gaze came back to the photo. Behind her stood

her sister. Caroline's gaze replicated hers, shining
with pure joy, luminous with belief in the future.
Caroline didn't look like that any more, either. What
had happened to them?

Life, said a voice in her head, and a cool whistle
of wind brushed her face. She whipped her head toward the window, but it was closed.

An image splashed in her mind, the chrome grille
on a green car, anger that grabbed at her from behind.
Despair reached through the fog in her mind. She
gasped at a physical blow that made her grope for
the lip of the tall dresser. She reached for more, the
reason for such overpowering anger.

Why had Alan lied? How had he lied before that
horrible day?

But all that remained of the glimpse into her own
past was her certain knowledge she had to leave to
protect the life she carried in her body. She couldn't
force herself to live in a fabric of lies.

Her knees buckled. She caught the handle on one
of the bureau drawers and sank to the floor. A groan
seeped between her lips. She'd trusted Alan. She remembered accusing him. She remembered telling
him she had to leave. She couldn't face raising another child in a vacuum.

She remembered the shock that had stretched the
skin across his face, and his disbelief made her angry.
His previous deceit remained a mystery to her now,
but the truth about herself mortified her. Despite
Alan's unforgivable betrayal, in some heartsick corner of her soul, she'd wanted to stay with a husband
she couldn't rely on.

Cate cradled the mound of her belly. Her glimpse

of the past had literally cut her legs out from under her, but life continued to grow inside her. A connection, soul deep, never to be broken, twined between her and these two lives dependent on her.

The phone rang. Its abrasive trill screamed across down her skin. She waited through another ring before she climbed on aching muscles to her hands and knees. Finding her feet, she staggered to the nightstand and picked up the portable telephone. A female voice spoke before she brought the receiver close enough to hear the woman's words.

She muttered a sound.

"Cate?"

Caroline's urgency frightened her. Cate glanced at the clock that blinked 4:32.

"Cate, are you there?"

"Is something wrong?"

"I don't know. Are you all right?"

She slumped onto the bed. "Why did you call, Caroline?"

"I shouldn't have at this hour of the morning, but I woke up and I desperately needed to talk to you." Caroline broke off, but her shaken tone bound them.

"I remembered the accident," Cate said. "And arguing with Alan."

"You need me. I'm on my way."

"No." It was too close to the middle of the night. She didn't need that much help. "Have you always known when I was in trouble?"

"We've both always known. A lot of twins know about each other. Were you thinking of me?"

"I looked at you in the photo on my dresser, and I wondered why we've both changed."

''Do you really want me to fill in the blanks in that story?''

''I think I have to know.''

''But not tonight. It takes too long to tell. You must have been looking at your wedding picture.''

''Why? Because you were already cynical by the time you got married? Wasn't it just a couple of years after my wedding?'' If she ever found enough strength to cross her room again, she'd look for a photo from Caroline's ceremony.

''Ryan and I married after Shelly was on the way. From the start, we chose to be together for the wrong reasons. Not like you and Alan.''

''Mmm-hmm.'' She didn't want to talk about her own marriage. ''I think I should go, Caroline. I'm exhausted, and I feel a little sick.''

''I'll go, but wake Alan up. Is he there with you?''

He might never join her in their bedroom. ''He's home.''

''Go get him if you don't feel well.''

''I'm just tired.''

''You've had another shock. I'll hold the line while you ask Alan to come in.''

''No, Caroline. Did I let you push me around before?''

''You were usually in charge, but I'm suggesting you wake Alan because you and the twins need him. For once, I want you to listen to me, because this time I know best.''

''Good night, Caroline.'' Best or not, she couldn't face Alan tonight with her memory of those moments at the office so clear and painful in her mind. ''Thank you for calling.''

Her sister's hesitation made for thick silence. "I love you, Cate."

A roiling burst of emotion exploded in her heart. She believed in the link that had prompted Caroline to call. "I'm learning to love you, too."

"I'll call again in the morning."

Cate pulled the portable phone away from her ear and pressed the off button. Almost immediately, a knock shook her door.

She looked toward the shadowy corner, where the door led to the house's narrow, upstairs hall. Her slump to the carpeted floor must have made an awful thump above Dan's head.

"Who is it?" She'd given Dan enough to worry about. If a champion had come to her rescue, let it be her lying husband.

"Cate." Alan's tone topped Caroline's for urgency. "Did you hurt yourself?" His concern set her teeth on edge.

"Go to bed," she said.

"Can't do that. You and Dan woke me. Did you just fall?"

"I don't want to talk to you."

Naturally, he opened the door. Still in darkness, he stopped on the threshold. "What did you remember?"

She curled her fingers into the rumpled sheet to keep herself from shoving him bodily from her room. "You recognize the signs of a fight?"

"You've been angrier with me than this."

If he'd lied to her consistently, he deserved more than anger. "What about that day in your office?

Have I ever been more upset than I was then? What else have you lied to me about, Alan?''

He came a step closer. ''That's what you remembered? Not the first time we made love or our wedding day? Not the day Dan was born?''

''I only remember believing I had to leave because you don't let me trust you.''

''That night at your aunt's, I told you the truth about the business. That's the only kind of secret I've ever kept from you.'' With both hands, he pushed his fingers through his hair. ''I've kept business secrets over the years, but I never lied to you about any other part of our life.''

''How am I supposed to trust you?''

Coming into the dim lamplight, he pressed the heel of his hand against his right eye. ''The same way I trust you. A hellish amount of faith. You aren't the woman I married. I'm not the man you trusted.''

A chill raced over her skin. She imagined telling Dan she was divorcing his father. She pictured bringing two newborn babies home to a house Alan didn't live in.

She couldn't let herself remember the savage love in Alan's eyes as he'd looked at their son this afternoon.

''Are you ready to give up?'' she asked.

He clenched both fists at his sides. ''I sat by your hospital bed for nearly four full days, and Cate, I prayed you'd come back to me. I don't give up, and you never have, either. I want to find out who you are.''

''What lies am I remembering?''

''Are you asking if I was faithful to you?''

She shook her head, her stomach growing even more restless. "I didn't get that far. All I remember is disbelief that you'd lie again and dread that I'd have to leave you, because I couldn't raise the twins by myself in a marriage I didn't believe in. I don't understand what all that means. Memory is usually a building block, but only one scene in my life flashed through my mind. I don't understand what happened before that day we argued, but I know I planned to leave you." She rubbed her belly, taking strength from her need to protect the twins and Dan.

He read her gesture. "I don't want you to stay for the children. I'm vain enough to believe my wife should live with me because she wants me."

"What else might I remember?"

Tiredly, he crossed the room and sat beside her on the bed. His scent, undeniably Alan, reminded her just how badly he could make her want him, but he kept a careful few inches of distance between them.

"I can't live with any more ultimatums," he said. "I've told you everything. The last thing I want is for you to give up on our marriage, but I can't make you believe me."

Instead, his quiet declaration made her respect him. Her missing memory had felt like a fresh start that let her choose to stay married or leave her family behind. Life wasn't that simple.

"I don't have all the facts, but I can't believe leaving you was an impulsive decision." She heard her own softened voice and resented the way it betrayed her. Something deeper than memory bound her to this man.

"How do you feel about taking the biggest risk of

our lives? I'll believe you can learn to forgive me, want to be my wife again, and you'll believe I can be the husband you need.''

"Can you?'' She broached a sore subject. "I'd like to take a job and contribute even a minimal salary.''

He swallowed. His throat worked harder, and he swallowed again. "Why do you need a job?''

Her heart went out to him, but she wasn't selfless enough to let him control her in the interests of his mangled ego. "I want to be with the people I used to know and learn about the town we live in and bring home wages I earn.''

"Do I have a choice?''

"I don't think so.'' She smoothed her fingertip along the frown line that ran from his nose to the corner of his mouth. "This is what you mean about my having changed, isn't it? Before the accident, I would have given in?''

"I never realized you gave in.'' He caught her hand and held it to his chest. "I don't care what happened before or how I felt about who you were then. I want you to stay now.''

"Please don't sound humble.'' She flattened her fingers against his T-shirt. As her palm relearned the hard muscle that warmed her skin, her breathing quickened. "Can't we compromise?''

With his fingertips, he traced the length of her thumb. The words they spoke bore little resemblance to the conversation he effortlessly initiated with her body.

"Promise me you'll give up the job if it's too

much strain. You were twenty-one when Dan was born. You're thirty-eight and you're carrying twins.''

Cate drew her hand from beneath his, her agreement rueful. "You're a sweet talker, Alan.''

His green eyes darkened and his mouth thinned with an almost feral intensity. "I care about you. Meet me halfway.''

She had no choice. She wanted a life with him. "You have to tell me if I'm going to remember anything else I can't live with.''

"I can't help the way remembering makes you feel.'' The muscles in his throat tautened again. Sliding away, he stood, as if he couldn't stand the intimacy between them. "Uncle Ford asked me to change the lightbulbs in his barn tomorrow. Do you want to come with me?''

Exhaustion confused her, but it might be best to see him with her family around her. Their unconditional love for Alan reminded her he'd adopted them as his own. He'd found a way to help Caroline raise her child as a single parent. A good man went to such lengths. "I'll go with you.''

She curled into the sheet she'd abandoned earlier. She was suddenly so tired breathing became an effort.

"Good night, Alan.'' Groping for bedclothes, she missed the warmth of his body close to hers. "If we're starting our marriage over, I wonder if we should have a second honeymoon.''

He was so quiet she thought he'd left. "Cate,'' he said at last, "are you talking in your sleep?''

Surely she was already asleep. She must have dreamed that unromantic response.

CHAPTER ELEVEN

"MORNING, DAD." Dan breezed around the kitchen door as Alan sat down with his fourth cup of coffee and the newspaper. "Did you and Mom settle your argument last night?"

Last night? He hadn't closed his eyes since he'd left Cate asleep in the room they'd once shared. After she'd suggested a honeymoon and apparently blacked out, he'd had to curb his own ignoble need to wrap himself around her and hold her until she woke again.

He'd lied when he'd told her he couldn't live with ultimatums. He couldn't think of anything she could ask him to do that he wouldn't attempt. Had they worked out their problems? He hoped so, once and for all.

"We're together, Dan. Don't worry."

"Could you stop telling me not to worry?"

"Sorry." He hated his terse tone, but without sleep, without faith in himself, he no longer knew what kind of father he'd ever been. "Did you have fun last night?"

"Yes, I had fun. No, I didn't drink. I took part in no drug-induced orgies, and I came home without the aid of the local police force."

He left Dan's verbal gauntlet exactly where the boy had thrown it. "What's your plan for today?"

"Phoebe and I rented a sailboat. We're going over to Saint Simons, and I'll probably come back late tonight."

Alan set the paper on the table. "I don't want you sailing after dark."

"I won't, but we'll probably eat somewhere after we sail back."

"Call me when you turn the boat in." He lifted the paper again. "We'll be at your Aunt Imogen's. Maybe at Uncle Ford's." Cate's uncle usually did his entertaining at his sister's house—using his sister's food as well as her good cooking.

Dan fished a box of dry cereal from the pantry and a bowl from the cabinet. "Are you sure that's a good idea? Every time you go over there, you end up planning a divorce."

"Uncle Ford asked me to help him change some lightbulbs in the barn. Not even your mother and I can argue about how to do that." He sipped his coffee as Dan poured himself a bowl of cereal. "How would you feel if your mom took a job?"

"Why ask me? I'm leaving for school in a few weeks. I feel bad for the twins, though."

"What do you mean?" Cate's voice, from the stairwell behind them, startled Alan.

Alarmed, he kept his gaze trained on Dan. Cate, before her accident, would have disliked his discussing her plan to work with their son.

"I always liked knowing you'd be home when I got here," Dan said. "The other guys liked coming to our house, too. You made us food. You didn't talk down to us, and you got out of the way when I wanted you to. You even tried to keep up with the music we liked.'' He snickered, as if she'd failed a bit there. ''You were kind of fun, and I knew I came first with you.''

Cate came closer. Over her nightshirt, she wore a huge, faded blue sweatshirt that belonged to Alan. He sat up, intrigued at the thought of his clothing next to his wife's skin.

She hauled a chair back from the table and sat, delicately draping his shirt over her knees. ''I wonder if you two are making a big deal out of nothing? You're not used to thinking of me as someone who isn't an extension of you, and the prospect worries you.''

''Nice diagnosis, Mom.'' Dan scooped up a huge spoonful of cereal. ''I disagree. How about you, Dad?''

Her suggestion annoyed him, but she might be right. ''I'll concede your mother needs more room than we're used to giving her.''

Dan shoved the spoon into his mouth. ''Whatever,'' he muttered around the cereal, and then wiped off milk that dribbled out of the corner of his lips.

Alan tried not to laugh, but Cate whipped a paper towel off the roll beneath the cabinet. She glanced at Alan as she passed the sheet to Dan and subsided in her chair.

''Don't we own napkins?''

''Not at this moment.'' Alan tossed the newspaper onto the counter and rose from the table to fetch a cup he then set on the table. ''We'll pick up staples on our way back from Aunt Imogen's. Coffee?''

Cate shook her head. "Can't." Her satisfaction with her pregnancy locked warm fingers around his heart. "And I'd rather not tempt my stomach to turn on me again."

Dan stood, his spoon dangling from his mouth. He opened the fridge and took out a carton of juice. The spoon still between his lips, he dropped into his chair and shoved the carton across the table.

Alan stood to catch the juice before it hit Cate, but it stopped inches from her hand. She stared as if the container had burst into a celebratory aria only she could hear.

"I remember that." She flashed Dan a happy smile. "You always throw the juice at me."

Dan finally removed the spoon from his mouth. "Not at you—to you. Do you really remember, Mom?"

She leapt from her chair and chased around the table to wrap her arms around him. "I remember admiring your skill at stopping the carton, as if you'd put the perfect spin on a chip shot. I love you, Dan."

He patted her hand, the one closest to his, and leaned out of her embrace. "Love you, too, Mom, but I'm kind of hungry. If you don't mind, I'm trying to eat breakfast."

Humming yet another tune, Cate backed off. Crossing behind Alan, she slid her palm over the top of his head and tangled her fingers in his hair. He caught her hand and brought her palm to his mouth.

She stopped, still as a breath not taken. Could she possibly understand how much her smallest touch affected him?

With a small, faintly wicked smile that made his

heart beat faster, she slid her arms around his neck. He breathed her in, the jut of her full breasts, the mound of the babies they'd made together. Soon, she'd want him to love her again.

ALAN TURNED INTO the gravel lot in front of Uncle Ford's house, but he frowned toward Aunt Imogen's place.

"What's wrong?" Cate studied the other cars in front of her aunt's house.

"My father." He pointed at a black Corvette. "Aunt Imogen must have decided to test your cease-fire."

"I promised to be polite." Richard didn't seem as important as her relationship with his son.

"I don't care what you do to him." Alan turned off the engine. "I don't want him to upset you."

"I can take care of myself." She lifted his hand to her cheek. "But I like knowing you're behind me."

Lightning flashed in his eyes. He leaned across the seat and kissed the corner of her mouth. "Thanks."

"I mean it." She had to. This might be their last chance.

"I mean it, too," Alan said. "I won't let you down again."

"You aren't the only one who's made mistakes. I'm afraid to commit. I don't want to get hurt, and I don't remember how it feels to be completely happy." She paused, her mind on Dan. "Although this morning, when our son shoved that juice across the table…"

"That was close?"

She loved his teasing tone. Lifting his hand again, she pressed her mouth to his knuckles. Strands of sparse black hair tickled her lips. Alan's gasp rattled her composure as he cupped the back of her head and lifted her face to his.

His mouth was a whisper away when she panicked. "We'd better go in." Pictures of his hard, lean limbs wrapped around hers frightened her as much as they seduced. What if she'd forgotten how to please him? What if he didn't want her the way she looked now?

"Why are you afraid, Cate?"

She reached for the door handle. She'd leapt into this relationship as if she had faith in Alan. She thought she could learn about faith, but surely her more unnerving fears still belonged only to her. "You're misreading me."

"I know your expressions even if I can't figure out ahead of time what you should feel."

"I'd rather discuss this at home."

"No, Cate."

He couched his refusal in a tender voice that undid her. She turned back to him, aware of the rustle of her dress on the car's leather seat, the bump of an insect against the window beside her head.

"I have no memory of making love." She didn't add she was afraid to undress in front of him, afraid she wouldn't make him happy.

He wrapped her in his arms. "I won't mind showing you."

"But twenty years together—I probably knew what you liked."

His voice, low and lecherous, brushed her temple. "Lucky for you, I still know what pleases you."

"I don't want you to be dissatisfied," she said.

His body shook against her. At first, she leaned away from him, afraid he might be laughing at her. She felt no better when she found she'd been correct.

He couldn't seem to stop laughing, and once she'd seen him, he made no effort to keep it quiet.

"I've just confessed one of my deepest fears," she said.

He sobered, sort of. "I'm weak with hunger for you, and you think I'll be dissatisfied? I trembled like a scared virgin when you touched my hair this morning. What say we assume I'll enjoy—the proceedings?"

Nice of him to spare her delicate sensibilities.

Shaking his head in mock despair, he tipped her chin. Passion arced from his gaze, and Cate sank against the seat. So much desire frightened her until she realized he'd let down his guard. He wanted her to see all the way to the truth of his feelings for her.

She closed her eyes and opened to the stroke of his tongue against the seam of her lips. Anxious to return his humbling gift, she leaned into him. His groan, earthy and naked, robbed her of conscious thought.

She swam in their mutual need, but her husband's strength kept her from drowning. He caressed her shoulders, his hands restless. He mouthed her name, and for once, his possessive tone thrilled her as he slid his fingers beneath the sleeves of her dress.

With his mouth a whisper above her skin, he followed the curve of her cheek. She tilted her head to bare her neck to him. Goose bumps ran the length of her body as he suckled the pulse in her throat. Inexorably, he made his way to the rise of her breasts against her scooped neckline.

She pressed closer, her pulse pumping in her ears. He seemed too far away. She needed to be nearer. He held her body, maybe even parts of her soul, in loving hands.

"We should have tried this from the start." Alan lifted a heavy-lidded gaze that almost covered his arrogant thought.

Almost. Not quite. She touched her fingers to his lips. Still warm from hers, they melted her resistance. "Don't say anything to ruin it."

He pulled away, his smile scorching. "Come with me to the barn. I'll reintroduce you to the loft."

A tap on the window behind her head cut off her answer. She turned, and Alan leaned over her to see their intruder.

"Dad," he growled. "Naturally."

"What do you think he saw?"

"Not a thing. The man's oblivious." Alan stretched a few inches more to open her door and push it wide before he moved back to his side of the car. "We'll explore the loft some other time."

Cate prepared herself for another of Richard's inappropriate jokes as she clambered out on shaky legs, but her father-in-law grabbed her hand.

"That cut on your leg still bothering you?" Richard asked as he hauled her to his side, but he didn't wait for her to reply. "When Alan mentioned you were coming to help Ford, I asked Imogen to invite Meg and me for dinner. I've been thinking pretty hard about this, Cate. You and I can't put off our talk. I don't want bad blood to ruin my marriage ceremony.''

Positive her own marriage would be better off if she had her mouth wired shut, Cate managed an acquiescent shrug. ''I'd love to talk with you, Richard. Alan, how long do you think you'll be?''

He popped out of the other side of the car. ''Half an hour maybe.'' Doubt glittered in his eyes. ''Why don't you two wait for me?''

His concern made up Cate's mind. She could talk to the man without starting a world war. She turned to Richard. ''Why don't we walk down by the river?''

''Perfect.'' Richard offered his arm again.

She accepted his chivalrous gesture and rested her hand in the crook of his elbow. ''See you later, Alan.'' She looked back to reassure him. If Richard pushed her too far, she'd simply shove him into the river. ''Take your time, and don't let Uncle Ford climb the ladder.''

Alan glanced at his watch. ''Good Lord, I'd better get in there. If he asks for help and I'm late, he does the work himself to make me feel guilty.''

She pictured her unsteady uncle slamming the ladder around the barn. Richard tugged at her.

''Let Alan take care of Ford. He's experienced in whipping an old man into shape.''

''You always know just the right thing to say, don't you?''

''The right thing to light your fuse.''

''Let's cut to the chase.''

He braced himself, reminding her of Alan. He

pulled aside a low-hanging branch to make way for her on the path toward Aunt Imogen's house. "Hit me."

"Were you as careless with Alan as those horrible stories you tell?"

Their feet disarranged the neatly piled pea gravel. A few small pebbles shot into the grass as they walked. Cate finally stole a glance at Richard's shamefaced expression.

"I was a bad father, maybe even before Heather left. I was so intent on giving her the things she wanted, the right house, the right car, the appropriate school for Alan, that I didn't notice we'd both stopped taking care of our son."

They crossed the cement path in front of Aunt Imogen's wide porch. Cate understood some of what he said. It dovetailed with her confusion over Dan. "But why do you act as if you're proud of the way you treated him?"

"You act as if I should have been prosecuted. I didn't beat him. I stopped leaving him alone once I sobered up."

Cate eyed him with horror. Once he sobered up? Still a few yards from the muttering river, she veered toward its shore. This man deserved a dunking, and she prayed the water was icy.

Richard caught her hand, but she jerked away from him. "Does Alan know how attached you are to him?" he asked. "I don't think he believes you love him."

Love? She wasn't sure, but she cared more than she could talk about with Richard. "I don't understand how you could take his childhood from him. I hardly know Dan, but I couldn't turn him into the kind of adult you made Alan—from the time he was ten years old.''

"You went to the other extreme with Dan. How do you expect him to take care of himself when you've babied him all his life? I didn't want my son to find himself in my shoes. Abandoned. Clueless. I tried to prepare him.''

"Toughen him up, you mean?'' What if he was right about Dan? Maybe there was middle ground to cover.

"Cate, I've tried to be patient with you, but you weren't in our house, and the way I raised my son is none of your business. You Talbots think you own some kind of moral yardstick, but your uncle has slept with every married and unattached woman in this town over the age of forty. And I wouldn't put it past him to start cruising for the younger set. He'd do a lot to prove he doesn't need that cane.''

"Leave my family out of this.''

"And what about your parents? Heroes in charge of our national defense. You know what? They craved an adrenaline rush, just like every Talbot before them, and they abandoned you and your sister just as Heather left Alan and me.''

Cate's injured leg, almost completely healed now, wobbled. She struggled for a memory of her parents. She'd memorized pictures of them from photo albums during her week with Aunt Imogen, but they'd never formed in her mind as living beings.

She turned toward the river to hide tears that stung her eyes. ''Whatever my family's done doesn't excuse the way you talk to Alan or the way you talk about him. Plus, I don't want Dan to hear about it.''

Richard heaved a sigh. Broken in the middle, it almost sounded like a sob. Cate whirled to him. He quickly averted his own reddened gaze. ''How weak-minded do you think I am? I know how bad I look. I'm sorry for what Alan put up with from me, but I can't change the past.''

His dejected shoulders tempted her to put a comforting arm around him, but she held back. She didn't know Richard. He might well try to con her.

''Maybe you could stop rubbing Alan's nose in it.''

''Like I just rubbed yours?'' Richard's hand landed on her shoulder. An awkward pat that matched his tone. ''I shouldn't have mentioned your parents, but I was angry. I don't enjoy having someone point a spotlight at my faults. That's why I talk about the years after Heather left. I know I was wrong, and I'd rather say so before someone else does.''

Cate gave in, as much as she was able. ''In a way, you're right. Your family's history is none of my business until you hurt Alan. You're making it his penance, too, and that affects *my* family.''

Richard buried the heels of his palms in his eyes. Cate stared at him. Give Alan some gray hair, round his shoulders a bit, and coat him with an unfamiliar air of despair, and there he'd be in another twenty years or so.

Not if she could help it. She wanted a healthy father to raise her children. She wanted a healthy husband to live and love with.

"I apologize if I went too far, Richard."

"You didn't. Alan should have given me his side before now."

"He believes he's made his own peace with you."

"You disagree?"

She shrugged. "You aren't yourselves with each other. What kind of peace is that?"

"And who are you now, Cate? Our damsel in shining armor?"

Their talk blunted his sarcastic edge. "I'm hunting down my own identity, but I can't seem to figure out who I am until I get a feel for the people I've loved. I didn't know how I could have loved you."

He squinted at her, as if he were trying to bring her into focus. "Like I say, I think you pulled a few of your punches before."

"Maybe I've changed."

"Poor Alan." This time, he used a chuckle to soften the blow. Then he turned her toward Aunt Imogen's kitchen. "Shall we go inside? Imogen promised me a fish fry. She drove over to Thunderbolt to pick up some flounder off the docks."

"Does she ever cook healthy?"

"You've only eaten in her kitchen on special occasions." Richard patted her shoulder again, but this time the gesture felt more natural. "For instance, today, I met my daughter-in-law for the first time."

"And I began to understand my father-in-law."

"Alan owes us both. Big time."

"So does Meg, but we won't tell them anything," she said anxiously. Now that she understood Richard a bit more, she was slightly ashamed of her overprotective baiting on Alan's behalf.

"Let's show them how much we can stand each other."

"Deal."

Turning, she held out her hand and he took it. After a hearty shake, he hugged her. She stayed in the curve of his arm as long as she could. A few seconds.

DAN SAILED ALONE to Saint Simons Island. Just after his parents left, Phoebe had called to say she still hadn't recovered from "graduation revelry."

He called a couple of the guys, but they'd put together a foursome and an early tee time. He couldn't reach any of them by pager or cell phone, so he took the boat out alone.

On the island, he strolled around the lighthouse, through a cemetery he vaguely remembered. One of Aunt Imogen's favorite authors, Eugenia Price, had helped to make the island famous with her books. Aunt Imogen kept copies of them. This trip had been more fun when he'd come with her and his mom as a kid. One turn up and down the tourist-ridden sidewalks, and he was ready to sail home.

He'd really planned the trip to have a few hours alone with Phoebe. He shouldn't have come without her.

He sailed back to Leith early, turned in the boat and left a message with his Dad's secretary that he was back. At home, he called Phoebe. Her mother said she'd gone out with friends. Should he look for her? He wanted to, but he wasn't used to feeling as if he needed to see her.

He played a couple of video games, watched a

little MTV and checked the time. He could drive over to Aunt Imogen's. They'd have plenty of food for him, but his dad would probably think to bring home leftovers. Nah, he'd go. He was leaving for college in three weeks. He'd like to see his family before he left.

Just as he picked up his keys, a large tan SUV careened into his driveway. Man, another corner of his mom's precious sod, destroyed. Not that she noticed any more. He went to the door as six of his best friends piled out of the vehicle, all carrying brown paper bags.

"Hey, Palmer, whassup?"

"Kevin, what are you all doing here?" Guessing at the contents of their paper bags, he dreaded his parents' response to the party.

"We ran into Shelly and Phoebe playing disc golf. Shelly said her mom was going to a family dinner, but Phoebe said you'd be home alone."

"Are they coming over later?" He stood aside to let his friends troop in.

"No. Phoebe's going out with a friend of that guy Shelly's dating." Kevin pulled a long neck out of his bag. "Want one, angel boy?"

He'd always said no before. Tonight, he didn't feel like "no." Tonight, he was the sappy son of parents who couldn't decide whether to divorce or make *little baby siblings* for him. And he was pissed because a girl who'd once seemed like his sister preferred to be with his cousin's friend.

He reached for the bottle. "I'll take it. Come on in." Raucous laughter rose from the living room. Something made of glass shattered in the kitchen.

Dan cracked the beer open and took a long, bitter swig. He wiped his mouth with the back of his hand to hide the truth. It tasted like crap. So he drank some more.

CHAPTER TWELVE

TWO NIGHTS LATER, Alan parked in the garage and used the remote to shut the door. As soon as he got out of the truck, the scent of beer hit him. Damn. He maneuvered around his truck and Cate's SUV to lift the lid on the garbage bin.

About a dozen dead soldiers nestled in pillows of white plastic bags. Alan's gut knotted. Either Cate had craved beer, or Dan had hosted a party while they were at Aunt Imogen's.

He put his money on Dan. His fear came straight from the memory of seeing his own father disappear in case after case of cheap beer.

Alan dropped the lid and headed toward the kitchen walkway. As he opened the door, acrid smoke covered the taste of malt in his mouth. At the stove, Cate was whaling on an open fire with an ineffectual dish towel.

Alan unhooked the fire extinguisher from the cabinet door beneath the sink. Nudging Cate out of the way, he sprayed the pan flaming on the stove.

"We'd better check the fire alarms," he said as she breathed heavily behind him.

"Why?"

He nodded toward the ceiling to indicate the silence. "Don't you think they should have gone off?

Why don't you stand outside and breathe some fresh air while I open the windows and clean up this mess?''

"You don't mind?" she asked between coughs.

"Not a bit." He glanced at her belly. "I don't want you in this smoke."

He opened the window above the sink. Should he tell her about Dan and the beer? He'd rather talk to Dan first, though hiding his son's drinking broke the strictures of his agreement with Cate.

He took a clean towel from a drawer and grabbed the saucepan's handle to toss it into the sink. His distress over Dan's dangerous choice lent him elbow grease as he cleaned the stove. He was still scrubbing as his son strolled in.

"Hey, Dad. Mom said she started a fire."

Alan straightened. "I'd like to start one under you. Want to explain the beer bottles in the garage?" Dan didn't answer. His stiff expression gave nothing away. "Don't make me wait, son."

"Some of the guys came over."

"Which one is old enough to buy beer?"

"I don't know how they bought it."

"But you drank it?"

"Part of one."

"Then the others drank your share before they left here. You think not finishing it excuses your breach of our trust?"

"Dad, it was just a beer."

"I've heard that before, from my own father. It doesn't go down any better from you. It's against the law, Dan, and you clearly aren't old enough to handle alcohol responsibly, or you wouldn't have broken the law to drink 'part of' a beer.''

"You're overreacting.''

"You think? Because I don't. I should haul you and your friends down to John Mabry's office.'' He turned back to the stove. "I want to know who bought it.''

"I don't know. I'm not lying.''

"What if you'd piled into a car? You're driving, and you turn to laugh at some asinine, drunken joke one of your buddies makes. You swerve into a van, and when you wake up in the hospital, a cop's at your bed, because you've killed a two-year old girl, her pregnant mother and her favorite uncle, who happened to have taught your kindergarten class. How do you feel now?''

"Since I drank half a beer? I feel fed up with you for blasting me with this load of—''

"You damned well know who drank the beer, and you're going to write down all their names and their phone numbers. I'm talking to their parents.''

"I'll talk to them, Dad. This isn't your business.''

Alan stared at him. "Are you kidding me? You broke the law in my house. Now, tell your friends first if you want, so they can warn their parents, but I want the list by tonight.''

The screen door opened, and Cate came inside, her gaze curious. "What's up?'' she asked. "Why are you shouting, Alan?''

"Dan and his friends threw a little party.'' He turned to Dan. "I assume it happened while your mom and I were at Aunt Imogen's?''

He nodded miserably, avoiding Cate's gaze. At least she still had the power to shame him.

"You didn't drink?" Disappointment sharpened her voice.

Dan eased toward the other kitchen door, but Cate followed him. He stopped when he realized she wouldn't let him escape.

"I'm sorry." He flashed Alan a defensive glance. "I mean it. I had a bad day, and I was angry. I made a mistake, but it's not like I killed someone. What's the matter with you two?"

"You could have killed someone if you'd gotten in your car. We're your parents, and we're in charge around here." Cate eased toward Alan, building a united front. "If we can't trust you, your life will change."

"He did change his life." Alan said. "No driving, except for golf and school. If you aren't practicing or at school, I expect to see your keys on this counter."

"Wait a minute." Dan looked to his mom for help.

She wavered, prey to a natural need to be her son's rescuer, but Alan wouldn't bend on this.

"It was a mistake." Dan looked cornered.

"One you won't make again," Alan stressed. He'd watched his father wobble into their house too many times to take a chance with Dan.

Cate curved her fingers around Alan's. "I believed you when you said you wouldn't drink. Your father is right."

"One more thing," Alan added. "I have to ask

you to be patient about that golf school we talked about.''

Again, Cate looked as upset as Dan, but if Dan was old enough to drink, he was old enough to hear the truth. "I'm in financial trouble with the company, and I'd like to put the school off until spring."

"How many ways can you punish me?" As if he hadn't heard what Alan had said about the company, Dan stalked into the hall. "Man!"

Alan shouted after him. "I want that list, Dan. Tonight."

The front door slammed moments later. Cate pulled away. "Did you do that to punish him?"

"We can't afford the school." She'd offered her support. He needed it. "I have to tell Caroline and the other employees about the business. Jim's still on the run with our money. I still can't persuade the others to spend the extra money we'd need to hire a private detective, and I can't pay our bills."

"*We* can't," Cate said. "Why don't you let me tell Caroline?"

He hesitated, unused to letting her cushion him. "Thanks," he said finally.

She hugged him. "Are you all right?"

He locked his arms around her, surrounded by debris, a thin layer of smoke and an unshakable conviction his son was in trouble. "I don't know. We need to keep an eye on Dan."

"I'm afraid so."

"I don't think he's done it before, but how can we be sure?"

"We'll know soon enough if it's a habit." Her pragmatism startled him. "I meant are you all right about the business? Why won't the others risk the expense of hiring a detective who might help save their companies?"

"They're afraid even a detective could take months to find Jim. Add that expense to legal fees and we're sunk anyway. But I'm determined to tell our employees. I don't want them to lose anything because of me."

"Would it help if we worked on a letter to tell them what they can expect?"

He closed his eyes, breathing in the scent of her from her hair. She was asking him to become a man who let her help. "After dinner," he said. "We'll see how it goes." He nodded at the blackened saucepan. "What was this supposed to be?"

"Potatoes for potato salad."

"Maybe I won't ask how you burned boiling potatoes."

"Why don't you see if you can catch up with Dan and grill him?"

"On a spit? Good idea."

DURING THE NEXT two weeks, Alan put together a new business plan and Dan began to absent himself from home. Cate made an opportunity for her son to snub her at least once a day, as she tried to get through to him.

On the day of the beer bust, Dan had snatched up Cate's cell phone from the hall table on his way out of the house. He'd called one of his friends and arranged for a ride into town before Alan caught up with him. Since then, he'd treated his parents as if they'd tried to pass him a bad case of plague.

Cate had talked to Dr. Barton about her continuingly elusive memory, but he'd been pleased with the wisps of past that had come back to her. He'd cautioned her about building false memories based on her family's recollection of her life, but she kept thinking she might be able to reach Dan if she knew him better.

She'd asked Caroline to meet her this morning at The Captain's Lady for Saturday brunch, but first, she headed to Aunt Imogen's for a pep talk. Driving down the narrow road toward her aunt's house, she came upon her aunt and Polly in matching flower-strewn headgear, strolling down the packed-shell road. Cate eased up on the gas and pulled over behind Polly, leaving room so as not to spook the mare.

Aunt Imogen turned back with a wave of her sombrero as Cate got out of the car.

"I'll walk with you," Cate said.

"Is it too far for your leg?"

"Exercise reassures me it's all healed, and Dr. Davis told me I should walk." She locked the car and caught up with her aunt, for the first time feeling the weight of her belly as she jogged along the edge of the road.

Dr. Davis had also reassured her about the occasional cramps she'd felt. As long as she couldn't time them, they were nothing to worry about.

"I didn't expect you," Aunt Imogen said. "Something wrong?"

"Sort of. I need some more advice."

"Glad to help you." Aunt Imogen whipped a fan out of her pocket and fanned a fly away from Polly's face. "These vermin are getting thicker every day."

"I guess it goes with summer," Cate said. "Aunt Imogen, why the hats?"

"I told you, this gives people something new to chew on. Besides, I like my hats, and so did the children I used to make them for at the hospital. Before children grew too cool—or groovy—whatever." She fanned Polly again. "I'm hell with a hot glue gun, and neither Polly nor I like sun in our eyes."

"Hell with a glue gun?"

"Laugh at me. I know you love me enough to overlook my eccentricities."

"Do you know you're eccentric?"

The older woman nodded, and her silk flower petals waved up and down with the movement. "I've cultivated the reputation. I'm alone a lot, Cate. I volunteer, but no one needs me outside my scheduled work hours."

"So you make hats?"

"And a garden with you, and I dress dolls for the church Christmas baskets, and I read to children at the women's shelter, and I cook any time I can lure my family to come eat with me."

"Is this because you and Whitney decided not to stay in touch with each other?"

"Well, I'm not like Ford, tasting all the flowers in the field. I guess I never found anyone I liked as well as Whitney."

"Why don't you come to us when you need company?"

"Because you have lives of your own. Your job doesn't include baby-sitting crazy Aunt Imogen."

As they passed between two trees into sunshine that increased the fly populace, Cate took the fan and waved it in front of her aunt and Polly. "I think Caroline and I owe you."

"I don't want love based on a debt, and I didn't mean to whine. I just don't want wrinkles, I happen to glue an attractive flower arrangement together and I believe in saying what I mean. That, along with the stories of Whitney that refuse to die, makes me unwelcome in some parts of Leith society."

Cate glanced at today's strip of tape. Clear and disappointingly bland. "I won't beat a dead—" She eyed Polly. "I mean I don't want to nag you, but Aunt Imogen, please call me or come when you want company. Did you think I took you for granted?"

"You had your own family." She paused reflectively. "I wonder if you've distanced yourself from Caroline and me because you didn't want us to see your marriage was in trouble. You never were one for sharing the hurtful parts of your life."

"That sounds right." Cate fanned again. "I hope Polly won't take this personally, but I believe she's drawing these flies."

"Shall I fan?"

"No, I don't mind. Can I talk to you about my latest problem?"

"Absolutely."

"Our business is in trouble, and I have to warn Caroline."

Aunt Imogen stopped dead still in the road. "How much trouble?"

"Alan tried to handle it, but they haven't found the CPA who embezzled from us, and we're worried the business may fail."

"Are you going to be all right?"

"Alan has agreed we'll start over together. I don't know what skills I'll bring, but I think we'll salvage a living."

"You have a history degree. If Alan can get enough renovation work, you'll know how to research materials and furniture. He likes those jobs best anyway."

Cate waved her fan with more enthusiasm, proud of her aunt's faith. "I need to suggest Caroline might want to look at another company, but I'm not sure how she'll take it."

Aunt Imogen buried her face in her hands. "I should come with you."

"What are you afraid she'll do?"

"She's a single parent, and Shelly's due to start college in the fall. She needs a job."

"We should have told her first thing."

"I can see you'd want to save her from worrying if she didn't have to, but I'm glad you're telling her now. Let's put Polly into her stall, and I'll change clothes. Do I smell like a horse?"

Cate sniffed tentatively. Smells still triggered nausea that hadn't gone away as her pregnancy continued. "Not as far as I can tell."

Aunt Imogen changed quickly, and Cate drove them both to The Captain's Lady. Caroline rose from a table for two as Cate followed her aunt inside the diner's small entryway. Caroline flagged down the server, who was quaintly clothed in a modified version of a nineteenth century maid's uniform. By the time Cate and Aunt Imogen reached her, she was moving to a table with room for all three of them.

"I'm starving," she said. "I spent the morning at a fabric wholesaler's, pawing through the goods."

"There's your opening, Cate. Don't put it off."

Caroline looked alarmed. "What opening?"

Cate glanced reprovingly at Aunt Imogen. "I meant to ease into the subject, but I guess she's right. I have to talk to you about the business." She cast a look at the busy tables. "I should have asked you both to my house."

"Don't bother to go on. So the calls we've had lately from nervous creditors meant more than I thought?"

Cate tried to read her sister's mind. She sounded wary, but not frantic. Cate leaned across the table. "Jim Cooper embezzled company funds, and he's disappeared. The police haven't found him, and Alan's creating a new business plan. I wanted to tell you before you heard it in public."

Caroline nodded. "I won't pretend I'm not terrified."

Cate sensed a thread of electricity. "You hide it well."

Her sister looked around the room. "Never expose your weakness," she said. "Does the company stand a chance of surviving?"

"I don't know. I don't think Alan knows. He's working with the money and the bills day to day. He's arranged for a placement service to help the employees find work."

"Can he afford that?"

"He has to. You're all family or friends. How would he sleep nights if he left you high and dry?"

Caroline nodded with an air of distraction. "I've

considered working for myself. In fact, I've organized sample business plans of my own, but I didn't want to let Alan and you down.''

"Now you feel we've let you down?"

She shook her head vehemently. "How could you know a man we've trusted for twenty years would steal from you? But I have to look out for Shelly. She starts classes in about ten weeks, and her scholarship only covers part of her tuition." Caroline waved her arm at the server again. "May I have a glass of water?" she called to the startled woman. Apparently, her customers rarely hailed her from across the room.

"Why not a glass of wine?" Aunt Imogen suggested.

"I'm not ready to celebrate a new business venture yet." Caroline attempted a small grin that trembled on her wide mouth. "I'll call Alan and tell him my plans.''

Cate covered her sister's hand. "I'll warn him you're considering a business of your own, but you take your time. Talk to him Monday about what you want.''

"Thanks for telling me before I had to pretend to be calm in front of a room full of spectators." The server brought her water and Caroline slugged it back. "This explains Alan's sudden interest in my budgets. I thought he'd lost faith in me."

"In himself," Cate responded without thinking.

Caroline gazed at her. "You'll help him with that." She clapped her hands to her enviably flat stomach. "To be honest, I'm sort of excited about doing something completely on my own. Now why don't we put this meal off for another day?''

"Aren't you hungry any more?'' Aunt Imogen asked.

"Not particularly, and I'll bet Alan is a wreck. Cate may want to go home.''

"Alan can take care of himself,'' Cate said. "And I came out to be with you.''

"I know how he feels about the business. I'm part of his family, and if he's not able to provide for his family, he'll see himself as a failure.''

Cate tilted her head, a touch resentful of her sister's knowledge of Alan. "How do you know him so well?''

"After more than twenty years? I'm ashamed to admit I've wondered more than once why you married a man who's first concern is your well-being, and I chose a man who abandoned me. We're twins, after all.''

"The Talbot curse,'' Aunt Imogen interjected.

Caroline touched her arm. "I can't afford to joke about it. I have an eighteen-year-old daughter whose choices I influence. I won't abandon her future to fate.'' She skewered Cate with pain and anger and love and frustration, all concentrated in blue eyes. "Then I look at my identical twin. Half the time even our own aunt and uncle couldn't tell us apart. In fact, Alan's the only human being who's never mistaken one of us for the other. But why did you choose Alan, when I chose Ryan?''

"Did you want Alan?'' The suggestion weakened Cate, inside and out.

"I've resented your easier path in life, but I've

never been jealous enough to covet your husband.''
Caroline let her go, her mood lightening. "I didn't
mean to scare you, but rivalry comes with the terri-
tory. Sometimes I think it's those thirteen minutes
and twenty-seven seconds. When can I stop trying to
catch up?''

Cate stood, almost oblivious to their fellow diners'
disapproving glances. Drawn to her sister as if forces
of gravity pulled them together, she embraced Caroline and held on tight.

"I love you," she said against her twin's curls. "I
owe you for your comfort since I got hurt. You're a
loving, accomplished woman. Why would you need
to catch up?''

"I know I don't." Caroline's eyes glittered in wet
beds of tears. "But I'm not always sure I'm doing
all right on my own. Since your accident, I've felt
as if I lost my past, too. I want back what you lost.''

"It'll come." Cate straightened. "To both of us.''
She suddenly noticed everyone staring at them and
scurried back to her seat, to her aunt's obvious
amusement. "What's so funny?''

"You were always the decorous one. Hated my
wrinkle-reducing efforts. Despaired of my millinery.
You tried to persuade us to fit in, and here you are
dancing around the diner, making a spectacle of
yourself.''

"Could we stop discussing my stodgy do-gooding
ways? My halo is now officially bent." She liked
this less socially conscious version of herself. She
turned back to Caroline. "We're both on the mend
if we can talk about rivalry. Should I tell Alan you're
looking for jobs of your own?''

"But I'll be available to help if he needs me."

"You're wise to make sure you can provide for Shelly, and I'm glad you aren't angry with us for waiting to tell you."

"I wouldn't have wanted to hear this news for the first time in front of my friends at work." Caroline reached for both Cate and Aunt Imogen's hands. "I'm glad we're together again, and really, this news just forces me to make a decision I've waffled on for a year or more." She looked soberly at Cate. "I was grateful when Alan first gave me the work, and I've made a name for myself with the company, but I'm tired of feeling beholden."

"I don't believe Alan or I thought you owed us anything."

"Sometimes a benefactor's oblivion makes the gift more oppressive," Aunt Imogen suggested.

"Exactly." Caroline turned a surprised gaze on their aunt. "But how did you know what I barely recognize myself?"

"I'm Ford's sister." Aunt Imogen shrugged. "He gets into romantic scrapes. He bides by no rules, and he's crotchety, but he gets away with his poor behavior, because he's sensible in the crunch. People respect his decisions. Do you girls know he's on the hospital administration board? He's on several scholarship selection committees at the University of Georgia and Emory. He's kept our family land together, and his advice has saved me from myself more than once. I love him and resent him for the safety net he's given me."

Caroline nodded sagely. Cate looked from one increasingly beloved face to the other. She didn't always understand these women, but they were her family.

"Do you think there's a chance he's buried anything in mayonnaise jars in the yard?" she asked.

CHAPTER THIRTEEN

Two WEEKS LATER, Alan knocked on Cate's door as she was dressing for his father's wedding rehearsal and dinner. She pulled her silk tunic maternity blouse over her head and then stepped into the matching navy skirt.

"Come in." Warily, she waited for the expression in his eyes as he looked at her. She'd put off wearing maternity clothes until she'd strained her waistbands to their limits.

Alan opened the door and came inside. When he saw her, his gaze warmed. She laughed. His wanting her made all her choices seem right.

"You like me in this?" Ludicrous shyness provoked her coy question.

"You're carrying my babies." He made no apologies for his masculine pride. "I love the way you look."

"That's a relief."

He crossed the room, his crisp white shirt rustling with each movement of the lean muscles it covered. He'd tucked his shirt into black trousers, but his collar remained open.

"I need a tie."

She met him at the closet door, opening it. "Let me help you choose."

"In a minute."

He swept her into his arms, and Cate met his insistent, seeking mouth. His tongue moved against hers, intimating a longing she felt just as strongly. Except the final commitment terrified her. She broke away.

"What's wrong?" His thick voice reminded her painfully of her own body's needs.

She rubbed her hands over her forearms. "I don't remember how to make love," she admitted again. "Knowing you better, wanting you more every day, I don't want to disappoint you." She lifted her arms to display her pregnant body. "And I don't know if you'll be so enamored of the way I look when I'm naked."

His complete disregard for her worries disarmed her. "How can I convince you I'll be enthusiastic? I could show you."

She skirted his seeking hands and turned to his tie rack. "If you do, we'll miss your father's dinner." She chose a wine silk tie. "What do you think?" It complemented his dark complexion perfectly.

"Fine." He took the tie without looking at it. "But I came to fill you in on the company, too."

She lifted both brows.

"Shep, Brian and Howard finally gave in about hiring a detective when I said we were telling our employees the truth. We're interviewing tomorrow. We don't want to waste any time on a wrong choice from the Yellow Pages."

"How did you find the ones you want to see?"

"It wasn't easy. They mostly laugh when we tell them we want an interview. Shep knows a guy who tracked him down when he was having an affair with—'' He stopped. ''Never mind that. Howard Deavers knows a couple of men he's used when he's had pilfering problems at the hardware store, but they haven't handled a job this important—as far as we're concerned.''

''Your father's getting married tomorrow.'' Alan seemed less at ease with his father since she'd begun her tenuous reconciliation with him. ''You won't miss his wedding?''

He narrowed his gaze. His unexpected hostility hurt.

''What kind of man do you think I am? I won't miss my father's wedding. I especially won't give myself an excuse to skip it just to show him I don't want to be there.''

''I'm sorry. I didn't mean to suggest you would.'' But she had wondered if some deeper reluctance lay behind Alan's flair for missing family occasions.

''I'll be home in time to take you to the wedding.''

He lifted his collar and looped his tie around his neck. Watching him, Cate suffered a powerful and peculiar pang of physical need. She wanted to prove she was on his side. Would making love strengthen their tenuous bonds?

Ironic that she'd married a man who saw his worth in his ability to provide material goods, and now the only thing that held her back from him was her fear that she wouldn't be woman enough to satisfy him. Well, maybe not that unusual. From all accounts, her previous self sounded restrained to a fault.

ALAN WISHED he'd packed his tux in the car before he'd left home for today's interviews. He pointed his truck at the tall spire that rose so high above the other buildings in town sailors had used it to steer for Leith's port on sunny days.

He swerved around the empty schoolyard and skidded into the church's parking lot. Just as the bells began to clang.

He snatched his garment bag from the hook above the passenger door and ran for the vestry. Dan shot out of the church, his forehead knotted.

"You're too late," he whispered. "They're married, and they're signing the register."

Alan dug his heels into the gravel, guilt ripping at him. "How's Dad?"

"Happy." Dan unzipped the garment bag and then glared at the grocery shoppers staring at them from the Shop and Sack across the street. "I guess you can't change out here. You'd better sneak down to the Sunday school rest rooms. Mom's going to take you apart."

"I don't doubt it." After yesterday, she would be positive he'd missed the ceremony to show his father and her just how little he valued their places in his life. "I need to see Dad first."

"Not a chance. If you show up in jeans, Meg will kill me. Her bet was, you'd forgotten your tux." Dan pulled the bag toward the front of the church, and Alan followed, trying not to wrinkle his suit.

"Let me go in first." Dan eased one side of the highly varnished doors open. He waved his father up the steps. "No one's opened the inner doors yet. They must be waiting for Grandpa and Meg. Go on."

Alan slipped inside the Sunday school wing and

bolted for the rest room. He dressed as fast as he could and packed his street clothes in the garment bag. On his way back, he tucked the bag into a closet in one of the classrooms.

Exultant voices reached him before he opened the church door again. The last of the guests had bottle-necked in the entryway. Alan mingled, explaining his absence with his weak-sounding meeting excuse.

He would have left, if he'd looked at his watch in time to see he was going to be late, but John Mabry had attended their meeting, too, giving them dire warnings about throwing away more money to find a guy who'd probably spent or squirreled away all their funds. Alan had found himself arguing the same points all over again.

He wouldn't have insulted his father or Meg on purpose. Who'd taken his place as his father's best man? Dan must not have, or he'd have been with the rest of the wedding party.

Alan finally squeezed through the doors that were propped wide-open to let guests into the churchyard. The photographer had corralled his father and Meg for pictures. At his father's other side, Cate beamed for the camera.

The hectic flush on her radiant cheeks probably came from rage at his absence. He recognized fire in her eyes.

He was tired of defending himself. He was trying with all his might to keep his friends and sprawling family safe.

"Alan, you made it." The sound of an open wound in his father's voice made him even more defensive.

"I'm sorry, Dad. I'll explain." Aware of interested gazes from the wedding guests who'd arrived on time, he paused. "Later."

"Come stand beside my best man." His dad beckoned him, but only Cate and Meg flanked him.

"Who?" Alan asked, avoiding his wife's accusing gaze.

"Cate. I've loved her as if she were my own child. When you were held up, who else should replace you? Cate, let Alan in there beside you. I know you're rattled because you think he let us down, but he'll have a good excuse when we *get him alone.*"

His emphasis on the final phrase drew laughter from the crowd and irritation from his son. Alan put his arm around Cate, his fingers sliding easily over the high-waisted sky-blue dress that draped her full breasts and silked over her growing belly. She was so stiff he was afraid he might break her.

"Smile, Mrs. Palmer." The photographer straightened to prompt her with a grin. "A couple more, and we'll adjourn to the party. What's not to like about that?"

Cate turned her head toward Richard. "Sorry."

"No problem. I'm just as annoyed."

Alan forced himself to stare at the camera, but he was far more interested in the connection he appeared to have strengthened between his father and his wife. Meg smiled his way, as if she realized he was out in the familial cold.

The photographer positioned them for a few more shots and then released them so they could go to their cars. "We'll continue at the club," he said. More of a threat, in Alan's view, than a promise.

Inside the limo assigned to them, Cate refused to look his way, much less speak. She tugged at the collar of her short jacket.

"Are you hot?" he asked. They couldn't possibly finish the conversation they needed to have before they reached the Leith Beach Club.

"On fire." She turned toward him in an effort to exclude the driver. "Where have you been?"

"With Howard, Shep and Brian. John came to the meeting and tried to persuade us not to hire the detective."

"So you had to convince him and the others all over again?"

"Yeah. John hadn't been entirely honest about the status of the investigation. Police departments all over the country are still looking for Jim, but they think he's put the money into bank accounts we'll never be able to touch."

"Why didn't he tell you before?"

"The powers that be." His stomach churned. "The police department and the D.A. are still working up a statement that won't bottom out the local economy."

Cate drooped against the seat. "I'm so glad we told Caroline."

He slumped beside her. "I wish I'd already told the others."

She touched his sleeve. "When are you going to?"

"I've scheduled a meeting for Monday. They'll probably be as upset as we are with the police. We shouldn't have held back so long."

She tugged him onto her shoulder. "You can't

backtrack now. I'm sorry I was so angry, but I still think you shouldn't have met with Mabry and the others on such an important day for Richard.''

Alan shifted so he could pull her head against his chest. Her perfume danced into his senses, stealing his power to string a rational thought out of his confusion. ''What makes you my father's new best friend?''

''He's not my favorite guy, but I'm trying because you and Dan love him.'' She shifted. ''You're probably not open to any more advice today, but you might consider meeting Richard for your own showdown. He won't hold a grudge if you stand up to him.''

''Just when I was planning to crawl on my belly. You forgive me, Cate?''

''I can't get that mad and just forget it.''

''Will it fade over time do you think?''

''Let's see how you dance.''

He pressed a kiss to her fragrant hair, not sure what he was supposed to do with this completely new side of his wife. Guiltily, he realized she excited him now more than ever before. Without effort. ''You don't like to dance.''

Stillness held her as she seemed to contemplate. ''That was when I cared whether I looked like an out-of-control Talbot.''

''You don't care now?'' Should he be surprised? Probably not, after the past few weeks.

''Do you want me to care?''

He kissed her hair again and rubbed his cheek over the strands that had curled in the humid air. ''I don't think so,'' he admitted. ''I kept thinking I wanted our old life back. Not just the company being solvent, but knowing what to expect from you. But I like the way you lose control and then reign it back in when you see the important side of an argument. I like your passion now.'' He glanced at her. ''Does that bother you?'' She'd been restrained in her passion before, saving it for the quiet of their room.

She shrugged. ''I'm all right. I don't think I can go back to being whoever I was before.'' She shrugged, and her knowing smile all but curled his toes. ''Why shouldn't you be happy, too?'' she asked.

''I can't think.''

''You'll come up with something.'' She leaned into him, brushing his upper arm with the heat and firmness of her full breast. ''I have faith in you. Sometimes shaky faith, but faith.''

She'd also become a talker since the coma. ''I literally can't think when you're like this.''

She laughed at him.

He didn't mind. The wife he hardly knew had begun to turn him into a man he didn't recognize.

''We'd better enjoy this reception,'' he said. ''I doubt they throw dances in the poorhouse.''

AFTER THE wedding dinner, Cate suggested Alan take over her best man's duties to deliver the toast. His stiff delivery made her feel guilty for lecturing him about his relationship with his father, but she anticipated a better toast at Richard and Meg's first anniversary party.

Her husband had begun to change. With new honesty in their relationship, he couldn't seem to settle for treating his own father as an acquaintance.

After the toasts, Richard and Meg took to the floor. Watching them dance with their gazes locked, Cate grew impatient for the end of the song. She wanted Alan's arms around her.

As the last strains faded, Cate took Alan's hand, but she slowed as they came to the edge of the floor. "I wish you hadn't told me I didn't dance. I feel self-conscious."

He looked down at her, his gaze totally involved. He took her in his arms, and she relaxed against him. Moving in time to the melody, Cate molded her body to his with more intimacy than she'd ever allowed herself. This moment seemed right to trust, though trust felt supremely risky.

He held her, his touch a seductive whisper of cloth and limb. As Alan tightened his embrace, she slid her hands up his forearms, testing the rough weave of the material that molded his shoulders.

They didn't speak until the song ended, and then Alan only held her close. She stood, safe and tranquil in his arms, certain in her decision to move forward.

"I'd better ask Meg to dance," he said.

She loosened her hold on him. "I'll look for Dan. He seemed to think I was going to move out again when I was upset with you. I'd like to set his mind at rest."

"You must have been angry if you couldn't hide it from him."

She met Alan's gaze squarely. "I was so upset I thought crazy things—like this might be the only way you knew how to tell me you didn't want to be with me any more. Because I'd said I needed you not to miss any more family events.''

"I'm trying, Cate.''

His honesty about the business, his willingness to share work with her, proved how hard he was trying.

"I never meant to lay all the blame for our problems on your shoulders.'' She squeezed his hand. "Let's talk about this later. You find Meg, and I'll look for Dan.''

He held her when she would have let him go. "He's a smart guy. He'll figure out we want to be together.''

She smoothed her dress over her stomach. "I wish I'd stayed instead of hiding behind Aunt Imogen's skirts.''

His edgy smile transformed him into a provocative stranger. "Go ahead. I'll find you and Dan.''

Looking down from his startling height, he seemed more male than ever and yet more vulnerable. His intensity singled them out from the other wedding guests.

Cate didn't want to leave him, but she needed to speak to Dan. She hugged the edges of the dance floor until Uncle Ford's voice stopped her in her tracks.

"Here's the best man. How about a dance, Cate? I saw you and Alan. Never knew you could trip the light whatever.''

Cate hated to point out his cane and her mission to find her son. "I'd love to dance with you, Uncle Ford, after I chat with Dan. Have you seen him?''

"Matter of fact, I have.'' The older man prodded the floor with his cane and levered himself out of his chair. He waited to speak until he was close enough to shatter Cate's eardrums. "I saw the bartender turn him and that spiked girl away from the bar."

"He's not old enough to drink."

"A fact the barman apparently reminded him of. I'm sure they're around here somewhere."

Frustrated with his lackadaisical approach, she searched her uncle's gaze. "Why didn't you find me? You should tell me if you see Dan ask for a drink."

"The barman took care of the problem."

She shook her head. "He's not Dan's parent—or uncle. You should have told me."

"I told you as soon as I saw you."

"What if they went somewhere else?"

He pointed to the men and women, and, with any luck, one young couple, flitting around the polished dance floor. "Go out there. Check on them."

"I will." She hugged him. "Sorry I was testy."

"No problem."

She had to remember to lean away from Uncle Ford's booming voice the next time she apologized.

She wove between the dancing couples, feeling responsible for Dan's recent missteps. She didn't know what to do to reassure him.

Each face she saw raised a question in her mind. The happy couples smiled at her, or said hello or looked at her as if a woman alone shouldn't wander a dance floor.

At last, she spied Alan's head, inches above anyone near him. She backed around the couple between them and found Richard had cornered him.

"So I'm trying to tell you I'm sorry, son. I shouldn't have discussed your mother's and my divorce. I shouldn't have forced you to grow up so soon." Richard looked fondly at Meg, ice-blond and beautiful in her ivory gown, proudly holding his arm. "Most of all, I shouldn't have filled you with wisdom about women from one lousy experience that frightened me so much I didn't try again for over thirty years."

Alan's skin looked ruddy, as if he'd been out in the sun. "That's it, Dad? You're sorry—it's over. You made a big mistake, but we've recovered at last?"

"I am sorry." Richard looked as if he'd expected a friendlier response.

"I've based my whole marriage on what happened with you and my mother. I almost lost my wife because I believed you."

People stopped dancing around them. Cate wanted no one to pity Alan, and they had a bigger problem.

She moved to his side. "I need to talk to you."

Meg edged closer. "What's happened?"

Too late, Cate realized her mistake if she was trying to keep her family out of the public domain. "Not a thing." She plastered her best smile across her face. Dan wouldn't thank her for turning Richard and Meg's reception into an all points search for him.

Alan tightened his mouth. "In case I don't catch you again, Meg, I want you to know how happy I am that you're officially part of my family now."

"I'm sure we'll work things out." She kissed his cheek. "Your father loves you, Alan."

With a nod, he took Cate's arm. "Have a good time, Dad. Call us when you get home."

Cate welcomed his tight grip as he led her out to the club's veranda.

"What's wrong?" he asked.

"I can't find Dan, and Uncle Ford saw him ask for a drink."

"Not a soda?"

"I don't think the bartender would have turned him down for anything other than alcohol."

"You're probably right."

"Let's look in the parking lot. He and Phoebe may have taken something out to his car."

"Good plan. You go around the building, and I'll check the lot by the pro shop."

She didn't bother to answer. Alan's concern confirmed hers. The sound of the rising tide grew louder as she turned behind the building. She looked for Dan's car, but she saw two figures in a small antique-yellow sedan. Phoebe might have driven.

Cate drummed on the car's window before she made sure her son was inside. Her uncle, far older than his startled companion, twisted uncomfortably in the seat.

He rolled down the window. "Cate, did you find Dan?"

His quick conquest appalled her. "What are you doing in that car? You're going to shame the family."

He glanced at the woman who couldn't be many years older than Cate, herself. She tried to shield her face with her hand.

"That's my girl," he said. "But I don't think we've done anything shameful yet." He turned to his friend. "Do you, my dear?

"Nor will we now. Good evening, Cate. I haven't seen Dan, if you're looking for him."

"Thanks." She turned from her fast-working, careless Lothario of an uncle. She'd trust his friend to pry him out of that car.

She hurried around the front of the building. In the lot beside the pro shop, Alan had buttonholed their son outside his car. Alone.

Alan turned his head as Cate neared them. "Phoebe apparently doesn't care for underage drinking any more than we do. She gave him an earful and left after the bartender told him to go away."

"Thanks, Dad."

"You'll hear more when we get home."

Dan broke away and yanked his car door open. "This time I'm not going home. You can find me at Aunt Imogen's. She's a better cook than Mom, and she and Uncle Ford respect me."

"They won't if you keep going the way you are. Go to Aunt Imogen if you want, son, but you'll have to face us eventually." Alan gripped the car door. "And call us when you get there."

"Not a chance."

The extra strain in his voice reached Cate. "What's going on, Alan?"

He answered Dan instead of her. "I'm not eighteen any more, but I'm not naive either. You aren't going to your Aunt Imogen's house."

"I will." Dan's expression reminded Cate of a cornered animal. "After I see my friends."

"I ought to drag you home with us." Alan sounded as if he might.

''Even if you did tonight, what would you do next time? You have to trust me, Dad.''

''How can I? You promised you wouldn't drink again.''

''And I didn't, but I'm getting pretty sick of everyone treating me like I have more right to a pacifier than a bottle of beer.''

''You do, son.''

''Thanks again.'' He slid behind the car's wheel. ''I won't drink, but I'm not going to call you when I get to Aunt Imogen's.''

He slammed the door and started the car. At least he refrained from spinning out of the gravel lot on two wheels.

Alan planted his hands on his hips. ''What is the matter with that kid?''

''I don't remember him. I walked out. We're giving him two new siblings and we've reneged on his golf school.''

''If he's old enough to scout for booze, he's old enough to cope with his life.'' Alan stared over her head at the road Dan had taken. ''He leaves for school next Friday.''

''I feel as if I've failed him. It's too soon to let him go.''

Alan turned her toward the front of the club. ''You didn't fail him by yourself. Don't underestimate my contribution.'' He clenched his hand on her shoulder. ''His whole life isn't based on the past few months, and I don't think we've done anything bad enough to drive him to drink or to feel he has to escape his home.''

''Try to see through his eyes.''

"I can't find empathy for Dan right now." He nodded toward the club. Lights had begun to filter the dancers' shadows through the ballroom windows. "Do you want to go back inside?"

She hesitated. "Actually, I'd love a walk on the beach, but I'm exhausted. Can we go home and burn these shoes?"

He peered at the ice-blue pumps Aunt Imogen and Caroline had somehow browbeaten her into borrowing from her twin's meticulously tidy closet.

"They make your toes look kind of sexy."

"I wish I'd worn galoshes." She almost confided the pain in her swollen feet, but a peek at Alan's strong, handsome profile reminded her no one had ever written sonnets to a pregnant woman's puffy appendages. She cast one longing glance toward the ocean. "Do you mind if we go home?"

"Best place for us, in case our son relents and comes back."

"He's in charge now, isn't he?" A way to change the balance of power escaped her.

"For tonight. We'll wrestle the reins out of his hands. That's what parents do."

She leaned into Alan's body, and he was gentleman enough to ignore the extra weight. To think, less than an hour ago, she'd felt sublimely female, a regular seductress on the prowl for her man.

Now, what she really yearned for was a wheelbarrow, so her man could more comfortably transport her to their car.

CHAPTER FOURTEEN

IN THE MIDDLE of the night, Cate woke alone in her bed. She'd been so exhausted she hardly retained any memory of getting to her room, but as she sat up, she knew beyond doubt, sleep had finished with her for the night.

She scooted out of bed. Faint light from the bay window drew her across the room. She gathered the sides of the filmy curtains in her hands and pressed her head against the window, twisting for a view of the driveway. Had Dan come home? He'd probably park in the garage.

She turned her head, and the glass cooled her forehead. Across the street, the tide seemed calmer than usual in the moon's glow.

The quiet outside threatened to lull her into her own sense of peace, but she had to know about Dan. She'd managed to turn his life upside down. Unlike those waves outside, he couldn't seem to stop churning.

She crossed her room and eased the door open, being careful not to wake Alan or Dan if he'd come home. Starting down the stairs, she came face-to-face with Alan, who stopped so suddenly on the third tread, he almost fell on her.

"I didn't mean to scare you." Something about her own voice reminded her of Uncle Ford.

"He's not home."

"Dan?" Cate peered over his shoulder, as if their son might materialize because they both wanted him. "I guess it's too late to call Aunt Imogen?"

"Probably." Alan, wearing only khakis, with the waist button undone, climbed the rest of the stairs and maneuvered around her. "I'll call anyway."

She tried not to stare at the arrow of dark hair above his slightly parted zipper. "I don't want to upset her."

"She won't mind if we wake her up to find out about Dan."

He was right. "I'll call," she said. "She'll give me extra leeway, because I'm pregnant."

Alan grinned. "I wonder if you've always been devious, but you were hiding it."

She picked up the telephone and tapped out her aunt's number. "I'm not devious." After three rings, her aunt answered in a sleepy voice. "It's me, Cate."

"He's here," Aunt Imogen said.

"Dan?"

"Who else? I performed a sniff test at his request. He has touched no alcohol tonight, and you all might want to lay off him. May I go back to bed?"

"Thank you."

"Night."

Cate pressed the phone's off button and nodded at Alan. "She knew I was looking for him."

"You haven't changed that much. He's there?"

"We have to talk to him."

"We've both alienated him with talk. He's not in

a receptive frame of mind." Alan turned her toward her open door. "Did I wake you?"

"I don't think so. I was exhausted when we got home. I hardly remember you helping me to bed, but I'm not at all tired now." She fingered her nightshirt. Not exactly the garb she'd have chosen for this moment. "I didn't expect to sleep alone tonight."

Alan's gaze grew watchful. "You're absolutely awake now?"

Hardly the reaction she'd hoped for, either. "I'm not talking in my sleep this time."

"Maybe I should pinch you."

"No." She scooted around him and returned to the moonlight at her window. Her window and Alan's after tonight. "Come over here."

"Okay." He'd already followed her, so his "okay" dusted her cheek with warm breath. "What do you want, Cate?"

"You." She reached behind her back for his hands. He let her take them, and she pressed his palms against her belly. "I need you to know what you're getting into first."

"I do know. You're the one who forgot."

"You've decided you can handle the differences I can't change about myself." She laced her fingers through his and stroked his hands down the sides of her stomach. "But I'd like to know ahead of time you can make a physical commitment, too. My body can't look or feel the way you remember it."

"Your clinical approach makes me want to laugh." His voice, thick and distracted, scattered her sensible intentions. He followed the curve of her tummy. Her belly appeared to protrude more each

day, but Alan didn't seem to mind. With each sweep
of their hands, he stretched his fingers to touch more
of her skin. At last, he curved their hands around her
hips, and Cate gasped.

Alan spread his fingers to free himself from her
grasp, and then he reached for her shirt buttons. She
tensed. Their history lived for him. All the other days
and nights, all the times they'd made love, her other
pregnancy with Dan.

"You're trembling, Cate." He moved on to the
next button. His heart, tapping stridently against her
back, belied his assurance.

She stared at the ocean, white foam riding in on
dark shadows of movement. Natural motion, measur-
able time, but for Cate, the passing seconds built up
speed. Alan nudged her hair aside with his chin.

His lips, pressed to her throat, pulled her out of
her fear of what came next. Here and now, he made
her feel lovely and loved. His kisses felt reverent.
She only realized he'd finished unbuttoning her
nightshirt when he lifted his hands to push the material off her shoulders. It dropped to the floor between them, and Alan linked his arms beneath her
breasts to pull her more firmly against his chest.

She felt her nakedness in the careful distance he
maintained between their lower bodies. He knew she
wanted him, but he was less willing to reveal himself
to her.

She backed against him and turned her head for
his kiss. At last he unzipped his pants and let her
slide her hands down the sides of his thighs. The
khaki moved beneath her moist palms. His whole
body jerked as if he weren't ready for her to touch

him. She settled his hardness against the small of her back. He groaned and curved her forward, his hands in her hair as he thrust against her.

Such an intimate position startled her and yet, she wanted him more.

He slid his hands down her back and spread them over her belly again, caressing the swelling of the children they'd created together. The hunger he communicated with his seeking fingers eased her last anxiety. He wanted her, and her pregnancy definitely hadn't put him off.

A sudden fluttering he must have felt almost as strongly as she stilled them both. Cate straightened and caught her breath.

"What was that?" she said, too stunned to believe it might be one of their twins.

"Wait." He opened his mouth against her neck, but the flutter didn't repeat. "How often do they move?"

"If that was movement, it never happened before."

His breath lifted the fine hairs at her nape. "I love our babies, but I hope they settle back down and allow their parents privacy."

As he cupped her full breasts, she had to agree. His hands beneath the fertile weight gave her excellent relief. His quickened inhalation reassured her again that he found her anything but overweight and undesirable. He nudged his fingertips across her nipples. Sensitive to his slightest touch, she opened her lips and sound flowed between them.

"Did I hurt you?" She hardly recognized his ragged tone.

She rolled her head against his chest and covered his hands, inviting him to touch her with less restraint. He rolled her nipples gently between his index fingers and thumbs.

Longing buckled her knees, but when she sank against Alan, he turned her, and their legs tangled in a complicated dance that led them to the bed. Alan eased her onto her back and stood to take off his own clothes. When he stretched out beside her, he studied her face, his own thinned by desire that almost traveled through the air.

"I can't believe you're here." He dropped his hand on her thigh. "I've waited too long."

Catching his wrist, she lifted his fingers to her lips. She lost herself in his gaze as she kissed the tips of his fingers, enjoying the salty taste of him, salt that reminded her of the ocean at their doorstep. "Someday, can we make love on the beach?"

"Maybe I like this amnesia thing. We went to the beach the night you graduated, but after that, you were always too aware of being a Talbot to engage in sand dune sex. I'll find a private dune for you." He opened her mouth and stroked the pad of his thumb over the moist flesh of her inner lip.

"I wish I could remember," she said. "Alan, why did you choose me? I mean, rather than Caroline? I know you're good friends. You've been more reliable than her own husband."

"Caroline?" he said. "Why are we talking about Caroline now?"

"I have to know, I guess. The day I told her about the company, I was a little jealous of the way she talked about you, as if she believed in you more than I had.''

He shook his head at her. ''I didn't choose you, Cate. We chose each other. We fell in love, and I never saw Caroline the way I saw you. She's my sister.''

He burrowed his head into the curve of her neck. ''Can we get back to what we were talking about before?'' He made his way down the line of her shoulder, his mouth growing bolder, hungrier, and Cate forgot everything that worried her about the past.

As if he couldn't wait any longer, Alan raised himself to plant his palms on each side of her head. He kissed her, his control melting with each slide of his tongue against hers.

Need swept Cate's body and mind. She responded blindly, pulling Alan closer and closer still, when he tried to hold his weight off her. Indulging in the heady freedom of touching him, she explored the planes of his chest, the taut, quivering muscles of his belly.

Recognition quivered at the edge of her mind. Her hands seemed to know the muscles that trembled against them. As she dragged her fingertips up the muscles of his buttocks, he pressed her back to the bed and levered one leg across hers.

His concentration enticed her. He cupped her breast, holding her as if she were immeasurably precious to him. He lowered his mouth, and she watched him ring her nipple with his lips. Bathed in the heat of his mouth, her flesh tightened all the way to the pit of her stomach. She arched, begging him to take more of her.

The pleasure of his loving besieged her. A strange satisfaction spiked with aching need. He turned his head to suckle the curve of her breast. He brushed his mouth the length of her sternum, as if he were relearning her body.

She reached for him, but he held himself carefully over her, and she had to content herself with exploring the breadth of his shoulders and the strong, straining column of his throat.

"Alan," she whispered, and when he didn't respond, she spoke his name again.

He lifted his head. His ruffled hair lent his gaze an unfamiliar intimacy. Would they have struggled through so many problems, if she'd invited him to share their bed when she'd come home from the hospital?

"What?" He spread his hand over her belly. "Are you all right?"

She nodded, and even the crinkle of the crisp pillowcase beneath her head took on an erotic quality. "I can't reach you."

His smile brushed her lips as he kissed her. "You can touch me later. This is like your first time."

"I want you to feel..." She'd insisted on communication, but she couldn't explain she wanted him to feel the way he made her feel, happy, aroused, beloved. Her emotions were too personal, even to share with him yet.

He traced the line of her throat, his mouth alternately gentle and firm. He scraped his teeth over the bones of her shoulder, but he'd finally moved within her reach.

She cupped him, and he gasped in surprise. She stroked, unsure of what she was doing, but her instinct seemed to be right. He arched above her, and his moan puckered her nipples. He took her in his mouth again. She explored his body, writhing against him, meeting his thrusts with her palm until he parted her knees.

He grazed the length of her thigh with the back of his hand. Unlike hers, his touch was sure. He knew exactly how to push her toward a culmination that almost frightened her. She wanted him with her. She wanted him to be part of her. Tonight was for connections, not selfish love.

She whispered his name, a plea and a demand he seemed to understand. Gently, he entered her, waiting for her to show him with her body when she was ready for more.

She clung to him, her faith in him complete. Alan, her husband, wouldn't take more than she could give, nor force her to beg for him.

The way he held himself above her, caring for the children they'd made in just such a moment as this intensified her joy. Their rhythm came from memories gone from her. She opened her eyes and looked into his.

He curved his mouth, but this time his smile challenged her. She held back, teasing. He adjusted to her movement. She took control, but he took it back, as if, in this one part of their marriage, he read her mind. His knowledge of her sang an emotional accompaniment to their physical joining.

Without warning, her pleasure changed. Deepened, lengthened, from her thighs to her toes, to her scalp. She raised herself off the bed, into Alan's arms. Her whole body reached for him, and he answered.

His expression tightened. His eyes drifted shut as his lips thinned. She held him, her muscles still quaking, as he collapsed and pulled her to his side. Careful to the end, to protect their unborn children.

Cate slid her arm across his chest. She pressed her mouth to his skin, smiling as his pulse raced against her lips.

"Such a worthwhile husband."

"I love you, wife."

She lifted herself on her elbow. "Are you sure your hormones aren't talking?"

He grinned, and his rumpled hair and sated eyes made her happy. "Do a man's hormones talk after the fact?"

She slid her hand down his flat stomach. "Maybe, if they anticipate being reawakened."

He caught her fingers. "I'm a little nervous. We never made love while you were carrying twins before."

"I feel spectacular, divine, ecstatic, really good." She stretched, thrusting out her breasts for effect. She was bold now that she knew for sure how he felt about her body.

Indecision entered his gaze, but he raised his head to kiss her. "Get some sleep, so I'll keep feeling spectacular." He pulled her to his side again and curved his leg over her thighs.

Nestling against him, she wondered if she'd ever

really believed her life would improve without him in it.

DAN CAME HOME the next morning as Alan opened the garage to leave for work. Alan stopped his car and got out. Dan parked on the drive as well.

"Everything okay?" Alan searched his son's face for signs of a hangover.

Dan pulled a "not again" face. "I didn't drink, Dad. I watched a movie at my friend's house, and then I drove out to Aunt Imogen's."

"What's your plan for today?"

"Start sorting out my room, so I can pack for school."

"What makes you so angry, Dan?"

"I'm not angry, and I'm not in the mood to sit through an interrogation. Aren't you late?"

By about half an hour. Holding his nude wife had proven too tempting to resist this morning. He'd left her sleeping; if she'd opened her eyes, he doubted he could have left her at all.

"I have to go, but I want to talk to you." Dan needed to know his mother and father had sorted out their problems, but their shared bedroom would tell that story. "You know your mom doesn't need any extra commotion right now. Why don't you cut her a little slack from here on? If you're angry, talk to me, but let your mother off the hook."

Dan opened his door and stood, concern blanching his young face. "Did something happen to Mom?"

Well, he still cared enough to worry about her. "No, but let's do all we can to keep her healthy. She needs our support right now."

"So you won't cut out on her when she expects you at say—a wedding?"

Dan's bitterness surprised him. "You know I've never chosen to break a promise to you or to my father."

"And to Mom?"

Maybe he'd assumed, once or twice or twenty times too often that she'd understand. "Your mother's and my marriage is our business. Not your problem, son."

"I'm not involved if my parents divorce?"

"Divorce?" Alan strode around his car and grabbed his son's shoulder. "We're about to have two babies. We have you. We've shared a lifetime together, but we haven't taught you much if you think we can throw all that away without a second glance."

"You'll never convince me Mom didn't plan to leave you that night at Aunt Imogen's."

"But she didn't leave."

"One of you will change your mind, and I plan to be prepared." He shrugged off Alan's hand. "Forget about it. Why do we have to talk about this again?"

He stomped through the garage, unfastening his keys from a ring on his belt loop. Frustrated, Alan had plenty to say to Dan's stiff back. But not one word sounded productive, even in his head. Dan wouldn't believe until he saw for himself that his parents had truly started over.

TRASH FROM last night's Fourth of July fireworks littered the road as Dan packed his car. He searched the street for some sign of Phoebe. She'd promised to say goodbye to him in person.

She was his one regret about starting classes early. He didn't want to leave her behind. In fact, he'd asked her to drive to school with him. She'd turned him down.

Behind him, his own front door opened. His mom balanced a canvas bag in front of her big old belly. A grudging smile hurt his mouth. He had to credit his parents for the honeymoon show they'd paraded past him since his grandfather's wedding.

They acted more like lovesick kids his age than middle-aged married people who were starting a brand-new family. In the old days their silences had pegged out the battle zone for him. Now, if the room they occupied was quiet, he'd learned to knock before he opened the door.

The only thing worse than your parents having sex all the time was never knowing where they'd be.

His mom peered down the street. "I can't believe your dad's late today."

"I'll drop by his office. Wasn't he writing reference letters?" Forget it. He wasn't going to wait around for his dad and Phoebe.

If he hung around here much longer, his mom would start to blubber, and the last thing he wanted was his mom wailing all over him again. He'd just eaten the saltiest, soggiest grilled-ham-and-cheese a mother ever tearfully slopped onto a plate, and he'd had enough.

Besides, he'd finally begun to realize he wouldn't see her hovering over him every day. He'd miss her.

He wrapped her in a loose hug. The babies felt

funny, and her clinging arms worried him, too. "Bye, Mom. I'll be fine."

"Call me after you check in. Let me know what you think about your room." She pressed her fist to the small of her back. "I don't know why you refuse to let me drive you."

Because he'd hoped Phoebe would change her mind and come with him. "I'll survive on my own." He opened his car door and jumped behind the wheel. Why linger when the inevitable had to happen? "See you later. You and Dad can come visit in a few weeks."

"I love you, Dan."

He climbed out of the car, hugged her tight as he could and bit his lip to keep girly tears from shooting out of his eyes. "Love you, too, Mom."

This time he didn't look back. And he didn't drive by his dad's office, either.

ALAN PULLED INTO the parking lot at Whitlock College's library. He picked up the map an assistant at the registrar's office had marked for him. Myers Hall stood on the street that ran past the north side of the library. The side opposite the lot where he'd stopped.

He circled the library in the parking lot to turn onto the right road. Cate's voice spoke in his head. "Just go see him. You can take him the little refrigerator as an excuse. He must have been annoyed or he would have stopped by your office, but he's had three weeks to cool off."

Apparently, Dan had told her he was going to stop on his way out of town to say goodbye. He hadn't.

Was he annoyed or petulant? Why would Dan be upset with them now?

A sign in front of a square brick building identified Myers Hall for Alan. He parked Cate's SUV at the side of the street and trudged up the sidewalk. Tall Georgia pines and thick hardwoods sheltered the residence, accenting its exclusive atmosphere.

Would they be able to afford the tuition Dan's scholarship didn't cover if the business went as badly as he now feared? Alan scratched the back of his head.

He'd give a lot for a share of Cate's confidence. She just kept assuring him they'd manage together. He'd learned to trust the together part of her promise, but he couldn't feel as sanguine about steps they'd take to manage.

The employees he'd had to lay off had found other building firms, but their commutes had all extended. He tried to make himself feel better with the knowledge he'd helped them find something. They weren't waiting each morning on the side of a road for a chance at day labor.

Alan stopped at the stone posts at the end of the sidewalk in front of Dan's building. Dan might not be in, but Alan hadn't called first. He hadn't wanted to give Dan a chance to put him off.

He figured he and Cate would have to borrow tape from Aunt Imogen if they didn't sort out their son's problems soon.

He wove through a crowd of lounging adolescents who looked too young to drive, much less live on campus at a college. They stopped talking as one to give him a sharp once-over.

Immediately inside the loud, unoiled front door, Alan scanned the lounge for someone in charge. Not one of the inhabitants sprawled in any of the chairs or on the floor presented an air of authority. A kid about Dan's age finally looked up from his book.

"Who do you want?"

"Dan Palmer," Alan said.

"Room 324."

"Thanks."

The kid went back to his book, and Alan took the stairs two at a time. He reached the third floor about the same time he suspected he was having a heart attack. Another sign indicated which rooms went to the left and which to the right. Dan's room was on the right. Girls and boys eyed him curiously as he huffed and puffed down the hall.

He knocked on Dan's door, and his son opened up almost immediately. The second Dan saw him, wariness came into his tired expression. He stood aside and Alan crossed the doorway into chaos.

Clothes littered two beds as if a tornado had spilled them out of its spinning mouth. Books and clocks and soda cans and food wrappers added to the turmoil. Alan decided not to dig for one of the chairs.

"I hope a load-bearing beam runs beneath this floor."

"Are you telling me to clean my room, Dad?"

He ignored the sarcasm. "I brought you a refrigerator to add to the clutter. Your mother thought you might be able to use it."

Dan remained silent and sullen for a moment, but he finally twisted a reluctant smile. "Thanks. I'll help you bring it up."

He cleared a space beneath the double windows that let in the room's only light, and then they went to Cate's car. His fellow students eyed them with greater interest as they hauled the minifridge through the lounge. Alan turned toward the stairs, but Dan tugged toward the far end of the room.

"Why don't we take the elevator?"

Elevator? "Good idea."

Upstairs, Dan managed to balance his end of the refrigerator while he fished keys off his belt loop. Alan was relieved he'd remembered to lock the room. Cate would be glad to hear he followed safety procedures.

Grunting in unison, they managed to position the appliance beneath the windowsill. Dan picked up a pile of papers from the floor and dropped them on top of the fridge. When he leaned down to connect the plug, Alan glimpsed a printed schedule on top of the stack.

He frowned. Dan's name ran across the page's right corner. He was supposed to be in a Spanish class at this moment.

"Son, have you dropped Spanish?"

Dan shook his head. A hint of guilt passed through his eyes. "I slept in."

Alan waited for a less lame excuse.

"I stayed up late last night." Dan glanced around the room. "Unpacking."

"I'd laugh at a joke like that if I hadn't watched you make one increasingly serious mistake after another this summer. What's wrong with you?"

"My life."

Alan's skin crawled. "Are you depressed?"

"I'm angry."

He looked it, to Alan's relief. Angry, they'd find a way to handle. Depression opened up a whole new set of dangers.

"What makes you angry about your life?"

"Which issue do you want to lecture me on first?"

"I'm serious. I can't leave until I'm satisfied you don't need to talk to someone more skilled than I am at helping you handle problems."

With widened eyes, Dan almost seemed like the kid who'd once looked up to Alan with awe. "I don't think I've ever heard you admit anyone could do something better than you."

"Then I've been a pompous fool. What's wrong, Dan?"

"Not as much as you think, probably. Mom's accident, your arguments, golf school. The twins, when we're all too old for new babies in the house. Then I met someone I—thought I liked—a lot, but I don't know how she feels about me."

He'd met someone? Thank God that put Phoebe out of the picture. "You haven't explained Spanish."

"I honestly slept in."

"I want to be sympathetic, but you asked to start classes this summer. Sleeping through them is a waste of time and money." Dan's expression began to close again, and Alan backtracked. "Your mother and I are fine except we're concerned about you."

"And I shouldn't cause Mom any extra stress. You don't need to repeat the sermon, but I've seen how quickly you change your minds."

"If we split up tomorrow, you'd still have your own life to work on now."

"I am working." Dan turned toward the door, and
Alan went with him. "Don't worry about me. I forgot to set my clock last night, but I know how tight
your money is. I won't lose my scholarship."

"Hear what I'm saying to you. I'll take care of
the money. I'm upset about your Spanish class because you never skipped in high school."

"And I won't again, but you have to go, Dad. I
have Geology in about fifteen minutes."

"All right." Was he abandoning his son? "But
call me if you need anything. Call me if you want to
talk. No matter what you think about me or your
mother right now, we're available to talk to you or
to come here any time you need us."

Dan nodded, and Alan's spirits rose at his less belligerent gaze. "Thanks for the refrigerator." He held
out his hand. "Thanks for coming."

Alan yanked him close enough for a swift hug.
"Call me, Dan, if you need me."

He laughed, embarrassed, but more like the son
he'd been before he'd learned to doubt. "I need to
go to Geology." Then he turned and shut the door.

Alan faced the scarred white paint and discovered
he shared his son's doubts. About the business, his
ability to provide and his future. But not about Cate.

Since Cate figured prominently in his future, the
rest, he'd handle.

CHAPTER FIFTEEN

"I'VE HEARD OF false labor, Dr. Davis, but I don't remember what it feels like, and these cramps are starting in my back. Would I feel false labor in my back?"

Dr. Davis's confidence had lost its power to ease Cate's mind today. Besides, the other woman looked concerned. Worry for her children lay lock a rock in Cate's belly.

"Let's not jump to conclusions before I do an exam. You aren't feeling pain right now?"

Cate shook her head. But she'd called the doctor's office the second Alan had left for Dan's school because the cramps had unsettled her all night. "They're never regular, but they usually go away more quickly than they have this time. Usually, I feel a few, and then they stop."

"Let's do the exam."

Cate positioned herself in the stirrups, and Dr. Davis donned fresh gloves. Cate studied her doctor, searching for any sign of trouble. The woman certainly did a thorough search of things. She smiled an apology as Cate flinched.

"I'll finish in just a moment. Everything seems fine, but you may feel more cramping this afternoon."

"Because of the exam?"

"Mmm-hmm." Dr. Davis glanced at her, looked away and then zeroed in on her again. "Calm down, Cate. You act as if you think I might keep bad news from you. I won't." She backed away. "I can't give you any bad news. Everything is normal."

Cate sagged in relief. She felt like an idiot—a reassured idiot. She should have told Alan about the pains, but she hadn't wanted to worry him when Dan and the business were on his mind.

"Just in case—you are thirty-eight, and you are carrying twins—I'd like to do another ultrasound before I send you home, and then I'd like you to limit your activity."

"Limit how?"

Dr. Davis patted her shoulder. "I'm not talking bed rest, but don't take any exercise. Don't go out of your way to do anything different than your normal routine. Let cleaning wait for another time. And no sex."

Cate blinked. She didn't care for the last part. She'd have to worry Alan with news of her visit after all.

"Just until we know everything's progressing normally." Dr. Davis plucked a pen out of her pocket to write on Cate's chart. "I guess you and Alan are back on good terms."

Cate leered dramatically. "Excellent terms."

ALAN WOKE early the next morning. By the time he'd arrived home from visiting Dan, Cate had been asleep. He rolled to his side and gazed at her, overwhelmed with gratitude for the new understanding between them.

She opened her eyes, but didn't seem startled to find him staring at her. "Morning."

"I've fixated on you."

"Good." She kissed him and then settled her head more comfortably on her pillow. "How was Dan?"

"Touchy, but he liked the fridge and we talked. I felt better when I left him."

"Did he?"

Alan shrugged, a difficult procedure when leaning on his elbow. "Hard to say. I'd never challenge him to a poker game."

"But you aren't as concerned?"

"I don't think I am. He's up and down, and he blames it on us, but you can understand when you think what a steady childhood we gave him until this spring and summer."

"I have to talk to you, Alan."

Her serious tone shook him. "Okay."

"I saw Dr. Davis yesterday. Those strange back pains came back."

He grabbed her arm. Fear took a grip on his throat. "Are you—are the babies all right?"

She nodded. "Dr. Davis said everything looks normal. She ordered an ultrasound, and the babies were active. She wants me to limit my activity for a week or two, but she says she has no reason to think anything's gone wrong with my pregnancy."

"Is she sure?"

"She acted as if she were. She said we couldn't make love."

"But the babies are all right? And you are?"

She laughed. "I thought you'd be upset about the sex. I am."

He ignored her teasing tone. "I'm upset because you didn't tell me."

"I didn't tell you because our other son needed you, and I wasn't sure I had a problem."

"But you don't—we—don't have a problem?"

"Right." She snuggled into his chest, and he put his arms around her, even though her secrecy still annoyed him. "Except we can't make love," she added again.

"I don't care," he said against her hair, but what he meant was "I'll love you all my life." She just didn't respond well to "I love you." Yet. Someday she'd stop looking like a deer in headlights when he told her.

"I'm relieved, but I guess you're right. I should have told you. I got scared."

Fear still laced her voice, a sharp note that asked him for comfort. All right. He'd forgive her one secret doctor's visit. He'd kept enough secrets from her over the years. Finally, he understood how betrayed and unnecessary secrets made a person feel.

The phone beside their bed rang. Alan reached over Cate to answer it. Chief Mabry started talking before Alan put the receiver to his ear.

"Your New Jersey detective found Jim."

A huge, killing weight hovered unsteadily over Alan's head. "How do you know?"

"He alerted the police, and they asked me to notify all of you."

"Why did he call the police instead of us?"

"Jim's cruising casinos, and the detective was

afraid he'd lose him if Jim decided to switch to Nevada or Europe. Apparently, New Jersey isn't lucky for our crook.''

"Great.''

"I assume you'll want to join the others on a flight to Newark?''

"I'm getting dressed. Are you coming, too?''

"Out of my jurisdiction, and besides, I'd like to shoot the son of a bitch on sight. New Jersey will send him home. Don't worry.''

"I guess I'm not allowed to shoot him on sight?''

"Not a good idea for a family man, but you'll probably have to identify him. And I figured you'd want to be there when they took him.''

"I do. Thanks for the call.''

"Your flight leaves at ten-thirty. Can you make the airport in time?''

"If I have to build myself a pair of wings." He hung up and turned to Cate. "They've found Jim. I have to go to New Jersey.''

She sat up, pulling the sheet across her bare breasts. "Why do you have to go?''

"Because he stole from me and my family and my friends. I'll be back tomorrow." He cupped her chin, remembering the twins. "Unless you want me to stay? Are you still worried about the babies?''

"No." She kissed him. "Go and don't worry. I trust Dr. Davis. By the time you come home, we'll know where we stand with the business.''

"Chief Mabry thinks we'll have to identify him anyway.''

"You don't have to explain. Just go—but take a cheap flight.''

"Like we'll ever fly first class again."

Cate's mouth curved, a lush invitation to heaven. "I can't remember ever going first class."

With heartfelt regret, he left her in their bed. Alone and wastefully untouched.

She dressed and made coffee while he packed. He carried his bag down the back stairs and found French toast waiting on the kitchen table.

"You didn't have to make this, Cate." But he'd eat it if he had to swallow a slice whole to make his plane on time. "Thank you, though."

He ate with rude speed and Cate walked him to the door.

"Don't drive crazy. If you miss your flight, you can take the next one."

He brushed her lips with his. So sweet. She tasted better than syrup, better than any other sweet thing in his life. "Go back to bed and rest. Don't do anything until I get home tomorrow, okay?"

"All right." She pushed her hair off her face. "I'll call Dan later."

"Don't, if you think talking to him might upset you."

"I miss talking to him. Even if his conversation is mostly monosyllabic."

"I'll miss you." He kissed her deeply and she kissed him back. This Cate gave as good as she got. On a groan, he finally pulled away.

"If I don't go, I'll have to beg you to break doctor's orders." He smoothed his thumb over her lip. "Turn around, and let me watch you walk toward the stairs."

With ego-boosting reluctance, she went. Alan

stepped into the garage walkway and locked the door behind him. Then he turned his attention to the bastard who'd stolen from him and his family and his employees.

THE DAY AFTER his dad's visit, the atmosphere in Dan's car all but choked him. Phoebe clung to the window side of the passenger seat, her face furious.

"I can't love you, Dan. You're like my brother. I kept hoping you'd get over this infatuation you have for me."

"Infatuation?" Even Phoebe treated him like a child.

"Your parents think I'm the next best thing to a card-carrying cannibal, and you think you'll show them what a grown man you are if you and I become more than friends."

"Your major is Psychology?"

"I'm angry. You're determined to ruin a friendship that matters a lot to me."

"Friendship with you no longer satisfies me."

Phoebe slowly turned her head, a fire building in her gaze. "Satisfies you?" She opened her door. "I know what you want in the way of satisfaction. My virginity in no way affects my brain function. I am not going to 'satisfy' you, just so you can annoy your parents. I'll take the bus home tonight. And don't follow me down this road. I refuse to get in this car with you again."

That being her final word, she pushed her long, mouth-watering legs out of the car and uncoiled the rest of her body to leave him in the cold emptiness of their broken relationship. She slammed the car door, and Dan sat, trying harder than he'd ever tried in his life not to cry.

He gunned the car away from the curb. Tears burned despite his strongest effort as he squealed past Phoebe. He didn't plan his trip, but he ended up at the public golf course the college used.

The dark, closed golf course.

Taking a token for the ball machine out of the change slot on his dashboard, he got out anyway. He grabbed his driver from the trunk. They didn't build fences around golf courses. Just put a wooden gate up that kept the polite golfers out.

Dan jumped over it. At the side of the clubhouse, the ball machine didn't work. He punched the front of it hard enough to break the glass that covered the metal door. Then he realized someone had unplugged it. With his bleeding hand, he plugged in the machine and got a bucket of balls. The balls kept coming even after he'd filled one of the baskets from the side of the machine.

He walked away and left the balls thumping on the cement, rolling to the grass.

By moonlight, he teed his first shot on the driving range. His aim in the near darkness wasn't expert. His third ball broke glass somewhere. He kept hitting. Another shattered piece of glass made him hesitate, but only long enough to get really angry again.

He drove a ball into the darkness. His life had about the same sense of direction. His father had believed telling him he and his mom were staying together because of him and the new babies would make him feel good.

And now, Phoebe.

He hit two more balls in quick succession. He loved her. He hadn't known he could want a woman so much, hadn't anticipated wanting Phoebe, but like everything else he wanted right now, she'd put herself out of his reach.

He hit ball after ball after ball until he emptied the basket. Then he walked back to the machine and scooped up another basketful from the pile on the ground. As he stood, blue lights slashed the night air and striped the clubhouse walls.

He turned as the officer driving the police car painted him in a spotlight.

CATE KEPT her promise to stay in bed all day. She called Dan, but no one answered in his room, and no one answered on the public phone in his building, either. In the middle of reading her second book for the day, she noticed night had fallen, but she hadn't eaten dinner.

Not particularly hungry after a day on her back, she went downstairs anyway, but as she reached the kitchen, the front doorbell rang. Cate cinched her robe and hurried through the living room. Uncle Ford stood on her doorstep.

"I heard Alan's left to find Jim Cooper, and I thought you might like some company."

Cate stood aside for him. Uncle Ford had avoided her since she'd caught him making out at Richard's wedding. "I'm glad you came."

"Have you eaten?" He produced a white sack, printed with The Captain's Lady logo. "I brought fish and chips."

"Sounds delicious. I couldn't decide what to eat."

She led the way to the kitchen where she started setting the table. "Should you be driving this late?"

"I've got a bum leg, but I gas and brake with the other foot. I'm no invalid."

She waved the plates at him. "Okay, okay, I just didn't want you doing something unsafe."

"You're still hiding my Cate in there somewhere."

She took utensils from the drawer. "You mean I can't help mothering people? Dan welcomes my efforts about the same as you do."

"I'm sorry I embarrassed you at Richard's wedding."

She laughed. It was silly now. "I don't know how you packed yourself into that car."

He flashed a self-conscious grin. "It was a tight fit." He cleared his throat. "But more importantly, I behaved with a reckless disregard for safety and public decency."

Cate stared at him. "Did you rehearse that speech?"

"I'm ashamed. I guess I saw myself through your eyes. You're a good girl, Cate."

"Woman."

"Woman, I mean, but you don't know how I feel. I'm seventy-three years old, getting older and more infirm every year—well, maybe every five years," he said with a hint of his natural personality. "I want to stay young."

"You don't have to defend your actions to me."

"I do if you don't respect me any more."

A string of pictures shuffled through her mind, tugged at her heart. Uncle Ford, with the black hair of a much younger man, teaching her to drive, Uncle Ford, with a strong proud, loving arm around Alan's shoulders—Alan in the tux he wore in their wedding photo.

Cate dropped the silverware on the table and grabbed a chair back. "I respect you." She forced her head up. "I've always loved you, Uncle Ford."

He came closer, scraping his cane over the floor. "You remember?" His rough voice matched his embrace. "You remember me, Cate?"

"You were kind to Alan. Kinder than Richard."

"I'm not scared like Richard's scared. I worry about commitment to one woman and getting old. Loving a boy who needed a father came easy."

Cate gripped his arm. "I wish I'd cooked you a nice meal."

"Why don't you slap those containers in the microwave?" He turned away as the phone rang. "I'll get that."

"It's probably Alan."

"Then maybe you should get it."

He maneuvered to the microwave and Cate took the phone off its hook. The voice on the phone gave her another shock.

The voice asked her to accept a collect call from the Devon County jail.

"Jail?" Cate whispered. She'd forgotten nothing since she'd awakened from her coma, and she knew Whitlock College was in Devon County. "I accept."

"Mom? I've tried to call Dad's office, but I couldn't reach him. I'm in trouble."

She flattened her hand over her heart, to keep it from bursting. "Are you hurt?"

"No. They haven't even arrested me yet, but I had to ask you or Dad to come up here."

"What did you do?"

A rustling sound came through the wire, and then his voice was muffled, as if he'd turned away or covered the phone. "I broke into the golf course. And I may have broken the ball machine, and then I may have broken someone's window."

How had he convinced Alan he was all right? "When did you do all that?"

"Tonight, Mom. Can you come, or can you send Dad?"

"I'll be there in about an hour. Do you know the directions?" He gave them. As she wrote the jail's phone number in case she got lost anyway, Dan spoke again. "I'm sorry. Dad asked me not to put extra pressure on you. Are you feeling okay?"

She felt desperately sick, but whether the sensation owed itself to pregnancy, shock or her son's indefensible behavior, she couldn't say. Someone shouted in the background and scared her half to death. "Be careful until I get there. Dan, what possessed you?"

"Nothing that seems reasonable now."

"Don't be afraid. We'll take care of it." Probably the wrong thing to say to an eighteen-year-old, but he was her son. She'd do anything to take care of him.

She turned to find Uncle Ford sprawled in a chair, his face pale.

"What's wrong with Dan?" he demanded.

She relayed Dan's offenses. "I have to change before I go. Will you stay here in case Alan calls?"

"He'd kill me if I let you drive up there alone."

He worked his way to his feet. "Besides, who could strike a more sympathetic pose than a pregnant woman?"

Cate paused on the first stair. "What are you talking about?"

"When you show up on the trembling arm of an old man on a cane, they'll send Dan home to take care of us both."

She shook herself, like a bag full of weary bones. "I hope you're right."

She didn't want her son to face consequences. His pain appeared rooted in her accident and the twins Alan and she hadn't okayed with him first.

She managed to put on clothes and she yanked a brush through her hair. She hadn't dried it after her shower. It clustered in Caroline's curls around her face. She tamed it with a scrunchie and ran downstairs. Uncle Ford was waiting in the doorway, but the phone rang again.

Cate hesitated. Uncle Ford swapped a distraught glance with her. This had to be Alan. She debated letting the answering machine take his call.

"He'll worry if he thinks I'm not here." She grabbed the phone in the living room. "Alan?"

"How'd you know?"

She marshaled her breathing to keep him from hearing her gasp for air. "Who else? I've already spoken to Dan." Perfect opening, but the rest of the story refused to come.

"Well, we found Jim Cooper. It doesn't look good for the business. From what we can tell, he's gambled almost all the money away." Defeat flattened his tone, but Cate was so numb she couldn't find words to comfort him. "I have to go to the police station tomorrow, so I'll probably come home on a late flight. Do you want me to call you from the airport?"

"Yes, please. I'd like to know when you're on your way."

She paused. The truth about Dan clung to the tip of her tongue. What could Alan do from New Jersey? How could she add to his problems? Would either of them ever have conceived of Dan's being taken to a police station? Had he ever done anything like this before?

Their family life had suddenly collapsed around her feet. She'd tell Alan as soon as he returned, but she couldn't talk about it now. She could hardly face it, herself.

"Why don't you give me your phone number up there, in case I need to get in touch with you?"

"Do you have pen and paper?"

She noted the number. "Let me know what happens with the police," she said. "And, Alan?"

"Yes?"

She swallowed. Her throat constricted. "Alan, I love you." She meant it. The slow process of falling in love with her husband had finally come full circle. "I might never be the wife I was before, but I love you."

"Cate, I wish I were there to show you how much I love the wife you are now."

She glanced at Uncle Ford. He tapped his watch, and she nodded. "You can't know how much I wish that, too."

"Do you believe I've failed you?"

Pain in his voice kept her from getting upset at the conclusion he'd reached. "No. We'll work out our future, and you've already begun to help the employees." Uncle Ford tapped his cane, and she nodded again. "I just wish we were together. I'd better go—I left the shower running."

"Go back to bed. I'll see you tomorrow night, but I'll call as soon as I leave the police station."

"Thanks."

After they hung up, she couldn't take her hand off the phone. As at his graduation, Dan probably needed his father more than Cate. She still couldn't remember him. What if she let their son down?

"Maybe I should call him back."

"Why didn't you tell him?"

"We've lost the business."

"My God."

"I couldn't pile this on top of the business. He always worries he's failing us."

"I don't think you'd have been happy if he'd hidden something like this from you."

"I'll tell him tomorrow when he comes home."

"It's your choice, but I hope you don't regret it. Don't you trust him, Cate?"

"I trust him." But why bring up Dan's problems when they might be settled by the time Alan could get home? She tried to work up a smile. "I guess I'm a reckless Talbot after all."

"You chose a terrible time. Do you want to drive, or shall I?"

"I will." No need to tire him out. Besides, he might fall asleep instead of badgering her into deeper guilt.

CHAPTER SIXTEEN

THE FIRST CRAMP came more like a memory of past pain. Cate clung to the door in the surprisingly busy reception area of Devon County's police station. Pushing away, she pressed her fists into the small of her back. Had she imagined it?

"What's wrong?" Uncle Ford's lifted voice brought all police activity to an awkward halt.

"Nothing."

One female and one male officer broke away from the large reception desk. "Are you all right, ma'am?" the man asked.

"My son is here. Dan Palmer?"

"Oh, yeah." The woman beckoned with her finger, and Cate and her uncle followed her down the white hall—white walls, white tile floor, shot with threads of black paint like splashes. "Come this way. I parked Mr. Palmer in an interrogation room."

Cate stared at the woman's dark-blond chignon. Was Dan in more trouble if they considered him "Mr. Palmer"?

Uncle Ford leaned into her. "Skillful use of your pregnancy. I'm ashamed I didn't suggest it."

The woman must have heard him, but she didn't turn around. At a dirt-shadowed, closed door, she stopped.

"An official from Whitlock is with him. I've asked the golf course manager to wait in another room. I'd like you to hear what Mr. Palmer has to say, and then we'll decide whether I arrest him."

"Do you have a choice?" Cate asked. Hope shot so quickly through her body she could barely speak.

"He's a kid." The woman's dark-blue eyes coasted over Cate's figure. "Are you his step-mother?"

"Mother."

"Excuse me if I'm rude, but he's so much older than the baby you're carrying, I wondered if there might have been some trouble at home. A divorce and remarriage or something."

"I guess we have had trouble."

"Let him talk. Then you can give me your story."

Cate's hope dimmed. Her story? As in the version of events she thought most likely to get Dan off?

Who was she kidding? If she thought quickly enough, she'd try a good story to get him out of here.

The woman opened the door, and Dan bolted upright from his chair. Concern made him look older, and Cate struggled not to cry in front of the man from Whitlock and the policewoman.

Dan hugged her. "I'm sorry, Mom. I never thought this might happen. Are you okay?"

She wished people would stop asking. She nodded as she clutched at him. "How about you?"

"I feel like a jerk."

"So you should." The policewoman held out her hand to Cate. "I'm Officer Burke." She turned back to Dan. "Don't pretend this just happened to you.

You trespassed and broke private property. You caused everything that's occurred tonight."

"Maybe he did," Cate interjected, "but you don't understand."

"I'm ready to listen. Sit down, Mrs. Palmer." Officer Burke pulled out a chair. "Do you know Dr. Jared, Mrs. Palmer? Dean of Students at Whitlock College."

"We've met," the tall, overly thin man said. "Mrs. Palmer."

She shook his hand and nodded. Not even the faintest memory of him stirred in her mind. "Thank you for coming, Dr. Jared."

"I've been concerned about Dan."

"I skipped a couple of classes," her son admitted, "but Dad talked to me about it, and I won't skip any more. I've always done my assignments."

"He has." Dr. Jared assured both Cate and the officer. "I've verified his performance with his professors—none of whom were that glad to hear from me at this hour, Dan."

"I can do the work. That's not the problem." Dan glanced Cate's way. His face burned bright red, but he went on. "My mother had an accident in May, and she has no memory of you, Dr. Jared, no real memory of me. She doesn't remember my father, and she didn't seem to want to remember him at first. Then came the babies—I'm embarrassed and I feel out of place, as ridiculous as that sounds. After that, we couldn't afford a golf school I need because everyone at this level plays as well as I do. Add a girl I thought would make me feel needed—who doesn't love me, and I've lost everything that mattered to me." He broke off on a choking sound, as if he'd used the last breath in his body. Cate reached for his hand. He pulled away. "Mom, I'm humiliated enough. Just let me finish. I lost control of my life, and I was afraid. My past felt like a lie. I wanted Phoebe, but she didn't want me. I was throwing away school, when I knew how difficult it was for you and Dad to pay the nonscholarship part of my tuition. I'm sorry. I got extremely angry and I acted like a kid. I did some stupid things. Not just tonight."

"What do you mean?" Officer Burke asked.

Dan looked bleak. "Nothing you could charge me with, but my mom understands. Whatever happens here, I'm sorry, Mom."

Another cramp crept from her back to her groin. She concentrated on not showing how it hurt. "I never meant to make your life look hopeless."

"You didn't, but my 'perfect' childhood ended that day you got hurt." He turned to the police-woman. "I know I have to face the consequences."

"How much damage?" Uncle Ford asked.

"That's my problem." Dan's flush deepened. "Sorry, Uncle Ford, but I'd like to shoulder my own responsibility instead of making more for my parents."

Cate kept her attention on the woman who held her son's immediate future in her hands. Officer Burke studied Dan, but then turned to Dr. Jared. "What do you think, sir?"

The strongest pain yet gripped Cate's belly in a vice. She gasped, and the others looked her way. She shook her head. The pains might go away again. She needed to hear Dr. Jared's answer before she admitted she was in trouble. "I'm upset. I can't help it. He's my son."

Dr. Jared spoke to Officer Burke. "I'd like to give Dan another chance. I'll make sure he attends classes. He's been a good student—surprisingly, when you consider everything he's told us. I know the golf team values him. His coach wanted to come tonight, but this is my job. What can we do to help Dan through his trouble?"

Officer Burke stood. "I'll get Mr. Cory. He runs the golf course." She went away, and Cate eased in a deep breath as the tightening started again.

"Thank you for speaking up for our boy," Uncle Ford said to the dean. "I'm Ford Talbot."

"I've seen your photo in the paper," Dr. Jared said. "When you used to show horses. My daughter is a big fan."

"I didn't know you showed horses," Cate said.

"What did you think the barn was for, Mom?"

"My animals are old now, like me." Uncle Ford made himself sound pathetic, and even though Cate knew he was putting on a show, she wished she'd left him alone in that small car to prove he was still young.

Officer Burke returned. "Unfortunately, Mr. Cory received an emergency call from home. I spoke to him and let him go." She smiled at Cate, appearing more human than she had before. "His wife is pregnant, too. He left terms for Dan." She read from a sheet of paper. "He has to replace the windows he broke in a resident's house. He has to help Mr. Cory repair the ball machine, and he'll have to work off the cost of repair supplies. Then he has to work off the same amount of time it would take to pay for labor to do the repairs. Finally, as I mentioned Dan seemed concerned about his tuition, Mr. Cory said if he worked well, maybe he could continue in the job and receive a paycheck.''

Relief shook Cate. She wiped tears from her eyes as Dan sprang to his feet to hug her. She tightened her arms, a reflexive response to another pain, but Dan thought she was clinging and turned to Officer Burke. "Thank you. I know you went out of your way to help me."

"You looked upset enough to make me believe your story. You weren't aggressive." She shook his hand. "We don't get paid by the adolescent we slam into a cell. Besides, I'll probably see you at the golf course."

"You plan to check up on me?" His tone conveyed resignation.

She laughed. "I'm taking lessons. But, if you can handle the truth, I'd like to be sure I didn't make a mistake with you." She shook Cate's hand again. "I hope you soon recover from your injuries. Look after this boy, because I won't be so helpful if he comes back here."

"Thank you." Cate included Dr. Jared. "I'm grateful for the chance you're giving him."

The policewoman nodded. Dan thanked Dr. Jared, who cautioned him about missing any classes for the next four years. Cate restrained herself from hugging the man who'd helped save her son.

At last, she and Dan and Uncle Ford made it outside, where Cate clung to the metal pole that provided a railing on the steps to the parking lot.

"Mom, I am sorry. I hope you don't think I resent you or the twins."

She nodded. "We'll talk later about what's happened tonight. Right now, I need to go to a hospital."

Uncle Ford's cane clattered to the ground. "I knew you were hurting in there. What's wrong?"

She didn't know for sure, but she'd never been more terrified. Her son had barely escaped jail, and his siblings wanted out of her body. Her first instinct was to curl up in a small, fetal ball and shut out the rest of the world.

"I can drive, but Dan, you need to go home. Your father is going to call in the morning. He's going to a police station in Atlantic City to identify Jim Cooper, and then he'll call home."

"What's wrong, Mom?"

The latest contraction finally released her. "I think I'm in labor," she said.

"Let's call an ambulance." Dan grabbed his uncle's cane and handed it to him. "Wait with Mom."

"No." Cate straightened. "I could be wrong, and I'd rather go to the hospital in Leith if we can. I have the cell phone in the car, and if the contractions get any closer together, I'll call the closest ambulance, but I need to go now."

"Can you drive safely, Dan?" Uncle Ford asked.

"I'm scared, but I'll be careful." Dan dragged keys out of his pockets. "Let's get you into your car, Mom."

"Okay, but Dan, don't call your father tonight, and don't tell him tomorrow. I'm probably fine, and we don't have to worry him. Tell him when he gets home from the airport if I'm not home. Drive carefully. No speeding, and don't do anything reckless.''

She'd feel better when he was home safe. She didn't want a nurse to corner Dan in a waiting room and tell him something had happened to the twins. She didn't want to worry Alan long distance, when she might be suffering more false alarms.

"I'll do what you ask, Mom, but Dad will leave *you* this time." He took her keys and opened the driver's door on her car. He hit the lock switch and she went around to the passenger's side, while Uncle Ford climbed behind the steering wheel. "I should go with you, Mom."

"I'd rather you met your Dad at home to tell him. He'll understand when I explain. He has to see the New Jersey police, and I might be wrong. I was wrong before."

She watched him run for his own car. She reached for Uncle Ford's arm. "I didn't want him to come to the hospital in case something is horribly wrong. He shouldn't have to face it without his father."

"If I were Alan and Dan, I'd put all your belongings on the front lawn. Do you think he'll take it better at home?"

"I don't want to believe it might be real labor. I'm barely twenty-seven weeks along. Let's not invite bad karma. I'll deal with reality later."

Maybe Dan and Alan would understand she was doing the best she could. She acknowledged a stab of guilt.

She was trying to take care of her family, to save them from worrying needlessly, but she faced a deeper truth. Being alone to cope with her own panic felt safer.

They couldn't do anything to help her. She didn't know how to comfort her son, didn't know how to tell her husband she might be losing his children when she felt as if she might shatter in unfixable pieces.

How could she allow even Alan and Dan inside her desperate fear for her unborn children?

ALAN DRUMMED on the arm of his seat and checked his watch for the thousandth time. Two hours in the air. He'd probably reach the hospital and his wife in two more hours.

She should have called him to deal with the Devon County police. She shouldn't have asked Dan to wait until tomorrow to tell him about the twins.

Dan had called instead, waking him just after midnight. Alan hadn't tried to reach Cate from his hotel or from the plane. He was too angry. According to Dan, the doctors had stopped her labor, but at twenty-seven weeks along, she was going to be in bed for the rest of her pregnancy. As Alan had fought for control, Dan had sworn she'd thought keeping him in the dark was doing him a favor.

This favor he didn't need. He loved Cate, but had she changed so much she had to prove her independence at his expense? At their family's? How could she possibly have convinced herself Jim Cooper or the business was more important than her or Dan or the twins?

He'd been a fool. Cate wanted marriage on her terms. Either he shared everything, or she'd leave him. But she'd decided not to tell him when their family was in trouble. She seemed to think she knew best, and he should follow her wishes. Alan refused to live by Cate's double standards.

After the plane landed, he abandoned his luggage and hailed a taxi. The hospital entrance glowed faintly in six-thirty-in-the-morning light. Ignoring the security guard's curious gaze, Alan strode to the elevator.

He had to know for himself she was all right, and the twins were still safe. But he also had to tell her he didn't want to pretend they were sharing a life together.

Dan had given him Cate's room number, and he found her easily on the maternity ward. Hell of a place to put a woman in danger of losing her babies.

The sound of footsteps from the direction of the nurse's station pushed him inside Cate's room before he was ready. She opened her eyes and actually smiled at him.

"You're here." As if he'd come to the rescue. She'd denied him that privilege.

"Dan called me." He shut the door and pressed his back to it. Anger pulsed in his head, his shoulders, his fingertips.

She looked impossibly young. She'd left her hair in curls and secured it in a ponytail. Her face, bare of makeup, was pale with worry. He felt for what she'd been through, but she couldn't expect him to take what she'd done without a complaint. He felt as if she'd tricked him.

"You could have lost the babies, Cate."

Her frown carried a hint of surprise. "You're upset with me."

All around her bed, monitors pulsed and printed tapes that recorded his unborn children's condition. "You decided I didn't need to know until everything was over."

"You had the business—the police—"

"And what about the police here, with Dan? Why did you expect me to share everything? You hid an emergency concerning my children from me. Our children, Cate."

"I thought—"

"Stop. I don't want to upset you more. I don't want to cause the labor to start again, but Cate, I can't live in this kind of marriage. I'm always on probation, and you have no rules."

"I tried not to make your problems worse. I assume you'll have to go back to New Jersey now?"

"When our family is safe. How could you think the business meant more to me than Dan and the twins? More than you?"

"I planned to tell you." She held out her hands. "Dan was supposed to bring you here the moment you arrived tonight."

"You still don't get it?" His head throbbed, but he bit down on resentment that felt like a wild thing trying to escape his body. He was terrified he'd start her labor again. "Are you all right?"

"Yes. And the babies are fine. They want me to stay for a few days, and then it's bed rest at home." She shook her head slightly, but her bewilderment only made him realize how far apart they were. Had she really expected he'd understand? "Will I be in our home, Alan?"

"That's up to you." He turned, and gripped the door handle. "Do you understand you wanted to leave me because I hid business issues from you?"

"Yes, but—"

"It is different," he cut in, "because it's worse. This was about our family. This was about you and Dan needing my support. I am your husband and his father—I need to be with you both when you're in trouble. Even though you were fine without me, I'm not fine."

He had to get out of here before he voiced the threats that formed in his head, because he wanted her to hurt, too.

Threats such as she would never make decisions for him again. She would never control him.

He didn't intend to parallel the years his father had spent, slicing himself to ribbons on the shards of a marriage. He turned back to Cate before he opened the door. "Let me know if I should pack your things or come pick you up."

He turned away. He despised the ache that nearly rendered him helpless in front of her. He prayed she'd stop him and admit she'd made a mistake.

She didn't.

"Alan?" a gruff, loud voice called.

He turned. Uncle Ford, on his cane, stood just in front of the waiting area. He'd probably been there all night.

"I don't want to talk to you, Uncle Ford. You should have known better. At the least, you shouldn't

have saddled Dan with the responsibility of calling
me.''

"I only followed Cate's wishes.''

"I thought I was also your family.''

HER OWN HEARBEAT tapped out a song of panic.
Could Alan be right? Had she decided he wasn't important enough to come home and then assumed he
should thank her?

No.

If Dr. Davis hadn't stopped her labor, Cate would
have called him.

But what if he'd arrived too late? What if the police had put Dan in jail last night?

Why had she been so afraid to tell Alan about the
children? He might be right when he accused her of
wanting marriage her own way. Not because she believed she knew how to arrange their lives, but because she hadn't known how to share her deepest
self, her fear for Dan and then her panic that the
twins might die.

The complexity of day-to-day relationships with
Dan and Alan had overwhelmed her. She hadn't seen
her fear coming. Maybe it dated from before her accident, one of those implicit memories.

Caroline had told her she'd never shared the truth
about her marriage. Alan implied she'd always hidden parts of herself from him. The truth was worse.
She hadn't felt capable of trusting him with her grief.

A small cry that escaped her own mouth startled
her. She'd hidden her deepest feelings from Alan.
She hadn't meant to, didn't want to on a conscious

level, but until she could be honest with him, she couldn't ask him to come back.

No more push me pull you. For the last time—for the future, she had to look into her own soul and find out if she was capable of sharing her life in a real marriage. The kind of marriage she'd claimed she'd wanted.

DAN MET Alan at the door, his expression wary but resigned. Alan's heart unclenched at the sight of him. He put his arms around Dan and hugged him as tight as he could.

"Your mother's safe. The twins are safe. I'm more grateful than I can tell you that you called, son."

"I'm glad you're home."

They'd deal with the police issue later. Right now, Dan needed to hear his little sisters—according to Dr. Davis—were still growing and thriving.

Dr. Davis had also told him Cate had asked her not to reveal the girls' sex to her. The doctor had speculated Cate might be afraid of growing that much closer to the babies.

The possibility hurt him. He wouldn't have left Cate at the hospital if he'd believed he could have helped her. She didn't want his help. She wanted to do it all on her own. How ironic that she'd persuaded him to stop being the man who hid behind his own pictures of himself as a provider.

Now he walked in Cate's old shoes. He needed her to love him without boundaries. He couldn't have produced a concept of such love before Cate had forced him to live as if he believed in it. Maybe he should be grateful.

Grateful? He felt foolish because she'd convinced him, but he hadn't noticed she didn't believe.

"YOU'RE BACK ON TRACK." Dr. Davis looked up from the strip of paper the monitor continued to feed the next day. "We'll begin to wean you off the medication. If all goes well, you can go home. To bed."

Cate nodded. "How long before I can leave?"

"I don't think I'll make you any promises." Dr. Davis dropped the strip. "Still don't want to know your children's sex?"

Cate hesitated. No, she couldn't know any more than she already knew. "Not yet." What a coward.

"Okay. When do you think Alan will come by today? I'll try to come back in case you both have questions."

"He won't come unless I call."

Dr. Davis quirked her eyebrows in apparent understanding. "You'll call?"

Cate breathed in. "I think so."

"Well, let my office know when he arrives. If I'm available I'll come back."

Cate didn't answer. Did she have the courage to call Alan? She'd spent nights in his arms. She'd shared her body with him, as naked as a woman could be.

But not quite. She'd withheld a vital part of herself, the part that needed.

"Dr. Davis?"

The doctor looked back from the door. "What?"

"Did Alan let you tell him the sex?"

She nodded. "You don't like to think he might be braver than you?"

Cate gasped. She didn't want to compete with Alan. She needed to believe he would sustain her. In all ways. And that her support, emotional and physical, had become necessary to him. She asked Dr. Davis a rhetorical question, born of her epiphany. "Maybe a married couple is as strong as their combined strength?"

The other woman thought. After a moment, she shrugged. "I guess each couple has to decide about that. You let me know, because I'm no expert."

"No, I'm right," Cate said as the door closed behind Dr. Davis. She had to be right. She reached for the telephone and dragged it to her bed, but when she picked up the receiver she lost her nerve.

She couldn't be wrong again. Not for Alan, not for Dan. This time, she had to believe. No matter who she turned out to be when she regained her memory, she refused to turn back from being Alan's wife and Dan's mother again.

She dialed home. After all her angst, the answering machine picked up.

"Alan." She willed the tremble out of her voice. "The labor terrified me. I was so afraid for the babies, I needed to be alone in case something was wrong. I couldn't let even you feel how much I hurt." She licked her lips as that pain sprang at her again. "But you were right, and I was wrong. I don't need to be alone any more. I need you. Will you come back to me?"

After a few seconds, when she couldn't think of any message more important than her confession, she hung up.

ALAN PLAYED the message several times. The wobble in Cate's voice shook him. His whole body tensed in an instinctive compulsion to do something to take care of her, but his second instinct warned him to protect himself. He'd believed her too many times since the accident, only to find she didn't mean what he thought she'd said.

Alan turned away from the phone. After he'd left Cate, he'd gone back to the airport and picked up his luggage. Then he'd spent the rest of the morning with Chief Mabry, swearing out a new statement that included information the detective had uncovered about Jim Cooper and his spending habits. They'd faxed a copy to New Jersey.

He'd called Dr. Davis's office and demeaned himself, admitting he and Cate were getting along so badly he feared he'd bring labor back on if he saw her again.

She'd taken all his numbers and essentially told him to grow up. Good advice, except he had grown. Too old to believe in fairy tales his wife spun. Even if she spun them without a conscious plan.

But he remembered how it felt to do what she'd done. In the old days, he'd shared just enough information to keep her happy. How many times had he persuaded himself she'd understand when he explained his motives?

His anger toward her troubled him when he understood the kind of rationalization she'd used.

After he played Cate's message one more time, he called the hospital again. A nurse informed him Cate had finally fallen asleep. Which probably meant she hadn't slept well the night before. She never slept during the day unless she was ill.

A memory of her soft relief when she'd seen him piled on a little more guilt. What had he done to her to relieve his own fear?

He drove back to the hospital and trekked to her room at a slower pace this time. At her door, he hesitated. She'd claimed she'd been afraid.

He understood being afraid. All his mistakes had come from his fear of losing her. Why couldn't they both learn to risk themselves for the deep and abiding bond she'd convinced him they could have?

He knocked lightly.

"Come in," she called.

He went, illogically hoping for the greeting she'd given him this morning. Instead, she eyed him warily.

"Did you get my message?" Color slid over her ashen skin.

"Did you mean what you said?"

She swallowed, and she looked so frail, he fought an urge to pick her up and take her home where he firmly believed he could shelter her from any harm.

"I meant every word, and I won't change my mind."

"What do you mean, Cate?" He couldn't soften his rough tone. She'd rubbed his emotions raw.

"I truly didn't want Dan here, but I was so frightened I forgot how to be his mother. And letting you see how terrified I was—it felt like taking my soul out and handing it over. How could I let anyone see that deep inside me?"

He'd been as frightened many times, but he'd

never told her. "Before, when we argued, we didn't explain ourselves to each other. We just made love and started fresh."

"I don't think you can start fresh until you patch up old hurts. I knew you'd be in as much pain as I was, but sharing it with you made everything too real, the babies, Dan's problems. I didn't know how to lean on you. What if you let me down?"

"But, Cate, you made me believe we were in this marriage together."

"I lost my nerve. I knew we'd figure out how to work on houses without money, but could we survive Dan being in jail? If I'd lost the twins how could we look at each other without remembering?"

"I believed we'd love each other no matter what. You gave me that, Cate. For years, I thought love came with conditions. Over the past few months, I came to think that was wrong."

"What do you want from me, Alan?"

He thought as he went to the side of her bed. "I want you to let me in. Good times and bad, I want us to be together. If I'd come home and you'd lost the twins without telling me they were in trouble, I don't believe I could have forgiven you."

Tears wet her eyelashes. "I was so afraid, I couldn't reach for you. In my mind, I've loved you a few weeks, not all my adult life."

"Can you change that, Cate?"

"You've changed. You tell me the truth even when you look as if talking at all hurts. I guess I can change, too. I won't ever take the kind of risk I took last night. For a little while, the twins belonged to me, and only I was strong enough to save them. I'm so grateful they and Dan are all right. And you're here." She held out her hands. "I love our children, and I'd do anything to protect them, but I'm stronger with you beside me."

Her hands, in his, reassured him. "Are you sure this time? We can't go back again."

"I'm sure I love you, and I never want to fail you again."

He sat beside her. "I guess I've let you down a time or two."

"I remember snippets every so often, snippets of arguments, flashes of the love we made instead of making up." Blushing again, she met his gaze.

He leaned down to kiss her. He meant the kiss to be a chaste promise, but her lips stirred beneath his, and his body woke with desire for his wife. A sometimes traitorous, yet absolutely sure response to Cate's slightest touch. He pulled away, rubbing his index finger beneath her lip.

"We'd better not."

"But you love me, Alan?"

"More than my own life."

"This time I know exactly what kind of commitment goes with love."

He leaned across her legs, taking care not to tangle himself in any of her monitor cords. "I wonder when most people learn to let their lovers share their lives."

"I hope we're slow. I'd feel sorry for a whole world full of people shoving each other away." She yawned. "I'm awfully tired. Do you mind if I go to sleep?"

He took her hand and realized she might be uncomfortable under his weight. "Do you want me to move?"

Closing her eyes, she shook her head. "Maybe later, when I get used to knowing you're here."

"I won't leave you."

"Alan." She popped her eyes open. "Are we having boys or girls?"

He was ridiculously glad he got to tell her instead of Dr. Davis. "Two girls."

She flashed a brilliant smile. "How annoying that you're braver than I am. I was afraid I'd see them every time I closed my eyes, if something bad happened."

"You might have, but so would I, and when you have bad days, I'll be strong. Then you can take your turn at being strong for me."

Incredibly, she widened her smile, but tears slid out of her eyes. Alan maneuvered between the cords to pull her into his arms. He'd shelter her from everything, except life.

That, they'd face together.

"I'm thinking Mary and Melinda for names," he said.

"No." She dashed her tears off her face, the Cate he'd come to love more than he'd ever loved her before. The feisty fighter who'd hidden herself all those years. "No alliteration. It's not cute."

"I like Mary and Melinda." He snuggled closer, tucking her sweet-smelling head beneath his chin.

"We're never going to agree on anything, Alan Palmer."

"Probably not." He curved a protective hand over her belly. "Night, Mary—night, Melly."

"That's even worse."

Several reassuringly firm kicks mounded beneath his palm. Cate laughed, sharing his relief. "Daddy's girls, already," she said.

He hugged her. "You go to sleep. I'll wait right here for you."

EPILOGUE

ALAN WAS ALREADY holding Mary when Melinda came into the world—screaming. Dr. Davis held their second daughter high enough for Cate to see her.

"Good work, Mom. And they're both in good shape. I'll let you hold Melinda for a second, and then they both go to the nursery. At thirty-five weeks and their weight, I think they'll be fine, but your pediatrician wants a good look. Okay with you, Pop?"

Alan nodded. "Cate?"

Deeply involved with her second daughter, Cate still had attention left for Alan, who'd shared every second of this labor. She nodded at him as she cradled Melinda against her breasts.

"Let's not ever tell her she was five minutes behind Mary, okay?"

Cate laughed, jouncing the baby. "Whatever you say, husband, but I think we'll be lying for no good reason. They'll find out anyway. They'll both want to be the older one."

"I guess we'll have to live with the consequences."

She met his gaze as she pressed her mouth to Melinda's head. Some consequences might not be as sweet as these two morsels, but they'd learned the pain, the strain and the joy of sharing.

Dan had finally begun to work for a paycheck at the golf course, and the new, downsized version of Palmer Construction worked only on the renovations Alan had loved best anyway.

"Let us have your daughters now, please." Dr. Davis nodded at the two nurses who pushed clear bassinets next to Cate and Alan.

Melinda opened her eyes. She seemed to look into Cate's, but Cate had to blink hard so she could see. Melinda uttered a soft sound that probably meant she was starving. Cate took it as a love song.

"I can't try to feed them yet?"

"After they visit the nursery."

"Can I hold Mary one more time?"

"For a second. Alan, pass Mary to Cate, and take Melinda."

Already, Cate recognized Mary's face, though she'd held her for a scant few moments before Melinda burst onto the scene. She kissed her baby's forehead and read her husband's pride in Melinda.

A love more fierce than she'd ever known unfurled from her tired body.

Melinda stretched with a squall against her father's chest, and Dr. Davis signaled the nurses.

"They won't be gone long. You can see them again in recovery."

"You should tell Dan," Cate said to Alan.

He nodded. "And Uncle Ford and Aunt Imogen, but I don't want to leave you."

"Go put big brother in the picture. By the time you come back, I'll be finished with Cate, and you

can take some time for yourselves.'' Dr. Davis turned
to the nurse who was passing her instruments as she
stitched Cate. ''Could you scratch my nose please?''

Cate laughed, and Alan leaned over her for a brief,
yet passionate kiss. ''Wait for me,'' he said.

She tried not to cry more tears of joy. As the door
closed behind him, she looked wearily on her doctor.
''He's a real jokester, isn't he?''

''A proud dad. I'm proud of you both. Those girls
weren't kind to you. An hour of labor for every year
of your life. What do you think of today?''

Cate wrapped her arms around herself. ''I can't
think. I'm too busy feeling completely happy. And a
bit cold.''

Dr. Davis turned to the nurse. ''I can complete this
on my own. Find a warm blanket for Mrs. Palmer.
The shivering is perfectly normal, Cate. Your body's
been through torture.''

''Torture?'' Cate repeated.

''A male doctor wouldn't admit it, but then, maybe
he wouldn't know.''

''Melinda and Mary were worth every second.
They're gorgeous, aren't they?''

''Slippery, but perfect, as I recall. We do good
work together, you and Alan and I.''

''Thank you for everything, keeping the secret and
all.''

Dr. Davis scooted her chair back, stood and then
began to readjust Cate's bed. ''Did you ever remember why you kept them secret?''

''Parts.'' That much was true. The past and her
fear of it seemed inconsequential. Maybe she and
Alan had both been afraid, as empty as they'd both

felt behind the walls they'd built within their marriage. "I'm perplexed now when I think of how Alan and I behaved toward each other."

"Everything worked out for the best."

A platitude that covered the truth of her marriage now, but left out the happiness that grew in her life—in her family, each and every second of every day. Some of those seconds might tick by unnoticed, but at the end of each twenty-four hours, both she and Alan could recount plenty of minutes they hadn't taken for granted.

Alan backed through the doors. "I bring gifts."

He held out the warm blanket, but the real presents streamed in under their own steam behind him.

"They're gorgeous, Cate." Aunt Imogen kissed her cheek. "Caroline and I made the attendants bring Melinda and Mary to the nursery window. They're absolutely beautiful."

"They're just red," Dan contradicted and quickly kissed Cate's forehead. "But they'll probably grow on us."

Alan leaned over her with a private smile as he tucked the blanket around her. "They were both howling. I think Melinda set Mary off."

"That's bound to happen. We'll rope Caroline in to baby-sit if the going gets rough." She looked at her sister. "Where's Shelly?"

"Running late—that new boyfriend of hers had some sort of meeting after classes, and she wanted to wait for him to drive back. She'll come by when she gets back into town."

Caroline clearly didn't approve of Shelly's Romeo. Life went on. Cate made room as Alan sat on the bed beside her. "Uncle Ford, you're quiet," he said. "Don't you approve?"

He shot a tentative glance at Alan before he answered. "I tend to agree with Dan, but I'm so grateful to be back in the fold, I was afraid to offer my opinion."

Alan chuckled, but stood up to pull a chair close for the older man. He wrapped his arm around Uncle Ford's shoulders. "How am I going to convince you I was frantic for Cate and the children that day, Uncle Ford?"

"How about if we try this?" Uncle Ford edged closer to the bed and whipped a photo out of his pocket. A small bay foal that stood about as high as his cane. "I bought her for the girls. By the time they're old enough to learn to ride, she'll be old enough to belong to them."

The whole family laughed, and Alan shook his uncle's hand. "Deal. Come sit down."

"No." Dr. Davis broke into the crowd. "You all come with me. Alan and Cate need a few minutes to themselves, and then Cate goes to recovery. I'll treat the rest of you to the worst coffee ever boiled up in a public cafeteria."

"Who could resist?" Uncle Ford's interest sparked.

Aunt Imogen made a show of sisterly despair as she fell into the exit line. Caroline paused for a quick hug that Cate heartily returned, and Dan stopped to pound his father on the shoulder.

"I think I'll go look at them again," he said. "I've still got to put one of the cribs together, so I'll probably see you tomorrow, Mom."

"Are you sure it's okay with your professors that you're staying another day?"

"Jeez," he said rather loudly over his shoulder.

Cate turned to her husband before the door closed on their son. "I love him even more when he's impatient with my mothering."

"Me, too, but I'm glad Dr. Davis flushed them out of here." He smoothed her hair away from her forehead and bent until his mouth touched her ear. "My life is better because I love you."

"Do you think we wasted time?"

"I think we got here as fast as we could. I'm sorry you had to forget the past before we could find out who we could be. Not just with each other, but as separate people."

"I'm glad we kept on loving."

He kissed her and then held himself above her so that their lips almost touched. "Glad we found out that where it counts most, you and I are one."

* * * * *

You haven't seen the last
of the Talbot Twins.
In November 2001,
look for Caroline's story.

HARLEQUIN *Super*ROMANCE®

**To celebrate the
1000th Superromance book
We're presenting you with 3 books
from 3 of your favorite authors in**

All Summer Long

Home, Hearth and Haley
by **Muriel Jensen**

Meet the men and women of Muriel's
upcoming **Men of Maple Hill** trilogy

Daddy's Girl
by **Judith Arnold**

Another **Daddy School** story!

Temperature Rising
by **Bobby Hutchinson**

Life and love at St. Joe's Hospital are as feverish
as ever in this **Emergency!** story

On sale July 2001
Available wherever Harlequin books are sold.

HARLEQUIN®
Makes any time special ®

HSR1000

Harlequin truly does make any time special. . . . This year we are celebrating weddings in style!

A Walk Down the Aisle
WEDDING CELEBRATION

To help us celebrate, we want you to tell us how wearing the Harlequin wedding gown will make your wedding day special. As the grand prize, Harlequin will offer one lucky bride the chance to **"Walk Down the Aisle" in the Harlequin wedding gown!**

There's more...

For her honeymoon, she and her groom will spend five nights at the **Hyatt Regency Maui.** As part of this five-night honeymoon at the hotel renowned for its romantic attractions, the couple will enjoy a candlelit dinner for two in Swan Court, a sunset sail on the hotel's catamaran, and duet spa treatments.

A HYATT RESORT AND SPA

Maui • Molokai • Lanai

To enter, please write, in, 250 words or less, how wearing the Harlequin wedding gown will make your wedding day special. The entry will be judged based on its emotionally compelling nature, its originality and creativity, and its sincerity. This contest is open to Canadian and U.S. residents only and to those who are 18 years of age and older. There is no purchase necessary to enter. Void where prohibited. See further contest rules attached. Please send your entry to:

Walk Down the Aisle Contest

In Canada	In U.S.A.
P.O. Box 637	P.O. Box 9076
Fort Erie, Ontario	3010 Walden Ave.
L2A 5X3	Buffalo, NY 14269-9076

You can also enter by visiting www.eHarlequin.com
Win the Harlequin wedding gown and the vacation of a lifetime!
The deadline for entries is October 1, 2001.

HARLEQUIN®
Makes any time special ®

PHWDACONT1

HARLEQUIN WALK DOWN THE AISLE TO MAUI CONTEST 1197
OFFICIAL RULES
NO PURCHASE NECESSARY TO ENTER

1. To enter, follow directions published in the offer to which you are responding. Contest begins April 2, 2001, and ends on October 1, 2001. Method of entry may vary. Mailed entries must be postmarked by October 1, 2001, and received by October 8, 2001.

2. Contest entry may be, at times, presented via the Internet, but will be restricted solely to residents of certain geographic areas that are disclosed on the Web site. To enter via the Internet, if permissible, access the Harlequin Web site (www.eHarlequin.com) and follow the directions displayed online. Online entries must be received by 11:59 p.m. E.S.T. on October 1, 2001.

   In lieu of submitting an entry online, enter by mail by hand-printing (or typing) on an 8½" x 11" plain piece of paper, your name, address (including zip code), Contest number/name and in 250 words or fewer, why winning a Harlequin wedding dress would make your wedding day special. Mail via first-class mail to: Harlequin Walk Down the Aisle Contest 1197, (in the U.S.) P.O. Box 9076, 3010 Walden Avenue, Buffalo, NY 14269-9076, (in Canada) P.O. Box 637, Fort Erie, Ontario L2A 5X3, Canada.

   Limit one entry per person, household address and e-mail address. Online and/or mailed entries received from persons residing in geographic areas in which Internet entry is not permissible will be disqualified.

3. Contests will be judged by a panel of members of the Harlequin editorial, marketing and public relations staff based on the following criteria:

   • Originality and Creativity—50%
   • Emotionally Compelling—25%
   • Sincerity—25%

   In the event of a tie, duplicate prizes will be awarded. Decisions of the judges are final.

4. All entries become the property of Torstar Corp. and will not be returned. No responsibility is assumed for lost, late, illegible, incomplete, inaccurate, nondelivered or misdirected mail or misdirected e-mail, for technical, hardware or software failures of any kind, lost or unavailable network connections, or failed, incomplete, garbled or delayed computer transmission or any human error which may occur in the receipt or processing of the entries in this Contest.

5. Contest open only to residents of the U.S. (except Puerto Rico) and Canada, who are 18 years of age or older, and is void wherever prohibited by law; all applicable laws and regulations apply. Any litigation within the Province of Quebec respecting the conduct or organization of a publicity contest may be submitted to the Régie des alcools, des courses et des jeux for a ruling. Any litigation respecting the awarding of a prize may be submitted to the Régie des alcools, des courses et des jeux only for the purpose of helping the parties reach a settlement. Employees and immediate family members of Torstar Corp. and D. L. Blair, Inc., their affiliates, subsidiaries and all other agencies, entities and persons connected with the use, marketing or conduct of this Contest are not eligible to enter. Taxes on prizes are the sole responsibility of winners. Acceptance of any prize offered constitutes permission to use winner's name, photograph or other likeness for the purposes of advertising, trade and promotion on behalf of Torstar Corp., its affiliates and subsidiaries without further compensation to the winner, unless prohibited by law.

6. Winners will be determined no later than November 15, 2001, and will be notified by mail. Winners will be required to sign and return an Affidavit of Eligibility form within 15 days after winner notification. Noncompliance within that time period may result in disqualification and an alternative winner may be selected. Winners of trip must execute a Release of Liability prior to ticketing and must possess required travel documents (e.g. passport, photo ID) where applicable. Trip must be completed by November 2002. No substitution of prize permitted by winner. Torstar Corp. and D. L. Blair, Inc., their parents, affiliates, and subsidiaries are not responsible for errors in printing or electronic presentation of Contest, entries and/or game pieces. In the event of printing or other errors which may result in unintended prize values or duplication of prizes, all affected game pieces or entries shall be null and void. If for any reason the Internet portion of the Contest is not capable of running as planned, including infection by computer virus, bugs, tampering, unauthorized intervention, fraud, technical failures, or any other causes beyond the control of Torstar Corp. which corrupt or affect the administration, secrecy, fairness, integrity or proper conduct of the Contest, Torstar Corp. reserves the right, at its sole discretion, to disqualify any individual who tampers with the entry process and to cancel, terminate, modify or suspend the Contest or the Internet portion thereof. In the event of a dispute regarding an online entry, the entry will be deemed submitted by the authorized holder of the e-mail account submitted at the time of entry. Authorized account holder is defined as the natural person who is assigned to an e-mail address by an Internet access provider, online service provider or other organization that is responsible for arranging e-mail address for the domain associated with the submitted e-mail address. **Purchase or acceptance of a product offer does not improve your chances of winning.**

7. Prizes: (1) Grand Prize—A Harlequin wedding dress (approximate retail value: $3,500) and a 5-night/6-day honeymoon trip to Maui, HI, including round-trip air transportation provided by Maui Visitors Bureau from Los Angeles International Airport (winner is responsible for transportation to and from Los Angeles International Airport) and a Harlequin Romance Package, including hotel accomodations (double occupancy) at the Hyatt Regency Maui Resort and Spa, dinner for (2) two at Swan Court, a sunset sail on Kiele V and a spa treatment for the winner (approximate retail value: $4,000); (5) Five runner-up prizes of a $1000 gift certificate to selected retail outlets to be determined by Sponsor (retail value $1000 ea.). Prizes consist of only those items listed as part of the prize. Limit one prize per person. All prizes are valued in U.S. currency.

8. For a list of winners (available after December 17, 2001) send a self-addressed, stamped envelope to: Harlequin Walk Down the Aisle Contest 1197 Winners, P.O. Box 4200 Blair, NE 68009-4200 or you may access the www.eHarlequin.com Web site through January 15, 2002.

Contest sponsored by Torstar Corp., P.O. Box 9042, Buffalo, NY 14269-9042, U.S.A.

PHWDACONT2

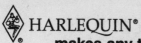

In August 2001

New York Times bestselling author

HEATHER GRAHAM

joins

DALLAS SCHULZE

&

Elda Minger

in

TAKE5

Volume 3

These five heartwarming love stories are quick reads, great escapes and guarantee five times the joy.

Plus

With $5.00 worth of coupons inside, this is one *delightful* deal!

HARLEQUIN®
Makes any time special®

Visit us at www.eHarlequin.com

HNCPV3R